falling in love with english boys

a novel by

melissa jensen

speak

An Imprint of Penguin Group (USA) Inc.

SPEAK

Published by the Penguin Group

Penguin Group (USA) Inc., 345 Hudson Street, New York, New York 10014, U.S.A.

Penguin Group (Canada), 90 Eglinton Avenue East, Suite 700, Toronto, Ontario, Canada M4P 2Y3
(a division of Pearson Penguin Canada Inc.)

Penguin Books Ltd, 80 Strand, London WC2R 0RL, England

Penguin Ireland, 25 St Stephen's Green, Dublin 2, Ireland (a division of Penguin Books Ltd)

Penguin Group (Australia), 250 Camberwell Road, Camberwell, Victoria 3124, Australia
(a division of Pearson Australia Group Pty Ltd)

Penguin Books India Pvt Ltd, 11 Community Centre,
Panchsheel Park, New Delhi - 110 017, India

Penguin Group (NZ), 67 Apollo Drive, Rosedale, North Shore 0632, New Zealand
(a division of Pearson New Zealand Ltd.)

Penguin Books (South Africa) (Pty) Ltd, 24 Sturdee Avenue,
Rosebank, Johannesburg 2196, South Africa

Registered Offices: Penguin Books Ltd, 80 Strand, London WC2R 0RL, England

First published in the United States of America by Speak,
an imprint of Penguin Group (USA) Inc., 2011

1 3 5 7 9 10 8 6 4 2

LIBRARY OF CONGRESS CATALOGING-IN-PUBLICATION DATA IS AVAILABLE

Speak ISBN 978-0-14-241851-2

Printed in the United States of America

This is for all the Goils
who dispense fierce wisdom
and ice cream,
and for a few in particular, through all the years:

Alex, Caroline, Carrie, Christina, Djenan,
Elizabeth, Jen, Jenny, Keri, Lesley, Luisa,
Margaret, Meghan, Michelle, Molly,
Sophie, Tessa.

Thank you. Love you.

The Cat's Cat-astrophic Cat-aclysmic Cat-atonic Summer Blog

June 22

Transatlanticism

Airplane bathrooms are only a step above the ones found in gas stations. Unless you're in first class, which I'm not. I haven't even seen first class on this plane. It's upstairs. Apparently you sit in your own private little pod. Which, when you think about it, must be kinda like sitting in the lavatory here in coach, but with your own movie screen and room service.

Airplane food (*"This evening, ladies and gentlemen, we are offering you a choice of spinach-stuffed chicken in a lemon-tomahto sauce or two-cheese ravioli in a spinach-chicken sauce."*) is disgusting. Unless you're in first class, which I'm not. Or flying Air France, which I'm not. I would much rather be going to Paris than to London. Paris has croissants and Dior and boys who look like Orlando Bloom but say things like *"eet geeves me such ennui"* and *"merde."* London has sandwiches made with cucumber and butter, guys with bad teeth, and the library where my (s)mother will be spending the summer trying to get to know some woman who did absolutely nothing of import and has been dead for two hundred years.

I so wanted to stay with Dad, but apparently the soon-to-be-stepmonster needs his spare bedroom for her "office." Like she can't keep her teetering towers of bridal mags, sample menus, and bad band demos in her own office until the wedding. But then, I've never actually seen her place of work. Perhaps she is not the on-the-rise cleaning-product executive she claims to be. Perhaps she is but a lowly soap-bar wrapper without so much as a cubicle to call her own. Wouldn't surprise me.

So then I'm thinking, I'm sixteen, totally old enough to stay on my own for a few weeks. Mom actually laughed when I suggested it, which wasn't entirely unexpected. Then told me it was a moot point as she was renting the apartment to a visiting professor from Kazakhstan, which kinda was. But I Plan B'd her and suggested staying with Grandma in the burbs. GM would have been happy to have me and offered to drive me to and from the SEPTA train station every day so I could get a job in the city.

Mom's response to that? According to her, since discovering Dr. Phil, GM has become "Freud with a chain saw." Whatever that means. Then she said that GM is also developing a "pernicious mochaccino habit that makes her a caffeinated hazard behind the wheel," and an even worse eBay addiction, which has resulted in a closetful of designer knockoffs made in Chinese sweatshops. (Mom is so obsessed with Third World labor issues.) With all due fondness, Mom sez, she wouldn't leave the dog with her mother for more than an afternoon.

As jolly olde, horsey-houndy England has never had a single case of rabies, there's this bizarre pet passport thing and the dog can't come with us because Mom missed the deadline. He's staying with Mom's teaching assistant. Apparently my passion for reality TV isn't the kind of "rabid" they fear, so here I am jetting over the Atlantic.

For the next ten weeks, while you, my beloved friends, have the CW and texting and weekends at the Shore, I'll have buttered cucumber and the Queen and this blog. Mom swears the apartment . . . excuse me . . . the "flat" has high-speed Internet access. Guess I'll find out when we land at 6 a.m. tomorrow.

Merde.

One pale, tiny glimmer of light has just pierced the gloom. (One other than the "Occupied" light over the lavatory door.) London might actually have Orlando Bloom.

June 23

Who Knew

I've learned these English things:

+ Their "ground floor" is our "first floor." Hence, when they say "third floor," it's actually the fourth. As in: "Charming third-floor flat a stone's throw from Regent's Park. No lift."

+ They say "lift"; we say "elevator."

+ They must all be champion shot-putters. I figure I could throw a stone to the park . . . oh, with the aid of a grenade launcher. If you lean all the way out the window—avoiding the copious pigeon *merde*—and think creatively, you can kinda see some green over all the brick chimneys.

+ When a girl with serious jet lag sleeps until three in the afternoon, the only sandwiches left at the so-called sandwich shop are egg-mayo (egg salad), yoghurt-prawn (shrimp), and chicken-rocket (I have no idea, but it was very yellow and very green).

✦ There is nothing on the "telly" at 3 a.m. except test match cricket (read: will test your viewing endurance with its endlessness) and reruns from the third season of *Friends*.

✦ High-speed Internet access here is an oxymoron.

June 25

Why Does It Always Rain on Me

Day 3 in London. It's raining. Hard. It rained yesterday. And the day before. I'm alone in the flat. Pix below. The distance between my bed and both walls, in case you're curious, is exactly twenty-two inches. The living-room sofa is, yes, truly that orange, the carpet truly that stunning brown. That row of books below the painting of the cows (and that third cow from the left is going to make me crazy—you just *know* it's going to go headfirst into the river) . . . *The Complete Guide to British Fungus, Volumes I–XVII*. Only *III* and *VII* are missing. Apparently the flat belongs to King's College's foremost expert on creeping mold. Who, according to Mom, is spending the summer doing research in the middle of some African desert. What is wrong with that picture, folks (not to mention the cows!)? And where are *III* and *VII*? Being dragged around by some poor camel?

Mom has been at the library since eight this morning. She was there from eight to four yesterday. I've been here, and here, and within three blocks of here. The "newsagent" down the street sells every magazine known to woman—except *InStyle*. And thirty-seven different kinds of chocolate. I counted. Mom tried to get me to go to the BM with her. Really. That's what they call the British Museum. She's working in some dusty back room, just her, some boxes of old papers, and the occasional presence of some old archivist named Mr. Reade. Really. She says I could entertain myself for days in the museum part of the BM, that it's the most famous museum in England. No *merde*. Ha ha.

My mother is full of BM. Ha ha. She loves that crap. Ha ha. Dusty papers, dusty old costumes. Stuff belonging to dead people, most of whom weren't even famous when they were alive. Like I want to spend the day with two-hundred-year-old shopping lists.

I could have done this in Philly, sat in the apartment for three days while it rained. But there it would be raining *and 80* degrees, which, while weird, has a kind of tropical vibe. Here it's 14 degrees Celsius, which means 58.

What I did today:

✦ Slept until 11:00.

✦ Put a sweater on over my pajamas. In June.

✦ Sent fourteen e-mails, including one to Adam the Scum, requesting the return of my DVDs. He has forfeited his right to ever watch *Eternal Sunshine* again. Or even *Borat*, for that matter.

✦ Took digi-pix of the flat (all four rooms; see below).

✦ Read *Elle*, *Vogue*, and something called *Hello!*, which is like *People* on meth.

- Ate one bar Aero (chocolate with little airholes), one bar Curly Wurly (chocolate-covered caramel), and one bag Maltesers (chocolate-covered malt balls).

What I would do if I were in Philadelphia:

- Wear shorts.

- Send three e-mails, because I would probably be seeing the four people who got the other eleven. Including Adam the Scum. But I wouldn't say anything to him, of course.

- Take Andouille for a walk, maybe all the way to South Street, because the Java Company allows dogs and Sophie and Jen and Keri would meet me there.

- Have some pizza, have some gossip, do some good browsing, because South Street has decent stores and miniature dachshunds will sit quite happily and quietly in your tote bag as long as you give them a regular stream of doggie treats.

- Go back to Keri's house because no one is ever there and she has a plasma screen. Watch an episode of *Grey's Anatomy* or *Ugly Betty*. Have a good Abuse Adam the Scum session. Slag him off with the help of my best girls. Probably cry.

Another English thing I've learned:

- "Slag" has rahther a lot of meanings.

Are We Having Fun Yet?

Help!

I have experienced boredom of the sort that numbs the soul and reduces the cerebellum to a desiccated and crunchy mass of no substance whatsoever. Kinda like an Aero without the chocolate.

O my friends, why hast thou deserted me? No e-mail since last night. No reports on Hannah's party and whether Adam the Scum was to be seen still in the company of that slag (*see?*) Mandy?

I did finally get e-mail from Dad, apologizing profusely for bailing on dinner the night before we left and promising to make it up to me in a Big Way when he comes to visit. So, what is an appropriate Big Way, do you think? Some Citizens jeans? A new iPod? Nah, I'll take just having him here without the soon-to-be-stepmonster.

Today the temperature has risen to a blistering 16 Celsius. Got math? That's 66 degrees, give or take. I need another sweater. I brought one. Twelve tees (Mom made me leave eight behind—as if she was going to have to carry them), one sweater. God, I miss H&M. Go, O my friends, and tell me what is on display. Even better, take pix. I walked by a clothes store this morning on the long way back from the newsagent (Cadbury Twirl). The sweaters had, like, plaid trim. Really. Help.

Mom says I need to get farther afield, expand my horizons. She also told me to go to Carnaby Street, where the Beatles used to hang out. Can someone please tell me where to go where the Ting Tings or Keane hang out???

✦ ✦ ✦

(later)

I found H&M. Resisted the urge to kiss the floor.

It stopped raining. Mom threatened to disconnect the Internet service, such as it is, if I didn't venture past the newsagent today. Sometimes I really hate my mother.

She pointed me in the direction of Oxford Street and gave me thirty pounds (about fifty-eight dollars). Sometimes I can almost tolerate my mother. Turns out that Oxford Street is pretty cool. H&M, Virgin Records, and Selfridges (kinda like Macy's with attitude). See pix. It's a lot like New York. Wiiiide street. Most of the cars are cabs—although their cabs look like everything around them should be black and white. Like Cary Grant should be getting out instead of guys with spiky yellow hair and girls with pink cigarettes. Half of the stores sell things with pictures of the Queen or red double-decker buses on them. Most of the others sell Rolexes. Everything is crazy crowded, everyone is carrying designer knockoff handbags, and everyone is making sure to look totally grim. Except the tourists.

H&M here is enormous. Shiny. Overflowing. Mecca, Valhalla, the Emerald City. I wandered. I basked. I worshipped.

I bought myself a boyfriend cardigan with Union Jack buttons. Most cute. See pix. If only finding a boyfriend could be accomplished in a similar fashion. "I'm looking for a medium in some variation of beige or brown. No, this isn't a good fit. Lemme try that one ..."

Tried on some jeans. I couldn't get them past my knees.

More English things learned:

✦ English clothing sizes are two numbers bigger. Like even a skeleton would need a 4.

✦ English shoe sizes are tiny. My size 9s? Here, I am a 6½. Go figure.

Mom and I went out for Indian food tonight in Soho. It's all Indian restaurants, where the Indian waiters sound like Colin Firth, and pubs, where everyone spills out onto the sidewalk and sounds like Adam Sandler. On the way we passed the house Mom's research subject lived in. Lots of the houses in the neighborhood have these round blue plaques on them. *"Frances Hodgson Burnett, Writer, lived here."* (For those of you who have forgotten your childhood, she wrote *The Secret Garden*.) Or *"Martin Van Buren, Eighth U.S. President, lived here."* What our president was doing living in London is a mystery. My fave (see pix): *"Beau Brummell, Leader of Fashion, lived here."* Leader of Fashion. Gotta like that. Mom says he lived at the same time as the woman she's studying, that if he didn't like the way a girl dressed, she could just about give up any hope of being a "success." She says he polished his boots with champagne bubbles. I get the idea she doesn't much care for Beau Brummell. He sounds okay to me. *What Not to Wear*, Regency Edition.

So we walked by the house Mom's Mary Percival lived in. Not so much as a tiny little blue bathroom tile there. Apparently her books didn't make her famous enough for a plaque. Pretty house, though, red brick with lots of windows and a fancy black stair rail that Mom says is definitely original. She touched it and got all emotional. Help.

Tomorrow maybe I'll stroll over to Clarence House. According to a very reliable source (*Hello!*), it's Prince William's official London residence. You never know . . .

Someday My Prince Will Come

No William. Too bad. He's on holiday somewhere, according to my knows-it-all source. (*OK!*— *Hello!*'s poorer and slightly funny-looking cousin.)

Mom brought home ("home," hah! Home is currently being occupied by the world's foremost expert on 18th century Cossack poetry) a photocopy of Mary's daughter's diary. She thinks I should read it. Apparently Miss Percival and I have a lot in common. So far, I've managed to get through the first ten pages. Her handwriting is almost disgusting, it's so perfect.

Here's what we have in common so far:

✦ A name (she's Katherine with a *K*).

✦ Approximate age (she's 18).

✦ (S)mothers.

✦ Fab dads who are really busy.

Here's where we diverge:

✦ Katherine is a bit of a twit. All she talks about is parties and some boy she calls "Mister" Whatever and who writes poetry.

✦ She never actually went to school. I keep seeing the word "governess." Think *Jane Eyre*. Or *The Nanny Diaries*.

+ She has big boobs. There's a b&w photo of a painting of her with the journal. She looks like Rachel Weisz.

+ She thinks dancing the waltz is naughty.

+ She gets to drink at every party she goes to.

+ She never saw a television, car, hair dryer, or flush toilet.

Yawn.

Onward. Thanks, Kelly, for the partay update and the pix. I especially liked the one of Adam being French-kissed by Hannah's pug. Who, as we know, is an inveterate butt licker. Most funny. And yeah, absolutely, I think She Who Shall Not Be Named must be taking diet pills. She's definitely got that pink, crazy, anatrim look going. Josh used to duck whenever she slid her Ford fender into the desk next to him.

I will acknowledge casting stones and glass houses, yada yada. My booty cannot help but expand if I continue with my experiments in English chocolate. They don't call it Bounty (same as U.S., chocolate and coconut, but so much better . . .) for nuthin'. So I took my booty out for a walk. I thought I would find a bookstore, see what Bridget Jones is up to. So, didja know they paint LOOK RIGHT on street corners to keep us dim-witted tourists from stepping into oncoming traffic. They drive on the left side.

Did I look right? Do I look right? Jeans, UPenn tee, my new sweater . . .

I walked past the American embassy today. Bit of a shocker there. It's on this really pretty square, one of those London–Jane Austen–Hugh Grant places with brick buildings all around and grass in the middle. But the embassy is this huge, hideous building with concrete barricades all around it. And there were all these people outside, waving signs and screaming about American troops in Afghanistan.

I'm starting to get the idea that they don't like Americans all that much these days. Lots of postcards of our former pres looking stupid and our current pres looking worried. And I think the guy who owns my chocolate store might have a picture of Saddam Hussein on the wall behind the counter.

Anyway. Keep the e-mails coming. Barring rain, and the BBC seems somewhat confused on the matter, I plan to devote much of tomorrow to Notting Hill. In the event of rain, it's just me and prissy Miss Percival here. Jane Austen she is not. I guess when you think about it, diaries then were the blogs of today. Think of it . . . *June 27. Met the hottest guy yesterday, but his 'tude makes him a total loser. I am so not going to go there. Fitzwilliam Darcy can go dance with himself for all I care.*

Farewell, gentle readers, until next we meet . . .

The Diary of
Miss Katherine Percival

6 May 1815

I do not care for Miss Luisa Hartnell. She laughs altogether too much when surrounded by young men. I do not understand why she is considered a Beauty. Her hair is so very <u>red</u>, after all, and of course there is the matter of those <u>freckles</u>.

Nor can I agree that she is nearly so accomplished as people say. She plays the pianoforte tolerably enough, I suppose. But there is no <u>style</u> to her playing, no <u>passion</u>. Miss Cameron always declared my playing to be passionate, which I quite liked, although I did not care for her forever telling me that I could temper that with proficiency if I were but to practice more. I prefer passion. What would a governess know of passion, after all? Poor unwanted thing, with her flyaway hair and beaky nose. And those ghastly grey dresses she wears! She has always put me in mind of a little bird whose nest has been caught in a gale—frowsy and twittering and fretful, drab wings aflutter. Mama says I must not be unkind about her, that Miss Cameron's family fell on great misfortune and, had matters but been a trifle different, she would have every bit as much of a fortune as I, and nearly as pleasant prospects.

I do not wish to write of Miss Cameron, however, as she remains in Somerset with her new pupil, and has no part in my story. I cannot help but wish, however, that she had been perhaps a better piano teacher. My performance at the Hartnells' last night was not met with quite the enthusiasm of Miss Luisa's. Had Miss Cameron's repertoire and skill been better, I'm sure I would have quite enthralled the gathering.

I especially did not care for Miss Hartnell's way of clapping. To an unbiased eye, she would have seemed all that was friendly and encouraging. I, however, know she was not so kind. Certainly she was gloating inside over her triumph, even as she played modest in refusing a second tune.

No, I simply cannot like her, even if others do.

I daresay, as Mama says of poor Miss Cameron, Money begets Beauty. Miss Hartnell has ten thousand pounds. Hence many people will find her quite pretty.

Then, too, it was her mother's party. Gentlemen are expected to partner their hosts' unmarried daughters in a dance. I wonder if perhaps in London, two dances are <u>de rigueur</u>. I suspect so, as seemed the way of things last night. I have ~~rather a lot~~ a bit to learn in my first Season. I am expected to be married by the end of this one, and brilliantly. At least Papa expects it. He teased that I must make myself useful somehow. Mama says I am to enjoy the experience, attempt to learn something of life, and not rush into an imprudent attachment which I will have cause to regret. As if I could possibly regret a brilliant match! Sometimes I simply do not understand Mama at all. She insists her writing is about such matters as imprudence and regret, yet she seems to know nothing <u>at all</u> about the way life truly is. Honestly!

I wonder if I danced with my future husband last night. It all went too fast. There was a Mr. Troughton, who had very pretty blond curls, but no chin. Mr. Pertwee wears a corset. Mr. Baker I rather liked; he is quite handsome, rather Grecian in his aspect, and called me an "ebon Aphrodite." I do wish he had not had two dances with Miss Hartnell. There were several others whose names I do not recall. All were young, all tolerable in appearance, all perfect gentlemen.

I believe I am going to like London very well indeed.

9 May

The weather these two days has my spirits depressed. It rains, and it rains. In truth, in the country, I do not mind the rain so much. I rather like a good walk outside while the water washes the air and the leaves clean, and makes things shiny ebon black like onyx.

On a day like this, I might walk to the vicarage to visit Annabel Jerrod, or perhaps cajole Phipps into harnessing the carriage and driving me to Highfield to see the Goodwins. Here, there is little to do but sit thumbing through the Ackermann's alone (which is a terrible tease, as I cannot purchase so much as a ribbon today!), wishing for half the dresses there, and be wearied by the pattering of the rain on the windows and my own foolish thoughts.

There are always puddles in the courtyard at Percy's Vale—all those hollows in the stone where three hundred years of carriages have turned and deposited their passengers. How I used to love to splash in them. I have a memory of Mama joining me once when I played in a puddle near the old castle wall. She was laughing and teasing Charles, who would have been ten or so to my four years and would not join us, telling him a bit of mud never injured anyone. Then Papa came out of his library and called us wallowing little sows. How pink Mama turned, as if he had just done magic and turned her into a piglet.

Papa is ever so proud of his beautiful boots, and he cannot bear a lady to be blowzy (he would insist on glowering so at Miss Cameron that she did flutter and twitter like the veriest peagoose on his rare visits home—how I giggled!). I find his compliments to me most gratifying. I stopped playing in the mud that very day, of course. Mama tried to make me join her once or twice after, but I would not. She very likely was trying to spite poor Papa. They were much at odds in those days, it seems. I wonder now if Mama was the one who always encouraged me; I had thought it my nursemaid, but I believe I was mistaken.

How I hate Mama today! She will not accompany me shopping and I cannot very well go alone. I am eighteen, after all, hardly a child, and I could take Becky. I have walked often enough into Sparkford with my maid for company. Mama says this is not Sparkford, Becky would likely faint at the first carriage to nearly run her down in the street, and I would no doubt be lost within minutes of leaving the house.

I do not like her any better for being correct on all counts.

Besides, it is raining. I would not wish to be spattered by a passing carriage and arrive home to find Papa on hand to see me muddied. I see him so rarely, not at all, really, since we arrived, I would not like to have a meeting where I've disappointed him and given him cause to call me a pig.

Still, my only outing since Monday's party has been to the very same house. Mama and I paid a call on Lady Hartnell to thank her. We were not there above ten minutes. Despite Miss Hartnell's presence, I would have gladly stayed longer. Lady Hartnell is all that is pleasing. She knows <u>everyone</u> who is in Town and all the parties that will be worth attending. She knows, too, the very best modistes and ladies' shops: where to buy gloves and ribbons and hats. Mama, of course, had very little to add to the conversation. She, handsome as she is, does not care overmuch for such matters. How very vexing, although I must acknowledge that she did not embarrass me by discussing her Work, as she so often is wont to do in company.

As for Miss Hartnell, she smiled very prettily, complimented my dress (sprigged white; hers of course, was yellow), and looked all the while like a cat in cream. I will not be fooled by her amiable mien. When she asked if there were any gentlemen I especially admired, I held my tongue. One cannot be too careful, after all, when it comes to such matters. An envious young lady may do untold damage to another's romance, even one yet to begin.

I must say, I did not entirely mind when she spoke of Mr. Baker. She asked if I did not find him very handsome and charming. I replied that he seemed pleasant enough. She then mentioned that he is a poet. Mama even seemed interested for a moment, until learning that he composes romantic verses. She does not care for anything without a moral or a lesson. I cannot help but think that is a <u>sermon</u>, not a <u>poem</u>. I will have the romance, thank you.

10 May

A trip to the modiste, at last! We sat and perused the very latest repositories of fashion (such fun!), and then I stood for what seemed like hours (not nearly so much fun; my feet ache abominably and one careless assistant stuck me with a pin!) while they draped me in fabric and pinned and tucked. What a funny little woman the dressmaker was, with hands that looked just like a mouse's and hair that was somewhere between black and red. She calls herself Madame Cambon and speaks like "zees" and "zat" and "la belle mademizille." Once we were back in the carriage, Mama had a good laugh and said she would "eat 'er stockeengs" if Madame were from farther away than Manchester.

I quite liked Mama today, even if she would not buy me an ermine muff. She rather likes ermines (oh, how she and Papa fought over hosting a fox hunt last summer!) and believes they should be able to keep their coats. Perhaps I will ask Papa when the weather turns cold. I confess I do not need a muff while the weather is so temperate.

Here is what we chose:

~ Three day dresses (white embroidered muslin, yellow silk—with the most delicious little puffed sleeves, white silk with tiny pale green stripes)

~ Four evening dresses (palest pink gauze embroidered with tiny white roses, white silk with a silver net overlay, gold lace with the loveliest rosettes at the hem, and white silk with gold tinsel embroidery)

~ Two spencers which, while they are certainly fetching, looking much like the short uniform jackets of the military, give me pause. I fear the manner in which my skirts billow beneath them makes my posterior appear . . . well, fat. I prefer shawls.

~ Three embroidered evening shawls in pink, white and gold silk

I will have matching silk slippers for all, new half boots in gold kidskin, and a dozen pairs of new gloves. I do like the elbow-length ones best. Mama calls my brown spots "beauty marks." I call them brown spots. The one on my left wrist looks distressingly like a tiny silhouette of a toad.

Mama says I must make do with the walking dresses we purchased in Bristol, especially as I do not often walk. Sometimes Mama finds herself most amusing.

Tonight we attend a ball at the home of Lady Everard, which should be quite pleasant. We have not met with her in some months. It has been just over a year since Sir Lawrence's death. Lady E. has cast off her mourning black and will no doubt host a lively evening.

It is a pity that Charles has not returned from the south, for Lady E.'s son, Nicholas, will be most sorry not to see him and will insist on playing the brother in Charles's absence. Perhaps if Nicholas Everard were less severe and less inclined to find me so ~~childish and wanting in sense~~ young, I should like him better. He is a war hero, after all, and not unpleasant to the eye. I should very much like to hear of his months in Spain and Portugal, fighting under Wellington. It all must have been so fierce and fervent. Charles says Nicholas saved his entire regiment from an ambush by French fusiliers. Yet when I have asked, especially about the scar across his brow, Nicholas (what a bother that I shall have to call him <u>Sir</u> Nicholas now, and without laughing) has merely scowled and told me not to pester him with my silly prattle.

Yes, a pity indeed that Charles is not here. More a pity that I shall not have any of my new dresses for a sennight at best. I suppose I shall make do with the cream silk.

I wonder if Mr. Baker will be in attendance tonight.

11 May

(three o'clock in the morning and I am yet to go to bed)

Charles surprised us and appeared at Lady Everard's ball. How very glad Mama and I were to see him (she cried) and how well he looks. His time in the southern counties has suited him, as the Continent last year did not. He was so very thin and pale then. Marching through the Pyrenees in winter and fighting with the French can do that, certainly. Now he is hale and cheerful and looks marvelous in his blue-and-silver uniform. He has been made a captain of his Hussars regiment, and at only four-and-twenty.

I saw many of the young ladies present eyeing him with the hope that he might request a dance. He did not, silly creature, instead withdrawing to some distant room with Nicholas Everard and some other gentlemen for cigars and, I am certain, endless talk of Napoleon Bonaparte's tiresome escape from Elba. I do wish our generals had done a better job of keeping him there. He caused such a terrible to-do on the Continent for so many years. Only yesterday, Lady Hartnell was reminiscing about how she had so missed French fashion during those sad times.

Charles says there will almost certainly be more battles, now that Bonaparte is tromping through France again. He also says he must leave for the Continent within the month (Mama cried), but he will stay with us until then. Hurrah! I shall have an escort and good company!

There is, of course, so much more to be remembered, and far better words to impart. I can wait no longer to record them.

> As stars do glow in darkling skies,
> Doth candlelight anoint the shine
> Of ruby lips and sapphire eyes
> The beauty, love, that is but thine.

I have copied that most faithfully. I think it the loveliest verse I have heard. How very clever Mr. Baker is! He was pressed by his comrades to compose upon the spot. After a few moments of protest, which the others cruelly disregarded, he demanded a bit of paper and a pencil, closed his eyes (the blue of sapphires themselves, I noted after), and within an instant had composed those four lines.

I do not think I shall forget that moment. Every sconce, every candelabra in Lady Everard's salon was lit, reflected again and again in the mirrors on the walls. I was standing near Miss Hartnell (one does not wish to be alone in the midst of a ball, and <u>everyone</u> below the age of five-and-twenty or so seemed to be standing near Miss Hartnell), listening to the gentlemen complaining about the food at Almack's Assembly

Rooms. Sadly, I would not know of the food or anything else, as Mama has not been able to secure vouchers for us to attend the Wednesday balls.

Then Mr. Davison and Mr. McCoy procured punch for the ladies (I do not ordinarily care for rum punch, but this was mixed with champagne and cherries and was quite delicious), and they began to quiz Mr. Baker and demand verse. I would not suppose it was written for me, but I venture to believe I saw Mr. Baker's own eyes fall upon my person as Mr. McCoy read the lines aloud. Of course, my eyes are not the colour of sapphires. Perhaps if a poetic gentleman were to gaze deeply into them, he might be put in mind of topaz.

"Well writ!" called out another of his friends, a fat young man I believe is called Roggut. I am not certain that is truly his name. "But to whom?"

I do so admire an abundance of curls on a gentleman. Mr. Baker's are the colour of bronze, and he tosses them in a most becoming way. "I leave that for you to guess," he replied, or some similar words.

It became a game then, ladies and gentlemen alike calling out names. "Miss Hartnell!" was the first, of course. She blushed, red from chin to crown, and laughed. It could not have been her and all knew it. Her eyes are green. "Miss Eleanor Quinn." "Miss Henrietta Quinn." And so it went. "Princess Caroline!" cried Mr. Davison, and how we laughed, for everyone knows the Princess of Wales is a coarse, ugly creature.

"Perhaps 'tis Mr. Baker, himself," teased Miss Hartnell, which I do not think pleased him at all, though his companions thought it most diverting.

Then, Mr. Roggut offered, "Miss Percival!" and the game was done.

Mr. Baker smiled, bowed to me, and announced, "The subject shall remain a mystery, but the dance, I believe, should be mine if Miss Percival will consent."

Of course I did, thinking all the while that he might perhaps have been waiting for someone to cry out my name, waiting so he could request the dance. Perhaps.

How I dread a Boulanger when one has a special partner. There is so little time to converse as one must dance with all the other gentlemen in the circle. It seemed that every time Mr. Baker took my hand, it was to pass me to the next gentleman. We were barely able to comment on the great success of the ball (it was a terrible crush; I am certain Lady Everard was delighted), the heaviness of the weather, and the pleasant prospect of another such gathering soon, when it was all over, and Mama was waving for me to depart.

I consoled myself with the thought that it was the final dance of the evening. The Boulanger is always the last, when it is danced. Everyone knows that. And Mr. Baker chose to dance it with me.

The drive home was endless, despite the fact that our house is but a few streets away. The crush of carriages departing the Everards' meant we all moved like garden snails. Then, too, I was soon thoroughly disgusted with Charles and Nicholas Everard, who were to deposit Mama and me at home before going off to one of their clubs or gaming hells or wherever tedious gentlemen go in nearly the middle of the night.

I could not contain myself in my giddiness, but told the tale and recited Mr. Baker's lines aloud. How I wish I had not! Mama covered her lips with her fingertips—I am certain she was hiding a smile. Charles laughed aloud. And worst of all, Everard gave a terrible snort and declared Mr. Baker's beautiful words to be "nothing more than a second-rate imitation of Byron." As if he would comprehend such talent as Mr. Baker's if it were to smite him in his decidedly large nose! I refused to speak another word for the remainder of the drive.

I shall go to Hatchards booksellers and purchase a book of verse so that I may drop a line or two when next I am in the company of a poet. Perhaps ~~Dunne~~ ~~Done~~ Wordsworth. I will work very hard at my recitation. Poor Miss Cameron did try. This time, I shall not say, "I wandered lonely as a sheep" and think it amusing.

Tomorrow we are to dine with the Fitzhughs, Mama and me. How lovely it would be if Papa would come, too, but he is so very busy with his own entertainments and quite scorns ours. I asked if I could perhaps accompany him on a night when we are not engaged. He laughed and asked what a silly girl would do at his club, even if they were to allow me in. I suppose he is right. I cannot simply trail after him into Boodle's in the same way I am wont to follow him about at Percy's Vale, prattling away until he tells me to spare his ears.

Mama says Lady Sefton will be at the Fitzhughs' and will grant me a voucher to Almack's. Absolutely everyone who is anyone gathers on Wednesday nights to dance and be seen. I <u>must</u> have a voucher or my Season will be all but ruined. Lady Hartnell says every brilliant match begins there. Charles says many very dull evenings begin there, but I am certain he is teasing. I wish to meet the Prince of Wales and the Duke of Wharton and to dance again with Mr. Baker.

How I wish we could waltz! I have never seen it danced, but Charles has, in France. There it is as common as a Scottish reel. Here, only the most daring hostess will allow it and only the most daring will engage. Charles says the gentleman holds the lady by one hand and at the waist—sometimes so close to his own form that her skirts might tangle about his legs—and twirls her about the room. How very delicious it must be, and how very naughty!

13 May

It ought to have been a lovely day. And here is why:

~ Papa promised to take me for a drive in Hyde Park. He says everyone who is anyone drives in the Park on a sunny day. If I am to make a brilliant match, I must be Someone.

~ The first of my new dresses arrived—the white with green stripes. With the matching green spencer, it is the perfect dress to wear to the Park.

~ Three gentlemen called to see me. Mr. Davison, who is charming; Mr. Tallisker, who, as it turns out, is Roggut; and a Mr. Eccleston, whom I suppose I did meet at the Everards', but who was only very slightly familiar. They were all perfectly pleasant. It is very gratifying that they paid calls so early in our acquaintance. Quite flattering. I do not think I shall marry any of them.

~ I received a letter from Sarah Goodwin. Everything is much the same there in Percy's Vale. I am missed. She has a new hat.

My day has been spoiled completely. And here is why:

~ Nicholas Everard was here for luncheon today and was positively beastly. When I mentioned how sad we should all be if French fashions are not to be had again, he gave me quite the most unpleasant look and said how sad the French might be if French food and other basic necessities are not to be had. Again. Oh, why can he not take his luncheon elsewhere—perhaps in Scotland!

~ Papa did not return from his club until evening, long after anyone who is worth seeing or being seen by has left the Park. When he did arrive, it was with the very worst sort of news: Lord Chilham is in London.

Ain't No Sunshine

So here we go again. Rain. "Heavy in the Midlands and south, tapering off to light drizzle by midday." (*BBC One*. Contrary to reputation, they lie. It's past midday and pissing from the heavens.) I owe my firstborn (okay, second—assuming the first will be the future monarch of England) to Djenan for sending the latest Pressing Question That Will Change the World. Otherwise I might have succumbed to the boredom and done something rash and inexcusable. Like clean the loo, which Mom is demanding that I do. Or write poetry, of which she would probably wholly approve.

Okay, so I'm feeling rahther sorry for myself. Wallowing, even, in my sad solitude. Which, the (s)mother always sez, is the perfect time to think of the good stuff. Like the fact that there's plenty of money. Like the fact that I'm healthy as a horse (a dubious blessing at best on those exam days when a bit of invalidism would come in handy). Like the fact that when I'm with my dad, there are no curfews or demands or "But don't you already have enough jeans?" Like I have the very very very best gal pals in the whole world. Like Prince William is somewhere on this same little island. Like I'm single and available to become the future queen of said island.

Which, of course, brings to mind the fact that I'm single. That I'm single because I had my heart broken by Adam the Scum. By e-mail no less. The scum. That I'm stuck on this island with my (s)mother, without my friends. And no indication whatsoever that someday-while-I-still-have-all-my-wits-and-teeth My Prince (of Wales) Will Come. I am girl; hear me grumble. I want to stick my head out the window and, at the top of my lungs, demand of all of London: I feel like Cinderella; so where the hell is my prince????

Maybe one of the royal cousins will respond. Or even a not-royal. Just a cute English dude with okay teeth and a comprehensible accent. Not Prince Right, perhaps, but Prince You'll Do in the Interim.

Or maybe I'd actually get some answers. People like to answer questions. The prob, as we know, O my friends, is that voice (read: me) that tells me it's not okay to ask some of the questions I really want answers to. Bizarre? I mean, you're supposed to ask questions, right? From Big Bird to Mrs. Jones in the first grade (you remember her . . . the one who looked like Nosferatu but smelled like sugar cookies?) to good ol' Mom and Dad, we're told that the best way to figure something out is to ask questions. Why, then, can't I ask . . .

Adam the Scum: Why e-mail? Why, period? I mean, on top of being gag-worthy clichéd, "It's not you; it's me" is just absurd. Of course it was me. Guys don't break up with girls because they know they're just not ready for commitment, or need Me Time, or want to get that novel finished. They do it because they're just not that into the girl anymore. So what was it? My butt? My complete disinterest in Xbox, Red Bull, and anime? My uncertainty that you were the one I really wanted to lose my virginity to?

She-Who-Must-Not-Be-Named, her posse of Mean-alikes, and their ilk: Beyond the obvious questions, like: Lindsay Lohan—*really*?

And what on earth could you possibly have to text to the person sitting right next to you? And why, oh why Uggs with everything??? But the big one is: When did Being Honest (as in: "Well, I was just being *honest*! God, don't you think you might be a little *sensitive* here?") come to mean giving yourself permission to criticize, rant, and say all the nasty things the person you're being *"honest"* with really didn't want to know?

To my dad (via e-mail, as the soon-to-be-stepmonster sticks her formerly hooked nose into everything else): Why? Why this vapid, self-absorbed, image-obsessed creature almost twenty years younger than you? Are boobs really that important? If so, I'm doomed. Are brains a liability? Mine is notably bigger than my boobs.

To the (s)mother: Is this honestly what you envisioned? Year after year of teaching hungover former prepsters who won't remember a word you've said once the exam is over? Who, the second they've graduated, will relegate you to a mental smoothie composed of all the enthusiastic but now-faceless teachers who can't help them get a job on Madison Avenue? A summer reading the laundry lists of a woman who no one else remembers? I mean, really, what's the point?

Why don't I ask? you ask. I guess maybe I think I can't handle the truth. Ack. Enough already. I can only wallow for so long without a mochaccino or quick cruise of eBay. You never know what gently used Chloe bag or vintage Ray-Bans might appear.

So on to M's Pressing Question:

What Are Your Top Ten Worst Nightmares?

1. I will stop looking like Claire Danes's slightly-less-pretty sister, and will start looking like Jack Black's slightly-more-pretty brother.

2. No one will fall in love with me.

3. I will consistently fall in love with guys like Adam the Scum.

4. I won't get into college, and will end up living at home with my (s)mother.

5. I won't get into college, and will end up waiting tables somewhere where snooty college students leave bad tips, all while living at home with my (s)mother.

6. My (s)mother will wait only until the day after my dad marries the soon-to-be-stepmonster before falling in love with one of her grad students, probably half her age, probably French.

7. My dad, having taken me in, will be fatally poisoned by the evil now-stepmonster, who will inherit the apartment, the Beemer, and all monies that might keep me from having to sling burgers and beer for bad-tipping college students.

8. My friends will decide I am a version of She Who Must Not Be Named and will suddenly start hating me.

9. My friends will not start hating me, but I will be dragged thousands of miles away from them.

10. They will forget me.

I miss you all. I really, really, really miss you.

15 May

He came for dinner. I do not think Mama wished to invite him, but Papa says we must respect the connection, so I suppose we must. I thought, too, that since Papa does not object to his company, I must not either. He is Papa's cousin, after all, and he has a title. Sadly, Lord Chilham's being a baron would be rather more exciting were he not so objectionable.

I tried. For Papa, who is so certain in his tastes and acquaintance, I did try. As Lord Chilham arrived in a shiny new landau, I thought for a moment as I watched from the drawing-room window that perhaps he might have improved somehow. But no, he was much the same as when he visited us at Percy's Vale: spotty, thin except around the middle, his hair like a black pudding bowl, in a yellow coat and black-striped waistcoat. He resembled a wasp.

He quizzed me incessantly about myself. He wished to know whether I sing well, whether I have read all of Mrs. Clarke's instructions for the improvement of young ladies, who I believe one ought to know in Town, what sights are best for a young lady. All the while, he played with his dinner knife, turning it this way and that. His hands are nearly as bad as his waistcoat. They are small and pale, and he has little black hairs on his knuckles.

I do not care if he is a relation. I did not like him any better than before, and I did not like his questions. I gave such replies as "I cannot say," and "I do not know," and tried very hard not to look at him. I would very much have liked to say "I will not tell," but could feel Papa's frown growing. I was perhaps being too sensitive. Perhaps I ought to have been more forthcoming, but I just cannot think it was at all correct of Lord Chilham to ask me my fondest wish.

I have been excused to come to bed. Chilham is with Papa in the library. How unfair, that he should have such access to my father when I do not. Perhaps if I had a shiny landau, or a title...But that is neither here nor there.

I do not sing well. I loathed Mrs. Clarke's instructions. She believes the arm should always be covered and mothers should accompany their daughters everywhere.

It would be rather nice to know the Prince of Wales, I think. One should always cultivate the acquaintance of whoever is likely to become king. I would like to meet the new Lady Byron. What bliss it must be to be married to a great poet. I am certain their union is all that is romantic and sweet. I would very much like to have an audience with the Duke of Wellington, to scold him for carrying my brother off to his silly war. Shame on me. My journal shall not be spoiled by talk of war.

I wish to visit Vauxhall Gardens, where women walk on ropes high above the ground and fire bursts in the sky. Charles says it is like a nighttime fairgrounds in the midst of London. I wish to see the Marbles depicting nymphs and centaurs which Lord Elgin rescued from their crumbling Grecian temple. I wish to see more of Papa.

So I could easily have answered Lord Chilham's questions. Even the one he should never have asked.

My ~~only~~ fondest wish is to be beloved.

I Want Candy

Thank you, ever so much, darling Madame Alexandra, for sending me the e-mail listing thirty reasons I should be thrilled to be in London. Below, please note all the ways it was helpful.

Oh, wait. There *are* no ways. Golly.

But seriously, you fab brainiac, what did you do, read the entire Wikipedia entry on London? I was reluctantly impressed. And I even recognized some of the names from prissy Miss Kitty's diary: Hyde Park (No. 3 on your list) is pretty cool. Enormous and seriously green. People even go horseback riding there, right smack in the middle of the city. How veddy English. The Duke of Wellington's (27) house is on the edge of the Park. Maybe I'll go have a look-see. There's this huge statue of Napoleon there that Wellington took and put where everyone could see it. I wonder if the duke and his buds used to get drunk and dress it in women's clothes. Frat-boy behavior, 19th century style. Apparently the current duke still lives there, in some apartment the public doesn't get to see. Apparently the current duke has a cute grandson.

The Elgin Marbles (21) are in the BM. Yes, Alex, I do remember that they were stripped from ancient Greece's greatest temple and brought to England. Yes, I know your Pappous wants them sent back. Give him a hug for me—your grandma, too. As for the marbles, haven't seen 'em. (And losing mine, btw.) I have been to

Hatchards (9). Books. All books. More books than you can imagine. I bought a map. There's still some cool shopping on Bond Street (19). Kinda old stuff, like Cartier and Hermès, but I peeked into Jigsaw and saw some killer jeans. Size 10. English size 10. Maybe if I stopped eating chocolate . . .

Speaking of. Mr. Sadiq the newsagent introduced me to a new one yesterday: Cadbury Flake. So I introduced myself. Turns out he has a cousin in Pennsylvania. In Bethlehem, of all places, which he said has been known to cause the occasional family argument.

He's a pretty nice guy, Mr. Sadiq. He didn't charge me for the Flake, despite the fact that I think I really offended him when I asked if the picture behind the counter was Saddam Hussein. It's his brother in the pic. He's still in Iraq. Which is all Mr. Sadiq said on the subject. I don't think he approves of *Hello!*, either. He kinda holds it between the very tips of his fingers when he's putting it in a bag, and he's always listening to BBC radio. He told me Cadbury Flake (imagine, if you will, a ruffle in chocolate-bar form) is really best when crumbled over ice cream. He's right. Maybe if I just go easier on the chocolate . . . So here's a question for you, O my friends:

We've all read interviews where skinny starlets say they *looooove* chocolate, but have you ever seen one where they say they actually *eat* it?

On that note. Or not. I betcha none of you knew that Lord Byron had an eating disorder. Yup, the Bad Boy of all Romantic poets used to binge and purge. Apparently he also went through days when all he consumed was green tea and soda water, and would often sit down to a pile of lettuce dressed with vinegar, hold the oil. And we think New York fashionistas are a 21st century phenomenon.

Can you say "The Devil Wears Knee Breeches"? So that's what I learned today.

Here's what I forgot:

✦ My keys. With an hour to go before Mom would be home.

✦ My "mobile" (cell phone). Ditto.

✦ That there really is a great big park a (shot-putter's) stone's throw away.

✦ Cute boys can frequently be found kicking around a football in a park.

✦ "Football" here is soccer.

✦ Soccer can be fun to watch for an hour. Especially when cute boys are playing.

And . . .

✦ Netflix doesn't deliver to the UK. Hence *The Lovely Bones*, *Say Anything*, and Season Two, Disc One of *Twin Peaks* are, as I type, in the Philly apartment with the rest of our mail, where they will remain, unwatched (unless the Kazakhstani professor is opening our stuff) for the next ten weeks. Sheesh.

That's me, the Cadbury Flake.

Smiley Faces

Lord Byron really was a hottie. Even by 21st century standards. Who knew?

Mom took the morning off from the BM and we went to the National Portrait Gallery. I gotta say, it was pretty cool. It's all about faces, really, famous ones. So you walk in and up these grand stairways, and it's just a museum: parquet floors, walls painted eggshell blue or eggplant or forest green, all these big gold frames. Then you *look*, and there's Henry VIII, fat and smug-looking, and you just *know* who it is because he's the second one you learn about in English History (after Queen Elizabeth I, his daughter, and looking at his face, you know it would have totally chapped his hide to know his daughter is the first). So there's Henry, surrounded by all his wives, including the two he had beheaded, and they're all in these heavy, heavy dresses covered with pearls, and none of them are very pretty, and I gotta say, after Anne Boleyn, they all look a little bit anxious.

More things gleaned from a day staring at portraits of famous British people:

✦ Shakespeare had an earring.

✦ David Beckham has two.

✦ If you look into Mary Queen of Scots's eyes, you can imagine her wanting to rule all of Britain.

- If you look into Elizabeth I's eyes, you can imagine her knocking off Mary without a second thought.

- You get the sense, judging from all the fur on everybody, that life in all those castles was a tad chilly. Small island, big ambition, big enemies. Hence a propensity for making themselves look as big as possible (you know, like a puffer fish or puffed-out cat). Big hats, big hair, big skirts, big codpieces (you look it up).

- Winston Churchill didn't always look like a bulldog.

- Queen Victoria kinda did.

- There's lots of really cool, bling-y footwear in English history. On the men.

- Queen Elizabeth II needs a stylist in the worst way.

So, Mom and I are walking through the galleries, and my heels are making this embarrassingly loud clacking against this pristine floor, and then we're in the Regency room, and there's all this Byron. Byron looking pensive, Byron looking exotic, Byron looking kinda pale (marble bust). And cute. "Mad, bad, and dangerous to know," one of his lovers called him. I think I get it.

Then there are these glass-topped display cases with big, black fabric flaps over them. You lift the flaps to see what's inside. Mostly little oval portraits Mom sez were painted so people could carry them around, like we do in our wallets (I really have to remember to take that pic of me when I was two and they'd put me in a ladybug costume out of her wallet before she shows it to one more total stranger). And there's the one famous portrait of

Jane Austen. Just a small sketch, a pinched little face above these faint, crossed arms. Like she's cold, or doesn't want to be posing.

Okay, okay, so I'm boring you. But go check it out. At least check out the cute poet: www.npg.org.uk

One more thing. Mom's subject, Mary Percival, is there, in that case. Not 'cause she was famous. She wasn't. But the guy who painted the portrait, J.M.W. Turner, was. Major art museum, back-of-playing-cards famous. Mom thinks he was in love with her. Maybe. Either she really was that beautiful—masses of dark hair and this look that totally says *I can teach you really important things*—or the guy with the paintbrush was seriously smitten. Kinda cool. It was painted in 1806. Mom sez she was 35. She died before she was 45. Kinda sad.

Anyway. Gotta go Google restaurants for my b-day. Dad will go for something "dead posh" (translation: "way fancy"). He'll be here for almost a whole week. I see some honest-to-goodness shopping in my future. What does one desire most at seventeen . . . ?

July 2

Say

And here's a golden oldie for all you hopeless romantics out there. This one goes out from "George" to his "Mysterious Lady." He wants to know if she'll meet him tonight under the statue of Eros in Piccadilly Square . . .

> *She walks in beauty, like the night*
> *Of cloudless climes and starry skies,*
> *And all that's best of dark and bright*
> *Meets in her aspect and her eyes . . .*

Wow.

Found that in the one book on the shelf that does not revolve around mushrooms. Byron soitenly had a way with words. I guess that might give me a little tingle if someone wrote it for me.

Off to the BM. Mom's got some toothless and decrepit descendant of the Percivals coming in, who, as it turns out, lives in London. She thinks I'll want to be there. Because I'm reading the diary, of course. I can wing it, right? It worked in Mr. Desmond's class when I'd only read the first three chapters of *The Grapes of Wrath*. Unlike Adam the Scum (hmm . . . betcha this bookshelf has a tome on his ilk), I didn't invoke the thematic significance of wine throughout the novel. This time, however, I'll mention rum punch a few times, invoke Byron, and no one will be the wiser.

Sigh.

My social life has really hit rock bottom when I start rhapsodizing about a guy who's been dead for almost two hundred years. And who probably quietly preferred boys to girls anyway. It's lonely out here, folks.

July 3

Eh, Eh (Nothing Else I Can Say)

Interesting turn of events. As it turns out, "descendant" does not necessarily mean "toothless" or "decrepit." As in, "The aforementioned descendant of the Percival family turns out to be a young gentleman, perhaps eighteen years of age, who might well, if one is neither completely blind nor utterly devoid of taste, be described as *not half bad*."

His name is William (*hee!*) Percival, known as Will. He is, by my estimation, six feet tall, remarkably blue-eyed, and has a real, honest-to-goodness dimple in his right cheek. Which I saw as the result of him laughing at me. Not in a totally bad way. I mean, he did actually help me up when I went flat onto my butt in front of him.

No, no, allow me to set the scene for you.

I'm half an hour late, having just navigated the recesses of the BM—starting from a notably small side door, down several corridors that would make a mouse dizzy, up two flights of stairs and down another (I'll say this for the people who work at the BM: unfortunate workplace nickname aside, they are *extremely* helpful; a very short, tweeded-out gentleman who looked just like a mole actually guided me through the last half-mile maze), to just the sort of double glass-and-wood doors you'd expect to see in the bowels of this particular museum. "Dr. Vernon's quarters," sez Mole, with a cute little twitch of his nose. He totally belonged in a BBC costume drama.

I figure, I don't have to knock. Dr. Vernon is, after all, my (s)mother. So I heave open the doors, take one step into the room (one dusty window, dust, dust, more dust, and a couple of dusty tables with dusty stuff piled on them), and *bam!*, my feet go out from under me and next thing I know, I'm sitting down—*hard*—almost at the feet of this demigod who, from the look of the open mouth and outstretched arms, either tried to catch the flailing behemoth (read: me) that came flying at him, or stop it (read: me) from bowling him over.

And my (s)mother, the one person who is supposed to shelter and protect me at all costs, to imply to all others that the sun shines out of my butt, doesn't miss a beat. "William," she sez, only just managing not to smile, "my daughter, Catherine. Cat, this is William Percival. He might be able to help me find Mary's missing letters, so we're being extra nice to him."

I think Tall, Dark, and Handsome tried not to smile. He failed. Then he said, "Old floors, terrible hazard," only it sounded like "flaws" and "teddible hazahd," gave me his hand, and pulled me up without even the tiniest grunt, and I swear I saw stars that had nothing to do with having gone down hard. Where *do* they learn to talk like that? And why, oh why, did I give up ballet in second grade?

What I really want to know is why nothing else in that place has been cleaned in a century—but someone decides to wax the floor.

Then Mom (and OMG, this was way worse than me falling!) actually said . . . *(prepare to cringe)*, "I'm going to leave you two alone for a minute while I talk to Dr. Furball." I think she added something about Dr. Furball being *impossible* to catch (and I think it's actually Firble), but that horrible roar of humiliation was filling my ears by that point and I was praying for the waxed floor to open up and swallow me.

We're used to smooth Englishmen in the movies. I expected this very very English dude to be smooth. So smooth and unconcerned by the (s)mother's unspeakably embarrassing behavior that he would whip out a chair for me and gracefully tell me all about his country estate, the mahvelous standing of the pound in the world economy, and why foxhunting really isn't so bahd, hence making me forget that I am the graceless spawn of a clueless she-devil.

He was grinning like an idiot. (*Oh, that DIMPLE!*) He did, however, clear off part of a desk for us to lean against, and ask me how I'm liking England.

I'm guessing Mom was gone for five minutes. Here's what he learned about me in that short time:

- I do not particularly like England (his home, the home of his ancestors, the home of the Queen, her corgis, and Cadbury).

- the names of my best friends, favorite chocolate bars, pond-algae ex-boyfriend, and dog.

- I think the National Portrait Gallery is kinda like looking at a yearbook from the school you didn't get into (do they even *have* yearbooks here?).

- my mother is a hostile alien and must be destroyed.

- my father is cool, but his habit of arriving forty-five minutes late to pick me up from ballet class every time somewhat hastened the demise of my balletic career.

- I currently inhabit a "flat" full of books on fungus.

- I am genetically incapable of keeping my mouth shut.

So I finally ran out of breath, or my brain kicked back in, or something, and I shut up. He smiled and maybe, maybe was going to say something I would like. Then his cell rang and he very politely, with the appropriate apology, answered it. His face promptly lit up and, although he very politely, and with the appropriate apology, told whoever was at the other end that he was busy, he arranged to call them back in fifteen minutes and hung up. As if on cue, Mom reappeared. The rest goes something like this:

William: "I'm afraid I have to be going. It was a great pleasure meeting you, Catherine."

Me: "Erk." (or something to that effect)

William: "Dr. Vernon, I hope those papers will be of some help to you."

Mom: "I'm sure they will. Thanks so much for bringing them. Are you sure you can't stay and join us for lunch? Catherine?"

Me: "Erk." (or something to that effect)

William: "I wish I could, but . . ."

And then he was gone.

Here's what I learned about him:

Nada.

I will never see this boy again. If he sees me, he will run screaming. When I see me, *I* will run screaming. My butt hurts. Ain't life just a bag of gummy worms left open in the sun?

16 May

Someone gave this charade to Mr. Pertwee, who gave it to Miss Quinn, who gave it to Miss Hartnell, who gave it to me. I confess I have been puzzling over it for quite some time, with no success. How very vexing! I believe I know well enough how <u>my</u> Season shall end, but I daresay I will find this riddle most diverting nonetheless.

<u>How Seasons May End, by A Gentleman</u>

My first may come before your Comfort or your Pleasure.
My second leads you, Miss, and begins your Vow.
My third, after your Needle, is a skill one might treasure.
My last shall be behind you should you Commit or Depart now.

Charles imbibed too much port last night and said one good riddle would quite do his head in. Mama is so clever at this sort of thing, but she is unwell and has taken to her bed with her chamomile tisane and her lap desk. With much reluctance, I showed it to Nicholas when he arrived to collect Charles (who is not so ill, apparently, that he cannot attend the races). He gave it the most cursory glance, and when I complained that I have been trying to work it out all <u>morning</u> to no avail, and that I believe I shall do best to put it aside, the wretched man merely said, "Not at all. In your case, you would do best to try harder."

He would do best to try harder as well—at any semblance of civility!

I am quite out of sorts now. I believe I shall take my needlepoint and go sit in the garden. I feel the urge to impale something.

(What's So Funny 'Bout) Peace, Love and Understanding

Part Un: Grosvenor Square

The scene:

Me. Still utterly humiliated by my disastrous meeting with the cute English boy. Thinking I'll go to Hyde Park and either drown myself in the Serpentine, the little river that runs through it (note to all who might care: the Serpentine is apparently only waist-deep at most points), or head farther south and gaze longingly at the Harvey Nicks cosmetic counters. I'm feeling a blue (liner) moment coming on.

And I gotta get some walking in. Cadburys, y'know.

So southward do I tromp. Right into Grosvenor Square, as usual, home of the American embassy and antiwar protests. There's one going on, as usual, but also as usual, I didn't pay any attention to the date when I got up this morning. Check the date, ladies. This was the biggest, loudest, angriest protest I've personally ever seen.

So I've kinda forgotton about eye shadow for the moment. I'm standing next to this incredibly pretty girl who looks like she should be in a Bollywood musical, only she's wearing cargo pants and a killer silver shirt with a peace sign on it, and thinking I would give up chocolate forever to have her boobs, and just deciding I had to ask where she bought her shirt when this crazy big black car complete with tinted windows and motorcycle escort comes driving out of some hidden orifice. The police (I dunno if they were all really the police or something far more serious, 'cause they had guns . . . like no bobbies the BBC ever showed us) are holding the crowd back. Like anyone's really pushing. Just lots of shouting, much of which I wouldn't repeat. Half because I couldn't understand what they were saying (I don't think "oigly" is a word, even in Cockney), and half because it was so angry (several possible new meanings for "slag" discovered) I felt it in my stomach.

Then I see this little tiny girl—not really a girl, I guess. Maybe eighteen, but *tiny*. Hair like a baby chick—you know, yellow, and fluffy and spiky at the same time. She had on this huge, shocking pink jacket that made her look even smaller, but totally made her visible. So she wiggles her way to the front, all five foot nothing of her. And heaves something at the car. At first I thought it was a bomb. I think a lot of people thought it was a bomb, judging from the number of angry folk who suddenly looked terrified and hit the deck. Then I thought it might be a paintball, 'cause it hit the windshield with a huge splat. An actual splat. And the car was covered with something wet and red, and people were gasping and laughing and cheering.

She threw a grapefruit.

Her aim was incredible. So was her arm. The Phillies could use her in center field. But what I kept thinking, *keep* thinking, is how incredibly *enraged* this little tiny person must have been to throw a piece of fruit with so much force that it was pulverized. Wow.

Of course the police were right there, shoving into the crowd after her, but more Bollywood: everyone squeezed in, a big, colorful, rippling wave of people moving inward, swallowing her completely. She was just . . . gone.

The minute after was the weirdest thing. Everyone stepped back, quiet and orderly, and so polite that you just knew you were in London. Then someone shouted, *"Hey, hey, U.S.A., you don't rule the world today!"* and it all erupted again.

Suddenly Hyde Park didn't seem quite so appealing. Fuzzy socks and a corner of the sofa, yup. Chocolate, absolutely. Eye shadow, not so much. I decided to pay a visit to Mr. Sadiq, stock up on Curly Wurlies, and comb the BBCs for some reruns of *All Creatures Great and Small*.

I don't know if it really was there, but as I headed back toward Oxford Street, I thought I saw an empty pink jacket crumpled on the ground at the edge of the square. People kept stepping on it. It's seriously un-sunny today. Someone that little will be cold.

Part Deux: Mr. Sadiq's shop

I was debating between Curly Wurlies and Bounty. Mr. Sadiq had, with a small smile and no prompting, put an *OK!* in a bag (I've already read the current *Hello!*), and was waiting patiently for me to make my choc choice.

"May I suggest something a bit different today?" he asked after I'd walked back and forth in front of the display for five minutes.

I never got to hear what his suggestion was. The door of the shop banged open, and a girl breezed in. The gorgeous, peace-chested girl from the protest. She didn't see me, but lifted herself half over the counter, smooched Mr. Sadiq on the cheek, and then started talking a mile a minute. I expected her voice to be lyrical, musical, full of cardamom and cinnamon and silk.

So smack me for stereotyping. She sounded like Keira Knightley.

"It was brilliant, Dad! There were thousands of people and

all the press, and I swear I saw Robbie Williams in the scrum. The police could barely hold us back, and then this titchy little thing chucks a grapefruit—"

"Elizabeth." Mr. Sadiq didn't raise his voice, but she stopped and followed his eyes. And saw me. "Catherine, this is my daughter, Elizabeth. Elizabeth, this is Catherine. She—"

"Was there today!" Her huge eyes literally sparked. "Wasn't it brill? The Yanks couldn't possibly ignore *that*! Didn't you just *love* the grapefruit?"

"Elizabeth," Mr. Sadiq said again, and this time we both heard the warning.

"What?" she demanded.

"Do you think she got away okay?" I asked. And her jaw dropped.

"You're American!" Not said in that *"Oh, cool, you must know all about hip-hop"* kinda way.

"Elizabeth!" Mr. Sadiq snapped.

"Well, she is!"

"I am," I agreed, in her defense rather than mine. I realized that as little as I knew about Elizabeth Sadiq, I knew she was someone I could be friends with. Maybe it was the fab clothing, or the gold streaks in her wild, endless hair. Or the fact that she had a Razor Apples button on her messenger bag. "Our chocolate is complete pants," I said. It's a line I took from last week's *Eastenders*. Only there, Stacey (resident biatch-just-needing-to-be-loved was referring to her husband's sexual prowess). "I'm emigrating." Then: "The grapefruit was pretty impressive, but your shirt is brilliant."

It was a long moment while she sized me up. Then she laughed. "Five quid in Oxford Street," she confided cheerfully. "Public objection is no excuse for bad presentation, but I'm not paying good money for something that might get ripped in the crush."

"My Elizabeth is changing the world one photographic opportunity at a time." There was pride in Mr. Sadiq's voice, behind the teasing. I wonder how Dad would respond if I were suddenly to go activist. Betcha he would laugh. The stepmonster-to-be would probably be confused by the similarity to the word "active" and try to get me interested in pink spandex and spinning.

"For all the opportunity I'll get to change anything in Aberystwyth." Elizabeth shrugged. "You at university?"

And I told her. About being a senior-in-waiting. About the (s)mother and the BM and this blog. I almost told her about Will, but caught myself. She's starting college in Wales ("West of Nowhere," she calls it) in August, is going to be a lawyer ("a barrister, as soon as they get rid of the god-awful wigs"), and is spending the summer alternating between selling processed food matter for her father and protesting several great evils. Today was the current situation in Pakistan and Afghanistan. I could tell she still wasn't sure about me. About my being American. I could tell she was dying to ask about my politics. I suspect her father's very polite, slightly formal influence was holding her back. Although considering the fact that she's got so much . . . *vavoom* (I dunno, do people say *"vavoom"* anymore?), I'm surprised she doesn't burst something. I doubt much constrains her.

I fingered a *Times*, wondering if it would just be too obvious a plea for admiration if I were to buy a newspaper. She can lift one eyebrow at a time. I've always wanted to be able to do that. *"Guardian* or *Spectator?"* she asked, a tad slyly, I might add. It took me a sec to realize she wasn't quizzing me on which I am in the workings of the world. I know one of the papers is liberal, the other conservative. But for my life I couldn't remember which is which. If I ever knew.

I snuck a peek at a *Guardian*. I recognized the face on the front. And took a chance. "I'm a *Hello!* girl, myself, but I think Al Gore's pretty fab for a grandad."

"Well, that's okay, then." Elizabeth grinned and I felt like an eight-year-old. I so want her to be my friend. *Pleasepleaseplease.* "Give me your number. I'll ring you next time I'm objecting to something."

I didn't notice till I got home that Mr. Sadiq had slipped a Dairy Milk bar into my bag.

23 May

There is little as wretched as a party that ends too soon.

It all began well enough. I was quite gratified by the persons in attendance at Mrs. Stuart's supper dance. I spied Mr. Baker immediately upon arriving. He was leaning against the mantel in the drawing room, looking far too handsome in his black coat and white breeches. Surrounded as he was by gentlemen all dressed in much the same way, he quite outshone all present. I confess the ribbon about my waist suddenly seemed to have been tied too tightly.

Why, I feel compelled to ask, do young gentlemen so often stand about in packs, muttering and chortling among themselves? They do it in the country, and I should not have expected them to do so as well in Town, but they do. I cannot imagine they have much of interest to discuss. Horses? Business? How terribly dull. But there they stood, for what seemed an eternity, appearing as comfortable as if it were their home and hearth, while I stood <u>not</u> comfortable, <u>not</u> quite chatting with Miss Winnie Stuart, who is perfectly pleasant but, I feel compelled to note, is just the sort of earnest, bookish girl one does not want to be standing with while hoping to attract the attention of the likes of Mr. Baker and his set. She would insist on recommending some Scottish novel called <u>Waverley</u>. Even worse, she must accompany her discourse with flailing arms. She looked as if a bee were trying to interrupt her tale of tartans and haggis. Her excitement probably matched exactly my embarrassment. I wished to be noticed, but not because of silly Miss Stuart and her imaginary bee swatting.

I was quite ready to ease myself miserably behind the nearest potted plant, when suddenly, at last, Mr. Baker glanced my way. I had thought he must have seen me before, but I had been watching him quite intently, and though he several times tossed his curls and angled his face in such a way that he should have spied me, he clearly did not. For this time, he smiled the most bone-melting, slow smile, and levered himself from the mantel. I believe I stopped breathing entirely as he approached.

I barely heard Miss Stuart say, "How very handsome he is! Just as one would imagine Waverley."

"Perhaps," I agreed, trying to sound ~~noncal~~ nonchalant, as if gentlemen such as Mr. Baker (and dramatic Scottish novels) were quite ordinary. Miss Stuart is hardly competition, but still—

He greeted her first, which I suppose was correct, as it was her home, but it rather rankled. Especially as the entire encounter lasted no longer than a blink and consisted almost entirely of the expected pleasantries anyone under the age of ~~five-and-twenty~~ five-and-thirty abhors and which any of the rabbit-eared matrons standing guard would demand to hear. He was delighted to see us both, wasn't the weather uncommonly fine, what better way to pass an evening than among such pleasant company? Then, finally, at last, he requested a dance. Of course, he had to include Miss Stuart, and she is not quite so silly as to refuse, but it was from me that he requested the quadrille. Which, while miserably short, allows for the most time with one's partner. The most conversation. The most clasping of hands. How I wish the waltz were not so scandalous! I think I should very much like twirling about the floor in Mr. Baker's arms.

My acceptance was far too quick and eager. I reminded myself immediately, and repeat now: I must not be eager. I <u>must</u> not be eager. <u>I must not be eager</u>. I must be cool and reserved and, like Miss Hartnell, behave for all the world as if Mr. Baker were just any other gentleman.

I might just as well try to pretend that diamonds are just another bit of rock.

"He is clearly taken with you," Miss Stuart said as he walked away. She said it quite wistfully, I believe, and in the moment I felt very fond of her, plain bookish creature that she is.

"Oh, nonsense," I managed to reply brightly. As if they were just words like any others. Yet I played them again and again in my head through supper, which I could scarcely eat for nerves.

He was true to his word. At the first strains of the quadrille, he was there to lead me onto the floor. He has a poet's hands, narrow and elegant, and meant to clasp objects like a pen without so much as bending the feather.

For the first several turns we exchanged more of those elderly, expected words. How well the musicians played. How pleasant to be on the floor when it is not overly crowded. How unfortunate that the quadrille is not a longer dance. I liked that exchange very well. He asked how I was finding London, if town houses such as this one did not seem overly cramped when compared with the splendour he had heard was Percy's Vale.

Then: "I have been looking forward to just such a moment in your company," he announced. "I seek an angel of mercy, Miss Percival, and wonder if you might be she."

"Mercy?" I answered. "Have you done me a disservice, sir? You have not yet trodden on my toes." Oh, to be Elizabeth Bennet now. It is near impossible to be clever at the moments when it is most important!

He did smile. "Well, at this moment, I may say only that my disservice is to Beauty. My most recent attempts at verse have been pale, ill-nourished things. Give me sustenance, Miss Percival, and I shall compose."

I must confess I am still not entirely certain of his meaning. Was he speaking of my beauty? Did he require words? Or perhaps a tea cake? How I wish I had a friend whose counsel I might ask! Even if Annabel and the Miss Goodwins were not so far away, they would have no answer for me. None of them have ever met the likes of Mr. Thomas Baker. There was something in his very, very blue eyes that teased, and I was terrified that no matter how I replied, it would be wrong.

"I am not an angel," I squeaked, and promptly tripped over my own feet.

He steadied me. "Even better," he replied, and the dance was over. He led me from the floor. "I believe we are not finished with each other yet, Miss Percival."

I did not mind in the least when he led Miss Stuart into the next set. It was, after all, her house. And her brother—a nice enough fellow if one does not mind his being extremely short—was right there to request the dance.

I would have floated, had he not turned the wrong way twice and stepped on my toes once. Then I was paired with Charles for one turn (he pinched me, as he has done every time since we were made to practice our minuets in the nursery), and Nicholas for another (smug beast, all he said was "Solved the riddle yet?" before swanning off back to the overblown earl's daughter with whom he was partnered). When I looked again, Mr. Baker was nowhere to be seen.

Yes, Nicholas, you arrogant toad, I have solved the riddle. And my Season shall <u>not</u> end in "Disappointment." Not while I have the brains and breath and nicely pink cheeks to prevent it. I am going to be a smashing Success.

Mr. Stuart kindly offered to fetch me some rum punch. As I waited, I tried not to look as if I were looking for anyone. I certainly did not mean to eavesdrop, but could not help but hear the conversation of two gentlemen behind me. I expect half of Grosvenor Square heard them.

"Where has Fenwick gone?" the first demanded.

"Off to hunt at Almack's," came the reply. I became quite interested then. "His cupboards are bare and the doors close at eleven. Fellow's got to feed himself somehow."

"Good Lord, why there? The drink is miserable and the food worse!"

"Not that sort of food, you noddy, nor that sort of hunt."

"Ah. Of course. Poor Fenwick."

More food that . . . well, wasn't. I could not make sense of their words, and certainly cannot see why anyone should pity a friend with an entrée into Almack's. I envy them so.

I noticed then that a small group of gentlemen were leaving through the far door. My heart quite literally dropped when I spied a shock of bronze curls among them. They were truly leaving. In that moment, I realised that several familiar persons remained absent from the party: Miss Hartnell, the Miss Quinns, Mr. Troughton. Just the sort of well-heeled, impeccably connected sort one would expect at Almack's. I had been too preoccupied to realise they had never arrived. No doubt they would soon be joined by the others, quitting a secondary entertainment for a better one. I should have recognised the Almack's required dress on half the gentlemen: black coats and white breeches.

I watched them go, chattering happily all the while: Mr. McCoy, Mr. Tallisker. Mr. Baker. A flock of magpies, ending the party for me, flying where I could not.

24 May

I cannot decide whose company I find more ~~uncomfortable~~ objectionable: Lord Chilham's or Sir Nicholas Everard's. They were both in attendance at the opera tonight, Chilham a guest in our box and Nicholas might as well have been, he spent so much of the performance there. I should have liked to have sat beside Papa, but he took the seat behind me, and when I looked back after the overture, it was empty. "Important matters," he said vaguely when I quizzed him upon his return at the end of the opera. "Trust me, Katherine, I left you in the most worthy of hands."

I would have been happy to send Nicholas off to be less than charming elsewhere. But that would have left me alone with the odious Chilham. He sat to one side of me, smelling of vinegar and looking like a frog with his tight green coat and bandy legs. He would not cease with his constant suggestions. I should accompany him to view the antiquities at the British Museum. The stone pots are most exquisite. I should raise my shawl and sit farther from the curtain lest there be a draft. I should no doubt prefer to be home with a nice book (to which I very nearly replied that I would no doubt prefer to be home with a nice cold if it meant being away from him). I should allow him the liberty of choosing those books most suited to a young lady of my stature.

Chilham: "May I suggest Crabbe?"

Nicholas, who thankfully has always smelled pleasantly of forest: "Katherine does not care for poetry unless it is composed to the perfection of her toes." I resisted the urge to kick him in the ankle.

Chilham, trying to get a glimpse, I suppose, of my feet, nearly leaning into my lap: "Well, as long as it is not that romantical drivel every man and his valet seems to be spouting these days. Terrible for the female mind." He leaned farther.

Nicholas: "I quite agree. Stop squirming, Katherine. You are not a child and you are spoiling the show."

As if anyone actually pays attention to the opera. Who on earth would want to? People in the pit below jostle each other, sing along badly, and watch those of us sitting above. We watch each other. I was nearly certain I had spied Mr. Tallisker in a box to our right. And where he is to be found—

Chilham: "A lady's mind is so much better turned to matters of deference and obedience."

Nicholas: "Give me back my glasses, Katherine. I need them."

He most certainly did not. He could at least have pretended that he wished to view the stage. Instead, I know perfectly well he was gazing at the ladies in the box opposite ours. One was the earl's daughter from last night. She has spots. I could see them perfectly even without opera glasses. When I suggested he might have a much better view from his own seat next to his mama, he had the gall to laugh. Then he guided my chin until I could see his mother. The seat beside her was occupied by a woman of her own age, with a rather sweet face.

Nicholas: "Maria Sefton. Patroness of Almack's, you know."

Chilham: "Allow me to lend you my glass, Cousin Katherine."

It was cold and slightly slippery. It gave me a very good view of the nicest of the patronesses, the one most likely to give a ticket to a desperate debutante. As I watched, she rose, kissed Lady Everard on the cheek, and wandered off. I tried to follow her progress. Without meaning to at all, I caught the eye of Miss Hartnell. She smiled very prettily at me. She insists on doing that. I still do not like her.

25 May

Mama ~~forb~~ did not wish for me to go to the Bellinghams'. She says they are a stupid couple, with stupider friends, and that their balls are overcrowded, uncontrolled, and attended by persons with whom an intelligent woman does not want to associate. She would not say more, but simply announced that we would not be attending.

I pestered Charles until he told me that the Bellinghams, while quite accepted among High Society, run with a "fast" crowd, including the Prince of Wales and his mistress. I have not yet seen the Prince, but two of his brothers were at the theatre last night. I was terribly disappointed. Both are fat with enormous whiskers. I know the Prince is fat as well, but he is, for all purposes, the King while his father descends deeper into his madness, and a king is a king.

Mama has met the Prince on several occasions. She says he put her in mind of an Arabian lamp: shiny, beautifully decorated, and not nearly bright enough for the job at hand. Papa and the Prince belonged to the same club for some years. Papa thinks him a splendid, fun fellow, and once lost his diamond cravat pin to him in a game of hazard. I do not know why Mama was so incensed; it was merely a piece of jewelry.

I, as Mama has frequently asserted, am more than bright enough when I decide to be. I wanted to attend the ball. Why should I not? Besides, I overheard part of yet one more row between Mama and Papa. She was obviously commenting on my immaturity and pale-lamp tendencies; he retorted that I am "eighteen, a woman, and more than ready for the responsibilities expected of a young lady in her place." I would have rushed in and kissed him, but did not want to give away that I had been eavesdropping.

As he said, I am eighteen. I know, as Papa so clearly does, that I am more than mature enough to decide what I shall wear, which parties I shall attend, and with whom I will associate. So when I told Charles that he must accompany me to the Bellinghams' tonight, as Mama had taken to her bed, I did so without the least guilt. After all, I was not lying. She was indisposed; I could not very well go alone.

Charles was rather cross with me, as I took a very long time to get ready. He'd intended to meet several of his fellow Hussars at some silly gentlemen's entertainment. But he had promised me first that he would escort me to the ball, and he does not break a promise. His regiment will have all of him soon enough. Charles is rather splendid, and I would say the same even if he were not my brother.

The carriages were so tightly crowded in the Bellinghams' street that it would have taken us less time to walk from our house. But I was wearing my new yellow silk dress and had spent an hour being certain my hair curled just so. I would not have either mussed, so Charles had no choice but to tolerate the hackney ride. Once there, I was nearly overwhelmed. Everything not moving in the house was draped with red fruits and gold chains and rather hungry-looking vines. Guests filled the halls and spilled from every doorway. I have never seen such bright colours and jewels on a gathering—ladies and gentlemen alike; with the many crystal chandeliers, it was nearly blinding.

"God help me," Charles groaned, and flagged down a footman with a tray of champagne. He downed his in a swallow. I would not be so crass. Champagne is delicious and must be savoured, ~~three sips, at least~~. "Well, come on, then," he grumbled, and pulled me through the crowd. There were more footmen everywhere, and more champagne.

Charles pointed out people as we passed. Yet another of the King's sons. A Russian duchess, an Italian prince. Beau Brummell, famous for being famous, and whose criticism of a lady's appearance may consign her to the social netherworld. Lord Gratham, who had married a great heiress and was suspected of driving her to insanity with laudanum. His mistress, Charles whispered, was reputed to be slipping bits of arsenic into his whisky decanters. I do love my brother.

I confess I merely gawked for the longest time. Then I spied the Miss Quinns with Mr. Eccleston. They all appeared quite pleased to see me. Soon, we were quite a jolly group, joined by Mr. Tallisker and Mr. Davison, who were so gallant as to make certain I danced my fill and was not without champagne. How merry we all were! Charles went off to drink with his friends, leaving me delightfully un-spied-upon. And then, none too soon, Mr. Baker appeared.

He looked very handsome, as always, and greeted me most warmly. Then, for the next hour, he did not talk to me at all. He laughed with his fellows. He danced with both Quinns. He bowed nearly to the floor when Miss Hartnell arrived, dressed in an aqua confection that made me nearly green with envy. He composed an ode on the spot to Miss Partridge's swanlike neck.

It was not his best work.

I was introduced to a Mr....Oh, bother his name. Brown, or White, or Black, perhaps. Perhaps none of them. But he was quite a bit older, six-and-twenty, at least, and very nearly very handsome. Blond curls, the brownest eyes (now I do not think his name could have been Brown, after all), a smile that curled up at the edges. He complimented my dress, brought me a lobster canape and an odd, greenish drink that tasted strongly of liquorice, and wished to dance.

It was then that Charles and his fellow Hussars decided to leave for other entertainments. He tried to insist on taking me home first, and would not be put off until one of the Misses Quinn—I confess I was suddenly having the oddest difficulty telling them apart—promised her mama would convey me home in her carriage. I still do not think Charles liked the matter, but it was so very noisy, we begged most prettily, and his friends were tugging at him. "No more champagne!" he said, although I thought he was teasing, and I stuck my tongue out at him as he went. Then he was gone, and I had another of the liquorice drinks, and although I know it was not at all proper, guided Mr. Whomever a bit when we were on the floor, so that we danced very near Mr. Baker and Miss Partridge. I laughed heartily at Mr. Whomever's jests to show just what a marvelous time I was having. I danced with more enthusiasm than I ever have. I made certain to swish my skirts and lift them just that tiniest bit higher to show off my ankles and Spanish silk stockings.

And I made quite certain we passed Mr. Baker as we walked out of the ballroom and onto the balcony.

"You'll do" is all Mr. Whomever said.

I cannot remember the man's name, but I remember quite clearly that the buttons on his waistcoat were wood meant to look like ivory, and when he pulled me against his chest, they hurt.

I suddenly did not want him to kiss me. I did not want my first kiss to be from a man whose name I did not recall, who wore built-up heels and had oily spots on his cravat.

His hands were everywhere at once, in several places they ought not to have been. I wished to scream, to call him every vile name I knew, but I was certain that if I opened my mouth, I would be sick all over him. I tried to pull away and felt my sleeve tear, heard that sad sound of rending silk. And then suddenly I was free and he was sitting on the stone floor of the balcony. I wondered for a moment if I had hit him, and then I saw Nicholas.

He was looming over the other man, looking quite fierce and completely disgusted. For a fleeting moment, I saw him as utterly splendid. My friend and hero. And then he turned to look at me, and his expression did not change a whit. He was just as fierce, and every bit as disgusted.

"Go inside, Katherine," he growled. "I will take you home."

"But how did you know . . . ?"

He jerked his chin toward the door. I saw Miss Hartnell then. She did not look smug, but decidedly anxious. "As lacking as you are in sense," Nicholas snapped at me, "you are fortunate in your friends!"

Miss Hartnell held out a hand. It did not occur to me to ignore it, or to be angry at her for tattling on me. She gently led me around the edge of the ballroom, toward the hall. For being so slender, she is surprisingly strong. I felt almost upright, until suddenly they were there in front of us: the Quinns, Mr. Baker's cronies. Mr. Baker himself.

I wished to sink into the floor. They must know, I thought miserably, that I have drunk too much, and behaved like a trollope, and been humiliated in front of . . . well, anyone with eyes. They will laugh at me and that is the end of my Season . . .

"I am feeling unwell," I heard Miss Hartnell inform the gathering. "Miss Percival is being so very kind as to accompany me home." For a few moments, they all made a fuss over her, petting and demanding to be the ones to see to her care. All the while, she held me steady, giving my hand an encouraging squeeze or two. Then, without quite knowing how we came to be there, we were in a carriage, where her mother was waiting.

Our house was silent when we arrived. Charles and Papa were still out, Mama asleep. Miss Hartnell helped me to my room, chatting with comforting cheer about nothing of importance as she did. She found a basin, held back my hair while I was vilely ill, and told the maid to be gentle. Then she left, with an encouraging smile and not a single word of reproach.

There is little as ~~pitif~~ wretched as a foolish girl who drinks too much and yearns for the most sought-after young man. I do not think I shall ever like liquorice again, but I think I am going to be very fond of Luisa Hartnell.

I Can See Clearly Now

Or, should I say, I can *breathe* clearly. I have had the worst head cold known to womankind. You know, the copious snot, then no snot no matter how hard you blow, sneezing, hacking, headachy, look-like-an-extra-from-a-zombie-flick kinda cold.

Leaving me to spend two dismal days in the flat, watching an impressive selection of veterinary and dog-training programs on the numerous BBCs, and reading the mags and rags the (s)mother collected for me. Among the mind-improving *Times*, *Guardian*, and *London Review of Books*, she did manage to include *Hello!* (reports of Prince William's demise . . . sorry, engagement might be greatly exaggerated) and, bless her maternal patootie, American *Vogue* (lose the skinny jeans yet again, ladies; yet again, wide-legs are coming).

It's a toss-up as to who's worse at our current positions, me as sickie or Mom as nurse. We both have a tendency toward surliness. Dating back to . . . well, my childhood, probably. In all fairness, I should probably take a smidge more of the responsibility. She's usually fine for the first day or so; I'm pretty cranky from the first sniffle. Which neither explains nor excuses her flat refusal to return the Hershey's she bought from Mr. Sadiq, and replace it with multiple Curly Wurlies.

"It's a chocolate bar, Catherine. You asked for a chocolate bar."

"That, Mother, is like presenting me with a dachshund, miniature no less, when I requested a pony."

"You like that dog more than you like me, madam."

Frequently. I adore that dog. But that's hardly the point.

We argue over matters of tremendous importance when I'm sick.

"'Look Right,' Ma. It's a Sign. A message to every girl in London."

"Absolutely. 'Don't get crushed by the big red bus with stairs.'"

"Please. Mother. Look deeper."

"Fine. It's saying, 'Catherine Vernon, wear the clean bra and panties, lest you get hit by the big red bus.'"

And, "That diary is living history, Catherine!"

"Correct me if I'm wrong, but doesn't the term *history* automatically imply *dead*?"

"Katherine Percival was a pretty, privileged teenager living in a big city, going to parties and chasing boys. How on earth could that not interest you? It *is* you!"

"Ditzy? Obsessed with yellow dresses and . . . gack . . . bad, soppy poetry? Not using a guy's first name—even in her diary?"

"It was the era, Catherine. Things were different."

"Wait, wait. You just explained how very *same* it was."

"Catherine, had I not been there when you were born, I would wonder who your mother is."

"Are you absolutely sure they tagged me correctly in the delivery room? I mean, what if Michelle Pfeiffer was in the hospital at the same time, and there was a mix-up . . ."

"Trust me, your father and I demanded a blood test when you turned two."

My mother can be a decent smart-ass in her own right.

✦ ✦ ✦

Elizabeth Sadiq called ... or rather, she *rang*. As in, "Oi, Cat. I'm ringing from Westbourne Grove. I'm here with the girls ... Can you hear me? My mobile's rubbish today." Imagine city street noises in the background: cars with bad mufflers and crashing gears, the bass beat of an old reggae song, much high-pitched female giggling.

"I can hear you." It sounded like heaven.

"So, we've had our shoe fix, and we're about to gorge on chicken tikka. Then on to completely unnecessary ... Hang on ... Don't you dare, Imogen! I mean it. No more Alice bands. God, she's so *Sloaney*. So, will you come, then?"

She has friends named Imogen. They wear headbands and are probably blond and skinny and take vacations in places that don't sound like they're spelled, like Gstaad or Ibiza. I would hate them. And love them to death.

"I'm sick," I moaned, with appropriate Victorian drama.

"Sick? What, like, vomming?"

"Well, no, but copious snotting ..."

"So come! Keep your knickers on, Consuelo. I'm almost done."

She has friends named Consuelo. They're impatient, probably Spanish, and gorgeously sloe-eyed with big boobs and brothers named Alejandro. "Now listen, Cat, get the Regent's Park Tube to Baker Street—"

"I can't."

"Of course you can; any berk can use the Tube. You just—"

"It's not the Tube. I adore the Tube. It's that my nose is red, my eyes are red, and my hair ... well, does Edward Scissorhands evoke a good picture?"

"Ah. Right. Saturday, then?"

You gotta love a girl who understands. And I didn't even have to mention the massive, red Mount St. Helens that erupted on my chin yesterday.

So, back to wallowing in self-pity for another half day. By the time this morning rolled around, I was ready to read the *Guardian*. The (s)mother's loving, concerned, nurturing comment as she trotted off to another day of fun and games at the BM? "Take a shower, Catherine. You look like something out of *Macbeth*."

Thanks, Ma.

No, really, thanks, Ma.

All of fifteen minutes after I'd reluctantly bathed and clothed my sorry bod, the doorbell went. Now, considering the fact that it's not really my doorbell and I wasn't expecting either guests or a care package, I debated not answering it. But I figured it might be Elizabeth, so I hit the intercom.

"Oi!" I've always wanted to say that. It's just so . . . well, cool when people like Elizabeth Sadiq or one of the Weasely twins use it.

"Catherine?"

Voice like velvet? Veddy English, veddy posh? Totally male?

Omigodomigodomigod!

"Will?"

No mirror anywhere near the door. What is the deal with Professor Fungus? Doesn't she check before she leaves the house in the morning, even if just to make sure she doesn't have some mold hanging out of her nose?

"Sorry to drop by without ringing, but your mum says you need releasing into the wild."

I'm torn. Do I love my mum? Or do I consign her to the circle of hell reserved for (s)mothers and gym teachers? Time will tell. In the meantime . . .

What can be done in the three minutes it takes a virile young Englishman to climb four flights of stairs:

+ Zit check and frantic application of heavy coat of concealer (didja know they call zits "spots" and makeup "slap" here?— works for me).

+ Equally frantic inner debate on whether eyeliner might not have been a better choice. He couldn't possibly remember that I don't have an Eva Mendes–esque mole on my chin. Could he?

+ Mental idiot-slap.

+ Scan of flat for the best places to sit where I can hide my chin in semidarkness.

+ Effect semi-semi-dimness by turning off the two closest lamps.

+ Shove *Hello!* under the sofa, dump the *Times* (opened and slightly crumpled for that been-read look) on the table.

What can't:

+ Microdermabrasion.

+ Streaky caramel highlights.

+ Tae Bo.

+ A quick skim of *Bridget Jones* or *Pride and Prejudice* for helpful hints and clever quips.

Okay. This boy is seriously adorable. (See pix below.) I discovered that, in the semi-semi-dimness, if I kinda squinted, made his straight hair curly and blue eyes brown, he kinda kinda looks like Orlando Bloom. Kinda.

Well, no, as you can see, he looks more like that incredibly suave actor who was in all those old movies with what's-her-name, but it doesn't matter either way. He's gorgeous in his own right.

Turns out he was dropping off some more dusty old family papers at the BM en route to meet a friend for pub grub. Friend canceled, (s)mother mentioned my recovery from pestilence, and so arrived this gallant swain on our doorstep.

He didn't stare at the zit. (Remember that chin-down, look-up-through-the-lashes look we all practiced to perfection in seventh grade? A modified version is fab for times like these.) He didn't sit across the room from my pestilence. He didn't even flinch at the blinding orangeness of the sofa as he sat down. Next to me.

And of course, there's that loooong minute where I'm thinking of and discarding all the right/wrong things to say, and debating whether to offer him tea (do people under the age of thirty drink tea? do we have any? what if we don't have bags, but just loose stuff, and I end up serving him sludge?), and trying to keep my chin down and eyes up without looking like a puppy who's just peed on the rug . . . Then, too, there's my determination not to say anything, just to ask questions. About him. And what interests him. And to look fascinated with every word he speaks in response.

"Tea?" I blurt.

"No," he replies, grinning. "Thank you." Then, after glancing around: "Remind me, whose flat is this?"

So I tell him about the world expert on creeping mold and we agree there is no remedy for the carpeting and then discuss the painting.

"Obviously the artist was a tortured soul," he says somberly. Not.

"Mad cow disease" slips out before I can decide it's probably not wise to mention it in the presence of an Englishman who might or might not like hamburgers. Then: "Tea?" And he laughs.

"All right. Let's have tea. Anyplace you'd especially like to go?"

Anyplace you'd care to take me. "Notting Hill," I hear myself say. It's cool, Elizabeth called from there, and it's far enough away that we'll have to spend at least an hour together.

He smiles approvingly. "Notting Hill it is." And unfolds all six-foot-something of himself from the sofa. Which means when standing, he's taller than I am. Like, *taller.* Which, as you all know from those years when walking around my bedroom with heavy books on my head had nothing to do with posture and everything with losing an inch or two, is a very good thing.

I had no idea, and couldn't exactly ask, if this little outing is to kill time or is a mission of mercy. And I don't care. Just call me Time-Killer-Charity-Case. I'm in.

I do love the Tube—the endless escalator rides that make you feel like you're heading into the center of the earth, the young men with guitars playing 80s covers in the tiled tunnels (Will told me it's called "busking," and he flipped a pound coin into the case of the one singing "Do You Really Want to Hurt Me"—maybe because people kept shouting "Yes!" from the platform), the veddy propah voice telling you to "mind the gap" as you step into the train. The sideways rocking of the cars that makes you bump up against the person sitting next to you. I made sure to sit so he was on the nonzit side.

He had one arm slung across the back of the seats, so it wasn't around my shoulders, but I could feel it if I leaned all the way back. With my chin still down, I noticed his shoes: brown leather oxfords, big, slightly battered, and infinitely classier than the silver-and-black Nikes Adam wears with such pride. And his jeans: faded and soft-looking over his knees and at the crease of his thighs. He wears his clothes like they're made for him, a totally comfy second skin. Wish I could do that.

So, here's what I learned by the time we got to Portobello Road:

✦ He finished a year ago at a place he calls "Charterhouse" (I'll assume it's a school and has nothing to do with steak) and just returned last week from a backpacking trip through Tibet.

✦ He would have given it all up to become a Buddhist monk, would he not have had to give it all up. "All," he mentioned, included bacon, Guinness, and the plasma screen he has come to worship after the last World Cup series. "All," I'm sure, also includes killer sex with beautiful women with names like Imogen or Consuelo. Boys like this have sex like that.

✦ He's staying at his family's flat "in Town" for a few weeks before going "home" to Somerset, then he starts university at St. Andrew's at the end of the summer. He wants to study philosophy. And finance. Clearly he's a compassionate corporate type.

✦ He doesn't like tea (which posed a minor challenge in Tibet), excessive perfume, or American football. He likes Reese's candy (a moderate challenge in the UK), English football, and Voltaire.

✦ His hair, in the sunlight, looks like polished mahogany, only way softer.

✦ ✦ ✦

We walked through Portobello Market. Will says it will be insane tomorrow, with half of London's dubious antiques and happy, conspicuous consumers cramming the street. But it's pretty cool on any day. Lots of people wearing funky clothing, buying funky clothing, and a veggie market that is colorful enough to make you blink. I bought a little basket of perfect, purple-black plums and a copy of a Stella McCartney hat (a copy, not a fake, I feel compelled to reiterate, although Mom gave it the evil eye nonetheless); Will tried on a Stetson—originally made, the vendor informed me, in Philadelphia—whaddaya know? (See pix.) He didn't buy the hat.

We ended up in a little café where the girl behind the counter had an inch of spiky green hair, a fishhook through her right eyebrow, and a tattoo of a dragon on her forearm. She demanded "Can I help yez?" with a friendly snarl. Will ordered our drinks and the two of us stood staring into the glass case, overwhelmed by the sheer excessiveness of the sugar-chocolate-pastry choices there. Green snapped her gum and waited almost patiently. I had to take a picture of the bounty. She leaned into the shot and bared her teeth. (See pix.)

Then this tiny, round woman with a face like a walnut came out of the back and handed Green a clean coffeepot. She rattled off something in a language that sounded like a cross between Russian and Navajo. The girl chirped back, the old woman patted her cheek and trundled back out of sight.

"My gran says to have the kugel. She baked it with love." Green rolled her eyes at this, but I could tell it was with love, too. We had the kugel. I wanted more. I kept that information to myself.

I picked the table. They were all tiny, but this one was in a corner, so we pretty much had to sit next to each other, instead of across. Clever, no? My cleverness does tend to have a limit. I couldn't not ask: "All this stuff you're giving my mom. Have you read it?"

"Some of it," Will answered.

"And? Dull as dirt, right? I mean, I know it's your family, but I've read the beginning of Katherine's diary, and it's better than Ambien."

He had his coffee mug (cream, no sugar; like the "berk" I am, I actually ordered tea, nuthin' in it, to Green's visible if amiable scorn) cupped in his hands. I thought that mug's gotta be hot, and that if he cupped my hand like that, it would totally disappear. "Not *Bridget Jones*, maybe, but a pretty straightforward account of her life."

"Tons o' fun for the fan of minutiae. But, who cares? Other than my mom."

He shrugged. "Maybe no one. Still, think about it. She didn't expect anyone to read her diary, so she was uncensored. Unself-conscious." Oh, that dimple! "Can you say the same about your blog?"

Smart-ass. Smart boy. It's fortunate I like smart boys. Especially ones with floppy shiny hair that smells like ginger ale.

"Blogs," sez I, "are our generation's contribution to the Great Global Village. Think about it. We share knowledge, commentary, threads to follow for even higher knowledge. Like, I link to the BM, and maybe someone follows it and learns that Lord Elgin stole the Elgin Marbles from the Parthenon in Athens, and maybe they find a reference to the fact that Lord Byron thought that was criminal, and wrote a poem about it . . ." Sadly, I had to stop there, as I had expended my knowledge of the Elgin Marbles and Byron's anti-Elgin poem.

"Impressive. How many people read your blog?"

I debated lying. Decided against it. "Only six. But it's password-protected. Private."

"Like a diary."

"Well, yeah . . ."

"Only censored."

"Maybe."

"And self-conscious." He reached out and lifted my chin, really gently with one finger. I wasn't about to tell him that I'd just put my face down because I'd remembered the zit. It got his hands on me. "We only tell the secrets we secretly want not to be secret, right? And learn as much from what isn't told."

So. Is that deep because it's deep? Or because the resident philosopher is brain-numbingly cute?

What we learned during the next half hour:

✦ I don't like tea, either. That made him laugh.

✦ My birthday is in two weeks. I want my own satellite. That made him laugh.

✦ I make him laugh. He told me so. I assume in a good way.

✦ I like catching people in unguarded moments for my pix. He has the same camera and hence was able to speedily delete the pic of him with kugel on his chin.

✦ I read *Bridget Jones* in one sitting, have seen the movie a dozen times (I didn't mean to tell him that Colin Firth is kinda hot; it slipped out—he laughed). He tried to read *Bridget Jones* last summer. Didn't get it. Went back to Kierkegaard.

✦ English is my fave subject, followed by French; history is my least.

✦ History was his fave until he discovered philosophy, but what's philosophy but pondering what dismal mistakes we made in the past and trying not to make them again? He acknowledges that we frequently fail and history repeats itself.

✦ I rest my case.

He sighed. Exasperated, but in that cute-guy-with-his-cute-companion way. "Dude," he sez. "Dude—" sounding totally American. "You're history. I'm history. Not yet, but soon enough. Don't you want someone to be interested in you?"

Yeah, I thought. *You. Now.*

His phone beeped. He politely ignored it, but informed me, "I'm meeting some mates in Kensington. Football match." He didn't invite me to come along. He asked if I wanted more tea. Politely. I hadn't finished the cup I had (some sugar would have helped, no doubt) and, agonizing as it was, decided to be wise and end the party while all parties appeared to still be enjoying themselves.

He did, however, rest his arm on my seat back on the Tube again. And he walked me up four flights of the stairs to the door of the flat.

"I'll ring," he said as he left. "We'll have tea."

Okay, so the debate begins: no mention of a girlfriend. Hence, no girlfriend. But guys like this *always* have a girlfriend. Hence, there must be one. He said he'd ring. No girlfriend. He said we'd have tea, not a night of dancing with wild abandon in some steamy underground club. Girlfriend. I'm an optimist. No girlfriend. I have absolutely dismal luck with the males of the species. All of them. Girl—

Oh, the hell with it. My friends, it is time. For that Question of Questions, ageless and timeless and all-important.

Do You Think He Likes Me???

26 May

Once, long ago, there was a lively, pretty girl who wished to marry a handsome prince. She did, but was not content. She desired a child, a little prince. One was duly born to her, yet she was not content. A princess, then, she decided, would make all well. Yet when the princess arrived, she brought no contentment in her tiny pink fists. On the contrary, her mother saw in her all the joy and promise she herself had squandered, and hence dedicated herself to being certain her daughter experienced nothing and was wary of everything...

I am certain I am not alone in living this tale. Perhaps there is something that is altered with motherhood, something which turns the pretty, lively girls we know only from portraits into these odd, mortifying creatures who alternately smother and bully us.

But I do not care to be philosophical. I would much rather be shopping. I am, however, confined at present to the house and, until such time as Mama sees fit to release me, must content myself with my diary, the occasional teasing presence of Charles, and the hope that Luisa Hartnell will call upon me.

Mama is being thoroughly unreasonable. Perhaps if she knew the truth of my behaviour at the Bellinghams', this ridiculous confinement would be justified. But she knows only that I went to the ball, against her wishes, and hence has decreed I should be allowed out only when she feels able to trust in my judgement (I really do not think she needed to add, "I wonder how you shall entertain yourself through the years, Katherine."), and only then with <u>proper</u> supervision. I gather Charles is not considered proper supervision. Mama did not scold him for his part in my downfall. It didn't matter a whit that he escorted me, and then abandoned me.

Perhaps I ought to have begun her tale with, "Once upon a time, there lived a wicked witch."

In truth, I only know she was a different creature in her youth because of very vague memories and the fact that I once heard Papa, near tears, demanding of her, "What have you done to the lovely, sweet girl I married?" My heart ached for him. I could have smacked her myself when she replied:

"Would not a better question be what <u>you</u> have done to her?"

I know she was beautiful. I suppose she still is. But she hounds me with her rules and her warnings—against Adventurers (men who shall court me for the three thousand pounds I have from Grandmother Cavendish), against Ignorance (my own, primarily, although she seems to feel there is an epidemic of sorts sweeping England), against Complaisance (or is it "complacence"? I am not curious enough to interrupt the lectures to ask). Then, of course, there is bad drinking water, heavy application of face powder, pickpockets, spoiled fish, immoral acquaintances, gin, gossip, and the colour chartreuse. Heaven help me.

I feel for Papa. It is she who keeps him away from home so often, I know it. She chases him out with her headaches and her waspishness and her writing, which is what he dislikes most of all. He cannot countenance a woman who cares only to speak of what she has read, or far worse, what she has <u>written</u>.

"There is nothing so deadly dull as a bookish girl," he has told me. "We men spend our youth waiting to be done with the tedium of school and governesses. Why on earth should we wish to repeat the experience with our wives? Be a fool, Katherine, be a vixen, but <u>never</u> a bluestocking."

I shall not. I shall not be bookish or dull. Nor shall I be changeable. I shall be steadfast in all things and shall be quite the same person at eight-and-thirty as I am now at eighteen.

27 May

Luisa visited this morning and was so charming to Mama and so persuasive, that I was allowed to attend a supper party at her house. I do love Luisa!

It was a lively evening. We were all gathered together at one table, the familiar crowd. Mr. Eccleston was most silly, telling us of the day he and Mr. Baker spent rowing on the Serpentine. It seems Mr. Baker is composing a poem about water nymphs and required water. Mr. Eccleston did the rowing.

"Why should he not?" Mr. Baker demanded of us all, his marvelous eyes alight. "He is the one with the brawn."

"And you with the brains, I suppose?" came Mr. Eccleston's retort. "What sort of brains are required to know that standing up in a narrow rowboat is simply asking to be upset, hmm?"

"It was a splendid line and needed to be cried aloft!"

"It was a lost line," Mr. Eccleston announced drily, "to water in my ears and your mouth."

Everyone laughed at the image of the pair of them flapping

about in the water. "And nymphs?" Miss Eleanora Quinn asked. She has taken to wearing funny little sprays of peacock feathers in her hair. Luisa and I have debated the kindness of telling her that she resembles a startled finch. I am in favor; Luisa against.

"We are all like birds, I expect," was her reasoning, "inclined to flutter and preen when a gentleman we admire is nearby." I have never seen her so much as flutter a lash. It would be most annoying if I were not secretly relieved that she shows no preference—in fact, she shows a disinterest—in Mr. Baker. I wonder sometimes, though, if she is perhaps interested She gets on very nicely with Charles, which is lovely, as it allows me to spend some evenings with two of the people I am most fond of, and even seems excess somewhat taken with Nicholas, which is quite beyond me.

This evening, for her part, Miss Quinn was fluttering and twittering away at all the gentlemen. I would have been quite put out, but she flirts with Mr. Eccleston and Mr. Davison quite as much as she does Mr. Baker. "Were there no nymphs about to rescue you?" she asked him.

"For water I go to Hyde Park," Mr. Baker replied. I nearly dropped my lemonade (I do hope I will soon like champagne again!) when his eyes caught mine. "For nymphs, I have come here. To be rescued."

"But there is no water, sir," I teased.

"There are many more circumstances requiring rescue," he answered.

"To be sure," said Mr. Pertwee. "Poverty!"

"Conniving mamas with available daughters!" from Mr. McCoy.

"Boredom," Luisa added, and yawned prettily.

"All true," cried Mr. Baker with a toss of his curls, "but none of those are what I fear most!"

"He's positively terrified of a badly tailored coat," Mr. Eccleston informed us.

"I am terrified," Mr. Baker began, and I leaned forward, "of nothing at all but solitude and an empty heart."

"What utter rot!" Mr. Eccleston laughed.

"Oh, but such pretty rot," Mr. McCoy added.

Mr. Baker laughed with them, but his eyes met mine again.

For the remainder of the evening, which went altogether too quickly, I could do little other than to ask myself, over and over again, "Is this how it feels?"

I cannot bring myself to say aloud what <u>it</u> might be.

As we all parted, Mr. Baker bowed low over my hand and he kissed it. I had not thought that the brief touch of lips to skin could feel so warm. I think I would very much like ~~Mr. Baker~~ <u>Thomas</u> to kiss me again.

I thought nothing could spoil the evening. I was, of course, wrong.

Papa is spending much time with the odious Lord Chilham and, appallingly, does not seem to mind. In fact, he seems entirely happy with the situation. I confess I cannot quite reconcile Papa's excellent taste in all matters with this odd friendship. His chosen acquaintances have always been from among the most elegant and discriminating crowd. The sort of persons he has always instructed me to emulate. Chilham is so much the opposite: boring, unfashionable, foolish. Yet Papa quite snapped at me when I suggested he might better enjoy an evening with the clown Grimaldi.

"He is my cousin, Katherine, and a far more important personage in Town than you! It would serve you well to remember that. You will treat him with all due respect, miss."

There is a quandary. How does one treat someone with due respect, when they are due none? After all, the man sports odd-coloured waistcoats and his stockings bag at the ankles.

I had scarcely arrived home from the supper party when Chilham burst from Papa's library and came at me like a wasp to a violet. He has now taken to wearing his cravat so high and highly starched that he cannot lower his chin. I suspect he is unable to see the floor, for a corner of a particularly dangerous and vicious pink silk carpet nearly felled him. He flailed for an instant, thin arms and legs windmilling, before recovering.

I did not laugh. My tightly laced corset helped. Papa's warning helped more. His just-visible presence in the library door quite sealed the matter.

"Good evening, Lord Chilham," I managed, trying not to fling myself backward when he reached for my hand. I feared there would be a terrible tug-of-war over my arm should he insist on grabbing me. The very idea of his putting his lips, or even his cold fingers, where Thomas's had been was unthinkable.

He reached, I twisted and curtsied. He reached again, then gave it up and bowed.

"Cousin. You are looking uncommonly well."

I think I probably am. I am happy.

He went on, "Do come and join your father and me in a glass of sherry and a bit of conversation."

How odd that when I so often desire my father's company more than anything, at the moment I simply could not be bothered. "I thank you, sir, for the very kind and generous invitation, but I am quite fatigued. I would certainly only bore you with the silly prattle of the evening."

What utter rot, as Mr. Eccleston would say. Yet it was pretty rot.

"Nonsense! I insist!"

And I am not some meek little miss to be commanded so. "I assure you, my lord, I am poor company and must decline." I am not certain I suppressed my yawn well enough; I caught sight of Papa scowling.

Chilham really is especially unappealing when he pouts. Beneath the pudding hair, his face resembles that of a petulant infant. Yet he was not deterred for long. "Far be it from me to deprive you of your rest. I shall not, however, accept a refusal for tomorrow night. It would be my great pleasure to escort you to Vauxhall Gardens. Your father tells me you are most anxious to see the fireworks."

Yes, I was. I was very much looking forward to going with Papa. He promised. We should engage a box and have supper there under the stars, and watch the people—the soldiers and tradesmen and women of questionable virtue—until the fireworks display began.

"I do not think—" I began. Father appeared fully in the doorway then, frowning fiercely. My goodness, he is intent on not offending this ludicrous—yes, <u>titled</u>—creature. "Oh, very well. Thank you, my lord."

"You make me the happiest of men, Cousin Katherine. I wish you the sweetest of dreams."

His collar points prevented him from merely bowing his head. So he bent from the waist and nearly toppled himself forward onto the floor. I quite laughed myself silly once I had closed my bedchamber door behind me.

July 8

Rich Girl

Well, Elizabeth's Imogen looks like Beyoncé, and is so posh and preppy I thought it was an act at first. She actually wears pearls. Over Petit Bateau shirts, it must be noted, but *pearls*. And Consuelo—sloe-eyed, Spanish Consuelo—is this elfin blonde who wears Doc Martens with a floaty little dress that I'm pretty sure I saw in last month's *Vogue*. They are both effortlessly friendly, in the way that only totally self-assured girls are, and effortlessly cool, in the way that almost no one is. I think it must have something to do with the fact that they both wear La Perla underwear. Not that they announced that to me, or anyone. It was Elizabeth, who told them to move their La Perla'd arses if we were to get to the park before July. Apparently Elizabeth hangs out with the rich kids.

They've all been friends since they were eight and starting at their Independent School in Kensington. I can tell that's London for "Expensive and Elite." They don't need to boast; their lives spill forth like caviar with no help whatsoever. Imogen's mother is a neurosurgeon with awful taste in men ("Wouldn't you think a naffing brain surgeon would have more sense than to take up with an unemployed actor? I mean, he left her in Portofino with nothing but the hotel bill . . ."). Elizabeth and Imogen spent last weekend at Consuelo's country house ("By the way, Lizzie, Daddy's buying you a new iPod. He feels just awful about the power surges, but it can't be helped. Most of the wiring in the east wing *was* put in for the king's visit in the thirties . . . ").

I asked if they know Will Percival. Consuelo thought for a moment. "Sounds a bit familiar. We might have had French lessons together, but I'm not certain."

Elizabeth eyed her skeptically. "And when might this have been, these lessons that are so clear in your mind?"

"Oh, well, I suppose I was three. Maybe four—"

"Would that perchance be William Percival the Tall, pupil at the Charterhouse School?" Imogen lazily waved her iPhone in my direction. "I can see why you would ask."

"Here, gimme." Elizabeth snagged the phone, studied the little screen for a sec, and let out a low whistle. "God, I love Google. Not half bad, Yank. And aristocratic. Which is not a recommendation."

It was Consuelo's turn to grab. "Oh, he's Lord Chilham's grandson." She looked up at me. "Does he speak French?"

"Yes, Yank." Elizabeth slung an arm around my shoulders. "How is his French?"

Chilham? I suppose I'll sort out that bit later. At the moment, I felt compelled to sort out Elizabeth. "You can wipe off that smile. I barely know him. He's just—"

"Yummy!" From Consuelo.

"Dishy," Imogen agreed, making the two of them sound like food wonks.

"Posh," was Elizabeth's comment, and it didn't sound like an endorsement.

She showed me the screen. It was Will all right, tuxedoed and tall, standing half a head over an older man I'd never seen before and a younger older man I definitely had. The caption read, *Lord Chilham, longtime Liberal MP for Wiltshire, celebrates his eightieth* birthday at the Reform Club. Pictured with the guest of honour are the Prince of Wales (r.) and Lord Chilham's grandson, William Percival (l.), now in his last year at Charterhouse, where both his father and grandfather were pupils . . . The rest, I saw as I scrolled down, was just a recap of the birthday boy's fifty years in politics. What I got from a quick glance was that he seemed to be in favor of preserving forests and red squirrels and against Walmart.

"I see your future," Elizabeth said solemnly, "and it is up a tree in Wiltshire."

"I don't like squirrels," I told her.

"If you say so," she shot back, and laughed.

We wandered over to the cricket field . . . excuse me, cricket *pitch* in Regent's Park to watch Consuelo's boyfriend play. He's named Bayard and he looks like a Viking. He's twice her size, has the longest nose I've ever seen, and has a jaw you could crush rocks with. He plays "deep midwicket," which Consuelo tried to explain to me, but all I got was that it has something to do with boundaries and damage control.

Cricket is incomprehensible. A bunch of guys in white pants and sweaters smack balls all over the place, then run back and forth and back and forth (and then back and forth) between sticks in the ground. They use words like "popping crease" and "cow corner" and "wicket," which very probably tells you everything you want to know.

It was endless. Consuelo pretended to be interested for the first hour. After that, even she gave up. Elizabeth and Imogen and I had gone from ranking the players in order of bone structure, shoulder span, and butts, to trying to see who had the largest . . . feet. Finally, Elizabeth groaned and flopped onto her back in the grass.

"God, this is deadly. Im, give me your *Tatler*." (*Hello!*'s aristocratic third cousin, who doesn't acknowledge any family connection.) She groaned again as she flipped through a few pages. "What rubbish. Who gives a monkey that Lady Finnuala Lennox is dating the Honorable Frederick Fremont?"

At this, Imogen raised one perfect eyebrow (is it something in the water here?). "Actually, considering the fact that *I* used to go with Freddie Fremont, I have a passing interest."

"Oh God, that's right. You did. He was a complete tosser then, and I sincerely doubt Lady F. has improved him much."

"Finnuala's not so bad," Consuelo protested. "We used to do dressage together."

"It's not about Finnuala, although you really might want to keep your dressage past to yourself. The point at hand is what Freddie used to want to do with Imogen when *they* were together. What was it again, Im? Clotted cream and the family cat?" Imogen did the eyebrow thing again. Elizabeth rolled over and brandished the *Tatler* at her. "Right, here's one for you. Would you rather sleep with Lord Voldemort or the Queen?"

Imogen thought for a minute. "The Queen, I suppose. Maybe she'd let me try on her jewels." Back at Elizabeth: "Would you rather lose your hair or your powers of speech?"

"Evil woman!" Elizabeth has fab hair. Have I mentioned her fab hair? Yards of wild black and gold. "Oh, take the hair, then. Consuelo . . . Would you rather never drink champagne again, or have to drink Pepto-Bismol at every meal?" I love these people.

"Pepto," Consuelo answered, "definitely! Doh! And now it's Cat's turn. Would you rather be married to Donald Trump for a year—no prenup, I might add—or have Jake Gyllenhaal sneak out the restaurant window halfway through your first date?"

I love this game. "Ouch, the humiliation, but Jake, I guess. I mean, can you imagine what Donald's hair looks like in the morning?" We all shuddered in unison. I should have quizzed

Imogen, but nice as she is, she kinda scares me. It's that utter perfection thing. "Elizabeth. Would you rather be banished for life to America or Siberia?"

"Too easy. America, of course. You disappoint me, Cat-Cat. You haven't seemed to grasp the difference between blaming a place for the idiots there and blaming the idiots for destroying a place that isn't theirs. But we'll make allowances for your excessive exposure to *American Idol*." Elizabeth did that slightly evil smile thing. "All right, then, Yank. Who would you rather have make every single choice for you for the next ten years: your intrepid Senate or your soon-to-be-stepmonster?"

She's good, Elizabeth is. She's really good.

Lucky me, I didn't get to answer. The match ended then, or went into hiatus, or whatever they do, and Bayard came loping over with a few of his still-remarkably-white-clad lads. Most pretty goofy and totally posh. Picture Hugh Grant really young and sweaty. Bayard scooped Consuelo into his lap and nuzzled her neck.

"Ooh, you're wet! And smelly!" she protested, but only halfheartedly. You could almost see their *togetherness*. I picture it as a small, rotund panda. Don't ask why. "You were brilliant."

"I was crap. You've been into the whiskey again, haven't you?"

Consuelo wrinkled her tiny nose and insisted, "You were sublime, my dearest darling."

"Got bored again, hmm?" He grinned at me then and I figured I wouldn't mind the hot and sweaty, either, if I had a boy like him to hold me in his lap and smile occasionally. "She hates cricket."

"I do," Consuelo admitted cheerfully. "It's the only thing about him I don't positively worship, including his utterly disgusting socks and Amy Winehouse fan-club shot glasses."

"I, on the other hand, detest absolutely everything about her, except the boots. I really, really love her boots."

"He loathes them," she told me, just as cheerfully. "They track dirt into his Porsche."

He kinda pinched her; she kinda squealed. I kinda hated them. Well, no. They're kinda extremely likable, even if they put one in mind of fat, furry bamboo chewers.

"So, Bay," Elizabeth demanded, breaking up the little lovefest, "would you rather Consuelo gained five stone or never shaved her legs again?"

"What?" He was busy smoothing Consuelo's hair into a perfect little ponytail. "Well, that's a stupid question, isn't it?"

Elizabeth rolled her eyes. "Of course it's a stupid question, you big oaf. That's the point. Humor us. Five stone—and that's seventy pounds to you, Yank—or eternal gorilla legs?"

"Ah, now you've gone and got me all horny, Bits. Come on, you." He managed to get from the ground to his feet without letting go of Consuelo. She wrapped herself around him, Docs and all. "I need a wash. You can do my back." And off they went. I think I might have sighed as they disappeared from sight.

I asked Elizabeth, "How long have they been together?"

"Fifty years tomorrow. We're buying them a monogrammed silver insulin dispenser."

"Seriously."

"Since infancy," Imogen announced. Then: "Consuelo saw Bayard across a duck pond when they were seven and decided to marry him. He never stood a chance."

Wow. I can't even imagine being fated like that. Well, yeah, I can imagine it. I mean, no matter how vehemently we deny it, we've all pictured ourselves in at least one Disney movie. And I don't just mean the (countless) ones where they kill off the mother before the opening credits are done.

"Consuelo does that," Elizabeth infomed me wryly. "Claims

people for keeps. Mind yourself—she'll do it to you, too." Like I would object. "She certainly sucked me in, poor, clueless scholarship girl that I was. Eight years old and scared half out of my wits."

Imogen gave a loud, albeit totally ladylike, snort at this. "Rubbish. You walked into the classroom as if you owned it. We all wanted to be you, or barring that, just sit next to you." I'm getting the sense that Elizabeth has that general effect on people. "But yah, Consuelo did gather us. I rather think she liked the way we looked as a trio."

"Love at first sight," Elizabeth said with high-drama dreaminess.

"Yes, it was" was Imogen's firm reply. And that, apparently, was that.

So here's one for you, Yanks:

Would you rather be loved unconditionally and not love, or be desperately in love and not loved in return?

28 May

So I went with Lord Chilham to the Vauxhall Pleasure Gardens. How unsurprising that it was something less than Pleasurable.

I was so very pleased when Papa said he would accompany me. I would need a chaperone, certainly; I could not be seen at such a place as Vauxhall, with its acres of outdoor walks and circuslike entertainments, alone in the company of a single man. To been seen anywhere in the presence of a man with pudding-bowl hair and a pink-and-orange waistcoat would be a tragedy. More than that, I was certain my father's presence would make the evening bearable. Where he is, I have always ~~thought myself~~ been happy.

Sadly, he was in a Mood.

"Do not even consider being contrary this evening, Katherine," he warned me as we climbed into the carriage.

I had not, but intent is only half of the way things go, after all. The entire evening was a show of contrariness, beginning with: I do hate to be a disappointment to Papa, but it seemed the Fates were determined I should. It is agony to imagine a Fate so perverse as to determine that Papa should be a disappointment to me.

The skies were perfectly clear, ideal for a display of fireworks. Yet there was a chill in the air. My pale pink dress with little silk roses scattered over the skirt is, I think, most attractive, yet I was forced to cover much of it with a shawl.

I think I could perhaps have been charitable about Lord Chilham's lack of appeal (we were, after all, going to a place I have been most keen to visit), yet he seemed to choose the occasion to showcase it.

He had a cold. And while one might politely, even eagerly, ignore watery eyes and a dripping nose, it is entirely beyond my capabilities to ignore honking, snorting, snuffling, and wheezing, all punctuated by the frequent trumpeting expulsions into his grubby handkerchief.

He thought to take my hand as we descended from the carriage. I thought otherwise.

"Of course, a man of lesser fortitude would certainly have taken to his bed," he announced as we walked through the grand gates, "yet I would not have disappointed you for anything." (In the moment, I would have given anything for that particular disappointment.)

And off he went: honk, snort, blast, announcing our arrival at Vauxhall like a trumpeter before a queen.

We could not possibly have been more conspicuous, and on a night when I wished to be completely invisible. I thought I should die if I were to encounter anyone I know.

Papa, completely unlike himself, said nothing at all as we went, merely followed Chilham, with his eyes in the distance, his mind clearly elsewhere. "Perhaps we shall see the Prince Regent," I suggested.

"Don't be daft," Papa snapped. "Why should he be here?"

"To see the acrobats, perhaps. Or the fireworks. I have heard he quite enjoys—"

"Be quiet, Katherine, and listen to his lordship."

Stung, I fell silent, which Chilham took as encouragement to continue the very discourse I had been trying to stem. For in between his enthusiastic nasal blasts, he was, with equal dedication, pointing out every small detail we passed as we walked along the lamp-lit paths.

I knew there was much to be seen beneath the hundreds upon hundreds of glass lamps lighting the tree-lined avenues: musicians and actors and tame beasts, sailors fresh from their ships and farmers fresh from the country. Luisa has told me of acrobats in Oriental costume with trained monkeys on leads. Charles spoke, though it was to Nicholas and he did not know I overheard, of Ladies of the Night in brilliantly red dresses that stop above their ankles. Mr. Davison swears he saw the Duke of York with a turkey upon his knee there a fortnight past. From the Quinns I heard tell of true Gypsics who read their fortunes—one who said Henrietta would be married before the end of the Season. Eleanora Quinn said she had a nose like a plum and curled hands with knobs and claws, like those of a very large rodent. I do not think Eleanora much cared for her, but I wanted to see that fortune-teller.

Here is what I saw, with Lord Chilham as my guide:

~ Six geese with ribbons about their necks, being led by a tired girl with dirty ribbons about her waist. ("Is she not charming?" Chilham insisted.) Her skirts stopped just below her knees. She had goose poo on her stockings.

~ A party of round-hatted rectors from some distant county.

~ A marble statue of Saint George.

~ Three yew hedges, two holly, and thirty-six elm trees. ("Note the deceptive strength of the Wych elm, named not for the magicking hag, but for pliancy or weakness. Like most females, it is to be found everywhere and useful for little save decoration. Hyaw. Hyaw.") I became closely acquainted with one yew and one holly hedge when I thought I spied Mr. Tallisker and dove in so as not to be seen. My shawl will not recover.

~ A man standing upon a box, playing a flute.

~ A pile of rocks intended to be a Grecian ruin.

I wished to see the acrobats, the actors, the murals of Greek gods revelling above the mortals. The mural in our supper box was of one shepherdess, eight scraggy sheep, and two ducks. Chilham found it "delightful," the music of the distant orchestra "stirring," the view "most excellent." I was huddled at the very back of the three-walled chamber, where I had chosen my seat so as not to be visible from the outside. I had a very good view of the appearance and disappearance of Chilham's handkerchief and my father's flask, and not a great deal else. It was not a well-positioned box.

I suspect, too, that Chilham chose an inferior menu. The chicken was like warmed wood; the potatoes tasted strongly of earth. I found a ragged-edged leaf amid my strawberries. It appeared to be from some sort of ivy. I had never taken Chilham for a miser, not with his vast array of silly silk waistcoats and enormous silver shoe buckles. I believe he must pay more for his hair pomade than he did for the food.

He did not hold back, however, on the champagne. There were three full bottles at the ready. We'd scarce sat down before he pressed the first glass upon me. Remembering the last time I had drunk champagne, both my mind and stomach recoiled.

"I fear I am not partial to wine or spirits, my lord," I told him, opting for politeness. "A glass of lemonade would suit me far better."

"Nonsense!" he replied. Honk. Snort. "You must have champagne!"

I demurred. He insisted. He was so close I could see the little patch of bristly hairs his valet had missed while shaving beneath his chin. I scooted my chair a few inches to the ~~left~~ right. He leaned farther, overfilling my glass, his knee bumping against mine. I scooted again, jostling the table, and upsetting my glass.

"You see, my lord," I said with forced cheer. My voice sounded shrill in my ears. "Champagne and I are a sorry match."

I thought I heard him grumble something about investments, but it was lost to a burst of laughter from the merry party in the next box. Then he was plying the bottle again, I was trying to discourage him, and suddenly Papa's fist hit the table, spilling yet more and startling me into stillness.

"Drink the bloody champagne, Katherine!" he snapped. They were the only words he addressed to me during the brief but torturous meal.

What have I <u>done</u> to displease him so?

Chilham gloated. He honked and snorted. I took to sipping (how sour it was!), then tipping out the contents of my glass when neither man was looking. I believe I emptied the better part of two bottles onto the already unclean floor.

I was altogether too glad to quit the box. I barely noticed the man in brilliant silks and brocades passing, a chattering monkey atop each shoulder. Nor could I find any pleasure in the knowledge that the fireworks would soon begin. I wanted only to be home, in bed, losing the memory of a dismal night to one filled with friends—and possible sweethearts.

I did not notice at first when Chilham quitted the brilliantly lit and busy avenue for a darker side path, much less occupied. The copious amount of drink seemed to have quieted his snufflings, leaving him free to drone on about the culinary joys of mushrooms.

By the time I paid attention, we were deep in shadows. I had heard of these paths. They are where couples go for their romantic trysts, where men behave not like gentlemen and ladies not at all like ladies. It was not a place I wished to be at all, and most certainly not with Lord Chilham.

I looked about, but Papa was nowhere to be seen.

I turned, ready to hurry back to the lighted promenade, back to where Papa was most certainly looking for me. But in the very next moment, my unwelcome companion had both of my hands gripped in his. His were decidedly moist. Feeling a bit alarmed and slightly ill, I tugged. He held fast.

"Katherine!" he breathed, much too close to my face. He smelled of sour champagne and onions. "Most lovely, most charming Katherine."

"Sir!" I jerked away and retreated until a prickly hedge brought me up short. "This is most improper!"

"Oh, but I have your parents'... well, your father's permis ..." He paused, head turning from side to side as if in search of something. "My intentions are not improper, Cousin." He peered intently into the darkness. "What ... ? Hmm." And back at me, as if I were somehow causing a distraction: "Ah, well. You cannot possibly mistake my intentions ... What was that?"

I had heard nothing, but glanced around, too, hoping

desperately to see Papa, hoping for <u>any</u> rescue from the moment. All I could detect was a soft rustling from the plants some yards away, and the soft giggle of someone far happier in her situation.

"As I was saying, Cousin Katherine. I do believe it is something of a certainty that we ... Confound it! What <u>is</u> it?"

I very nearly jumped from my skin when a hand clamped about my wrist and tugged me firmly away from Chilham and from the shrub. Heart pounding, hopeful, I turned to see not Papa, but a tiny woman peering up at me from under a broad head scarf. It was difficult to see anything in the dim light, but I could make out the shape of a bowed back beneath her shawl, and eyes glittering from deep sockets. The fingers about my wrist were gnarled, but had the strength of youth.

"'Tisn't safe for the likes of you in a place like this, missy." There was a hint of far-off lands in the soft cackle, and a touch of humour. "All sorts'll be thinking to take advantage."

Chilham noticed her then. "Take your filthy hands off the lady!" he commanded snuffily. "Begone, before I summon the watch."

She tilted her head and seemed to study him closely for a moment. Then: "Nay, thought not. Ye've no place in what's to come. Begone yerself."

He puffed up so visibly that I feared for his buttons. "Why, you vile old—"

She waved her free hand at him. Abruptly, his words were lost to a fit of sneezing.

"Does the young lady wish to hear her fortune?"

Mesmerised, I nodded, but it was difficult to hear much of anything above Chilham's noise. The old woman tugged at my arm until I was bent nearly double. "Cross my palm," she commanded into my ear. I knew she wanted money. I fumbled in my reticule and found a half crown. She folded it into her fist.

"Ye young chickies," she grumbled, "only wanting t'hear of love and marriage. Am I right?" Well, of course she was. "Even if 'tisn't what matters most. So be it. Yer beloved . . . Yer beloved is a man of words. Listen."

I did. Chilham sneezed.

I listened. "Well?"

"Not to me, foolish girl! To him. To your beloved."

She let go of my arm and started to turn away.

"Wait. Please. My beloved is a poet, is he not?"

"If so ye say . . ."

Suddenly there was a whistle and a crack, and the sky was briefly lit by a thousand brilliant sparks. All over the Gardens, people cheered.

"Mind those dear to you." The woman shook a finger at me. In the darkness, it looked skeletal. "Mind them good!"

More fireworks boomed and sparkled. I spied Papa then, standing at the branch of the path, calmly smoking one of his Egyptian cheroots. I hurried toward him, thinking he must have been there all along. Then, deciding I'd best be absolutely certain the old Gypsy had said "words"—rather than "swords" or something far less portentous (truly, soldiers are so very common, after all—Charles and Nicholas and the Goodwin brothers and the fat princes . . . and poets so rare), I turned back.

She was gone, vanished into the shadows.

I am not entirely certain, but I believe in the last flare of fireworks, her nose did appear veined enough to be almost the colour of . . . a plum.

Chilham's sneezing subsided after that, but he could not seem to regain his earlier vigor. Papa said nothing on the ride home, but it was clear he was in no better form than when we had left the house hours before. He and Chilham disappeared into the library as soon as we reached the house. Neither took leave of me.

Once in bed, I thought of Chilham's speech.

"You cannot mistake my intentions, Cousin."

I could. I could quite easily and with pleasure. I would very much like to mistake his intentions. I wish, too, that I could be mistaken in Father's desires on the matter.

Could he, could he <u>truly</u> wish to see me wed to awful Lord Chilham? Is a title worth so much? Or am I worth so little?

No. I am certain it is not. I am not. Yet, there are his lectures and scoldings and could it have been just that he was strolling too far behind us tonight to see what Chilham intended? I cannot think on the matter now. Perhaps tomorrow.

Mama came in just as I was falling asleep. She had been out, too, at one of her literary evenings, I would think. She looked unusually pretty, in good health and a new sapphire dress that glowed in the light of her candle. She did not look happy, though.

"Katherine." She ran one hand gently over my brow, as she had done when I was small and she would come in each night to be certain all was well. "Did anything . . . unusual happen tonight at the Gardens? Anything I perhaps should know?"

I was so sleepy. Different images flitted through my mind.

"A Gypsy woman told my fortune," I murmured.

Above me, her face relaxed. "Oh? And what did she destine for you, my lovely girl?"

"I shall marry a man of swords," I told her.

"Ah," she said, and smoothed my hair from my face.

I thought to tell her no, the Gypsy had said "words," but I must have fallen asleep.

Stronger

What doesn't kill us . . .

Mr. Sadiq was a science professor in Baghdad. I learned this over dinner tonight with the Sadiq family. And here is how that happened:

I was in the shop, keeping Elizabeth company while she worked, and trying to decide between Wine Gums (think Gummi Bears with serious 'tude) and Liquorice Allsorts. No chocolate this week. I'm bargaining with Fate:

If I am very very good and abstain from what I love best, the gods of love will smile favorably upon me, and Will will call.

Will hasn't called. It's been four days since I saw him. It could be nothing. ("I'm sure he has every intention of calling!" From Consuelo. "But they've such dismal senses of *time*, boys.") He didn't specify *when* he would call. It could be that he's been busy. And has a dismal sense of time. ("Prats. All of them." Imogen.) It could be that my heavy chocolate consumption has made my rear view appalling, and the fact that, if he's half as fab as he seems, I think I could really really like him has turned me into a blithering idiot, not fit for average company, let alone his.

"Cat, you pinheaded eejit!" Elizabeth, not mincing words, again, as I sigh over the liquorice. "You're fab. Losing your mind, but fab nonetheless. He's losing out. Period. If he has a single brain cell in that inbred aristocratic head of his, he'll come worship at your feet." I love Elizabeth. "Now, your mum's got that museum do tonight, right? Right. You're coming home to have supper with me."

It was true. Mom did have an event at the BM. A dinner for visiting researchers or something. She invited me. I declined. To her credit, she didn't push. Even my mother knows there's a limit to how much dust, real and figurative, that a girl can take.

So, it was whatever I scrounged up for dinner (note for future reference: "Pot Noodles," especially the "Bombay Bad Boy" flavor, are pretty yummy, colorful, and available one aisle over, two shelves down from the chocs) or a glimpse into Elizabeth's home life. "Your parents . . . ?"

"Think 'hospitality' is a sacred duty. They'll be chuffed. Dad likes you."

I hesitated. For like a second. "Sure. Should I . . . um . . . bring something?"

"Box of chocolates?" Elizabeth kept remarkably poker-faced for an impressively long time. She thinks my chocolate abstention is hilarious. She took pity on me eventually. "My mum likes lilies."

So three hours later, Elizabeth, the lilies, and I walked out of the Finsbury Park Tube station. The Sadiqs' neighborhood is famous, Elizabeth told me, for the mosque and the fact that Arsenal Football Club has its stadium nearby. There did seem to be a lot of red-and-white shirts around. It was my first trip to a part of London not found in most guidebooks and Hugh Grant movies. To be honest, I'd expected it to look a little more . . . exotic, maybe? Stop rolling your eyes, Djenan. I'm being *honest*, after all. Y'know, like Will said. *Uncensored*.

So I expected to see minarets and gold embroidery and women in burqas. They were there, sure. But so were belly shirts, gangsta hoodies, and a lot of very pale people in ugly jeans. A sociological polyglot, the (s)mother would call it, trying to expand my frame of reference. It just kinda looked like South Street to me, right down to the bling-y accessory shop sandwiched between the mobile phone store and the pub.

We walked for a few minutes, away from the shops and into a narrower street lined with identical orange-brick houses with supersize white trim and tall windows. The Sadiqs' flat is the whole bottom floor of one of them. As we entered the foyer, we could hear the only-slightly-muffled thump of drums coming from upstairs. In the offbeats, I could just make out a sort of garbled moaning. It wasn't a recording.

"Swedish medical students," Elizabeth told me, as if that explained everything.

We were barely through the door when two versions of Elizabeth, in descending size, came at us. "Mum's working late; Aunt Suha's on the phone!" the smaller one announced, bouncing up and down. She looked about twelve. "Dad's talking to her now. The wedding is on!"

"My sister Joanna," Elizabeth announced as she lifted her bag full of—chocolate, of course—what else?—out of her sister's reach. "Jo, this is—"

"It was still off until Wednesday," the taller cut in. She looked twelve, too, but the black Pink shirt made me guess at fifteen or so. "Then his parents gave Shaz a new car... well, not a *new* new one, but only a couple of years old, and said they'll give her a house when she marries Youssif."

"This is Sarah," Elizabeth told me. "She's obsessed with bad telly and the *Eastenders*-like drama of our cousin's engagement. Sarah—"

"Youssif's hideous!" Joanna proclaimed.

"A toad!" Sarah agreed.

"He's rich," Elizabeth said, "and he might be a perfectly decent bloke—"

"Ewwwww!" they both groaned.

"Fine, he's a toad all around. She won't end up marrying him." To me, Elizabeth explained, "Suha's my father's sister. She lives in Jordan, with her aforementioned daughter, who may or may not actually be marrying the rich but wholly unattractive son of a rich but boorish car dealer. It's an ongoing saga, fast losing its salacious appeal." She waved the bag like a hypnotist's watch in front of her sisters. "Now you will both pay attention to me. This is my friend Cat from the States. Do not eat this chocolate in front of her. She's bargaining with Fate."

Sarah got the bag. "Hiya!" she said to me. "Fate is an impervious foe."

"Brilliant!" Joanna announced. Whether to me or the choc, I have no clue.

"To the table!" I heard Mr. Sadiq call from somewhere down a hall.

Their flat looks like ours at home. Lots of books and comfy furniture and not quite enough room for everything in it. There were fashion mags on every flat surface. One gray cat was sleeping on the windowsill. Another one lay on its back, all four paws in the air, on one of the Middle Eastern–looking rugs. Kinda like Andouille does on our rugs. Only I doubt theirs are from IKEA. Theirs glow a little.

Elizabeth pulled me past her sisters. "Come on, then. If Mum's late at the hospital, Dad's cooking. So be warned."

"Warned . . . ?" I asked.

"He's an experimental cook. Tonight's menu is braised snake."

Okay, so I'm halfway into what's obviously the dining room, trying to think of how I can possibly explain that I go into anaphylactic shock if I eat legless reptile—without sounding like the lily-livered American coward that I am—and she lets me actually get to "I . . . er . . . ah" before letting out that killer laugh.

"You really are an eejit, you know." She sighed, slinging an arm around my shoulders. "We're probably having some form of pasta pesto."

I hate Elizabeth. I love Elizabeth.

We had rotini with turnip-green-and-walnut pesto. Mr. Sadiq watched me take my first bite as if I were, in fact, prone to anaphylaxis. It kinda tasted like garlicky turf. How do I know how turf tastes, you ask? Do please recall my brief stint at Taney baseball. (Ten points to whichever of you can find out what happened to Trevor Wilson. Haven't thought of him since he fell for that ballerina from St. Peter's and so ended my twelve-year-old aspirations of getting to first base.)

"Delicious," sez I. Actually, it really was pretty good. Mr. Sadiq beamed. The Junior Sadiqs rolled their eyes in perfect unison, and all was well in the world.

My dad cooks. Kinda. The soon-to-be-stepmonster talked him into taking a series of couples' cooking classes last year. He went to one. He learned to make stuffed baked potatoes. He makes them stuffed with canned chili. Or tuna. Or their innards mixed with canned soup. He gets a little grumpy when Samantha the STBS asks him to leave her potato unbuttered, unsalted, unstuffed. He stomped out of the kitchen once when I reminded him that I haven't liked tuna fish since . . . well, since forever, actually.

"There you are, Dad," Joanna said on hearing about my dad's culinary prowess. "You could mix potato innards with basil pesto."

"Or rocket pesto," Sarah added.

"Or potato pesto, perhaps," from Elizabeth.

Mr. Sadiq took it all with his familiar dignity. "There will be no sweet for any of you ingrates. And I have made Victoria sponge with—"

"Pesto!" all three girls said together.

"Yes, yes, most amusing." To me, Mr. Sadiq announced, "A chef I am not, but I like to combine interesting ingredients. I have not entirely left the science professor behind."

"You were a professor?"

"I was. Chemistry, at a technical college in Baghdad." He must have noticed my surprise. He smiled, a little sadly. "Ah, yes, I had a career before the shop, a life before London. But then, you could not have known that, and I daresay many of the shopkeepers in your Philadelphia look much as I do."

He's right. They do.

"How many Iraqis have you met, Catherine?"

"I don't know exactly," I admitted. "Two or three that I know of."

"And they were teachers? Doctors? Engineers?"

"No," I admitted. "They were driving taxis."

"Just so." Mr. Sadiq nodded. "In this country of opposite sides," he said, "I am not a good driver."

He wasn't talking about driving. As much of a Homer as I felt right then, I knew that. I felt about six inches tall, goils.

Mr. Sadiq didn't mean to make me feel bad. Or maybe he did, in a nice way. Maybe I deserved it. But the girls barely blinked. "No worries, Yank," Elizabeth assured me as she carried an armload of plates from the table. "We think all Americans are stone stupid."

"Complete pilchards," Joanna agreed cheerfully.

"Self-centered, egomaniacal, earth-destroying bullies," Elizabeth added with glee.

Sarah grinned. "With crap taste in music."

"And books."

"And television."

"And crisps."

"And chocolate."

"Enough!" Mr. Sadiq commanded finally, but with that last, sadly true pronouncement, I could only concede utter defeat and tuck happily, with everyone else, into a seriously excellent sponge cake.

They asked about America. Mine, anyway.

Joanna wanted to know if I'd ever met Miley Cyrus, Kevin Jonas, or Robert Pattinson. She took it pretty well when I said I hadn't. I didn't mention that, as he is English, Robert probably lives in London. Elizabeth grilled me about my vast knowledge of Washington, D.C. I told her everything I knew. Like how the Mall looks when it's full of PO'd librarians protesting funding cuts. Lucky, ain't it, our class trip to the Smithsonian coincided with that march? Elizabeth need never know we ended up in the middle of things only because we took a wrong turn looking for a Fourbucks. I think I still have the pix of Kelly holding the "Literacy Ain't Everything" sign she found.

Anyway, when she's done her duty in the UK, Elizabeth plans to come be civilly disobedient on our shores. Joanna thinks she's a pilchard (which, as well as being a synonym for "berk," apparently, turns out to be a sardine—who knew?). Joanna wants to go to Hollywood.

Taking advantage of this geographical clash, Sarah told us all that, not only did *she* want to go to Ipswich, but that she had a *plan*. As in the Ipswich, which would involve a train ride out to the coast with her best friend, and a night spent with the cousin of a friend of one of her posse's older brothers. Sounded like a good time to me.

Mr. Sadiq's response? "Not while there is breath in my body."

Note: he said the same regarding Joanna's plans to be in the next Jonas Brothers' video. He's reliable.

"They're all going, Dad!" Sarah insisted. "All my mates! Jacinta and Patrice and David and Hamid and Regina and Claire!"

"No."

"I'll be an outcast. A pariah!"

"Good word, 'pariah.' Your excessively expensive school seems to be living up to its exalted reputation. But still no."

"*Pleeeeease?*"

"No."

"You don't let me do anything. I might as well be in Baghdad!"

He gave her one of those looks that can stop the mighty Mississippi from flowing. She shut up, but it was a very noisy silence. "Has Jacinta promised her father that she will attain at least B grades in her GCSEs?"

(Elizabeth sez GCSEs are like our final grades and SATs combined; how well you do kinda determines whether you go to Oxford or serve greasy burgers to Oxford students.)

"Well, no ..." Sarah admitted.

"*Will* Jacinta attain at least B grades in her GCSEs?"

"No ..."

"And attend a university that does not specialize in alcohol consumption and cosmetic application?"

"Yes! Well, no. Probably not."

"So." Mr. Sadiq accepted a cup of tea from Joanna. So did I. What was I going to do—decline? Elizabeth smirked at me. "When you have completed your exams, when a parent can enter your bedroom without the aid of a shovel and biohazard waste bin, when I am reasonably certain that your iPod earblooms are not permanently fused to your ears, I shall entertain the possibility of you accompanying your mates to Ipswich. Fair?"

Sarah looked a tiny bit embarrassed, for a tiny second. Then: "All right, then. I won't go to Ipswich. Can Jacinta and I go the cinema Friday night? There's a midnight showing of *Harry Potter and the Deathly Hallows*. Her mum will drop us off and pick us up."

"Fine."

Sarah grinned at Joanna; they both grinned at Elizabeth. Mr. Sadiq smiled into his tea, and that, apparently, was that.

After dinner, Elizabeth and I hung out in her room. It is, of course, infinitely cool. Gold graffiti on the walls (RESISTANCE IS FERTILE, IMAGINE, STOP MAD COWBOY DISEASE), fab clothing everywhere, pictures all over the walls of Elizabeth and Imogen and Consuelo and the other beautiful people who, I guess, are satellites around their tight little solar system.

I wandered over to look at a pic of the trio in front of the London Eye. They're all holding airplane barf bags. Empty, I assume. "I should take my dad on the Eye when he comes," I decided. "He likes being at the very top of things." Yeah, yeah, Keri, I know. I *don't*. But this is my dad's visit. Besides, maybe Elizabeth still has the barf bag.

As usual when I thought about Dad's visit, my stomach did a little jiggle. I still haven't found the perfect restaurant for my birthday dinner. I like Indian; he doesn't. He likes *haute cuisine*; I don't wanna spend my b-day dinner worrying about using the wrong *merde*ing fork. Beyond that, I'm still not sure about the hotel (what does *"Caters to the fine character"* mean, anyway?). And, despite several offhand mentions to the contrary, I'm not completely convinced that he won't show up with the STBS in tow, rendering all of my concerns moot and plans irrelevant. He can be kinda hard to plan around. (Remember the New York fiasco, Soph? Of course you do. Although, to be fair, you gotta admit that the two of us taking the midnight Chinatown bus back to Philly turned out to be kind of a hoot.) The STBS likes four-star, white-glove, no carb, no character whatsoever. And what she wants, he gives her. The wedding? Prepare for really really expensive rubber chicken.

And back to the regularly scheduled program . . .

Elizabeth pointed to a pic of her with another crazy pretty girl, mugging for the camera in matching Rasta hats. "That's Shazia when they visited in April."

I peered more closely and saw the diamond ring on Shazia's finger. She looked like Elizabeth: bright and confident. "Why is she getting married if the guy's such a toad?"

Elizabeth shrugged and flopped onto her bed. It's covered with this gorgeous tapestry that feels like a pashmina and has all these little mirrors sewn into it. I don't think it's from IKEA, either. "They want to stay in Jordan. Things are still pretty horrific in Iraq. My uncle's been in prison there for eight years, my aunt can't find work, and Shaz can't shop." She said the last bit casually. But I know it isn't. Casual.

I thought of the picture on the wall of the shop. "What did your uncle do?"

"He was caught spying for your lot."

"*Really?*"

"No. Jeez, Yank, you really will believe anything." Elizabeth fished a bra out from under her butt (okay, I might actually trade any possibility of something with Will for the ability to wear something with lace *and* an underwire) and sighed. "Look, Cat, not to cast blame, but it's a crap life sometimes, being Iraqi. A fluke of geography, really, when you think about it. I mean, all the borders were drawn in 1922 by a Brit. A few miles difference and my grandparents could have been Jordanian. Or Syrian."

I must have looked confused. "Okay," she said. "Look at it this way. The Vernons are what? French? English? By ancestry?" I nodded. She got that exactly right. "But they landed in a place some Brits colonized and became pretty French-English people living in America. Americans. Yeah? So we're Sunni Muslims. Who lived in a place that some Brits colonized and became Sunnis living in Iraq. Iraqis. There are Shiites, too, and no matter what your intrepid Fox News people say, neither is good nor bad nor innocent, and believe me, Yank, no one in Iraq is happy. Get it?"

I got it.

She went on. Her parents saw bad things ahead and left a month before she was born. Her dad's cousin had a restaurant and sponsored him with a job in it. No one would hire him to teach, so when the chance came up, he bought his own business. Her mom was an anesthesiologist in Baghdad. The English wouldn't acknowledge her degree and there was no way she could go back to med school. She speaks four languages, so she's a translator at a hospital in the East End. The uncle stayed in Baghdad. He was arrested for refusing to put his chemistry expertise to . . . noneducational uses. There's hope he'll be released, oh, someday, when the good guys, whoever they are, notice he's still in there.

Elizabeth scooped a green Kate Moss cardi off the floor and put it on. "But I am a bloomin' English rose, aren't I? And I have just acquired a bootleg copy of Season Six of *Lost*, including the Unaired Episode. You in?"

Three hours, countless Black Smoke Monster encounters, and one huge bowl of popcorn later, we staggered out of her room so

I could get home. Elizabeth was all about coming all the way back with me on the Tube. Good friend. But I flashed the twenty-pound note the (s)mother had given me. Cab fare.

In the end, Elizabeth had to tend to Sarah, who was having a makeup disaster and had locked herself in the bathroom. Mr. Sadiq walked me out to the corner and waited with me. It was a busy street, even at nearly eleven: people coming home from late work or play, a handful of kids still not in bed, people my age going in whatever direction while they texted on their mobiles.

I wanted to say something. *Sorry about all the invasion stuff.* How could I possibly?

Suddenly, from a distance, I heard a long, musical call, rising and falling. It was a single male voice, singing words I couldn't understand, but they made me feel sad somehow. Heads turned; men picked up their pace, intent on reaching some nearby destination. A taxi pulled up in front of me, and Mr. Sadiq ushered me in.

"What is that?" I asked. "It's amazing."

"It is the *azan*, the call to prayer. I must heed it."

I thanked him quickly for dinner.

"You are welcome, Catherine Vernon." He shut the taxi door and said through the open window. "You are always welcome."

I could still hear the *azan* as we turned several corners and zipped away from the Sadiqs.

The driver had no chin and was wearing a Manchester United jersey. "Hate that bloody racket," he informed me.

He had something twangy and clearly American blaring on the radio.

Had I had any idea whatsoever where I was, I would have told him exactly what I thought of Manchester United football club. Instead, I just stiffed him on the tip.

Stronger, Part Deux

I woke up way too early (read: 10 a.m.) to e-mail from Kelly. (Thanks for the Adam update; I am certain that tomorrow I will be tickled fuchsia about the french fry debacle.) And one from my dad.

To: Me

From: Him

Subject: London Birthday Visit

(Crap, I think. I really gotta pick a restaurant. Like today.)

It was a real scorcher here today. 95 on ice. Went to the Phillies game with most important client. Thought I was going to melt. They did, in the seventh. Lost to the Mets 5-2. Client was not impressed. He's from Milwaukee. I'm giving up the seats after this season.

(That's what? The twelfth year in a row he's said that? Like he's ever going to give up third row, third-base line.)

I bet it's a heck of a lot cooler where you are.

(Honestly, Dad. The weather??)

Which makes me even sorrier that I won't be able to come for your birthday.

(I mean, I know we don't have the sort of deep, highly intellectual discussions you and the STBS have, like about Chardonnay and Labradoodles and whether glass tile works with oak . . . Wait. What???)

Samantha feels terrible about it, but she completely misread dates and arranged critical meetings with Realtors and caterers. I can't leave her alone for them, or I'll find myself living in the boonies—not to mention eating boiled twigs and flaxseed cake at my wedding.

You understand, Kitty Cat. We'll do something special when you get back, just the three of us.

Samantha sends smoochies.

Love, Dad

I *don't* understand. Should I? Is that the sort of thing I usually understand? Dad seems to think so.

I must have made a noise. A loud one. Mom came in. She managed to catch my laptop before it slid off the bed and onto the puke green carpeting in Professor Fungus's second bedroom.

"Oh, Cat. I'm so sorry." She knew. She already knew. "He e-mailed me, too."

"I'll live, Ma."

"Oh, Cat." And she climbed onto the bed next to me and kinda (s)mothered me for a while. It was the right thing to do. Then she left and went to buy me a Dairy Milk bar. It was the right thing to do.

I'll say this for Mom. She never bad-mouths my dad in front of me. Never has. Not on those Fridays when I sat next to the front door with my overnight bag—waiting and waiting until the phone rang and she would silently put my sleeping bag back in the hall closet and make me mac n' cheese for dinner. Not when he gave me a doll for my thirteenth birthday. Not even when he wouldn't pay his share of my TPS tuition for a year because he didn't like the new head of school. I'm not supposed to know about that. GM told me when she'd had a third mochaccino once and he forgot to pick me up from her house. She gets kinda feisty when under the influence of excessive caffeine.

So when Mom called Dad that one word we never expect to hear come out of our mothers' mouths (especially considering the fact that, when you consider moms, dads, and what he-did-to-she-to-make-we, it's a perfectly reasonable name to call 'em), it was kind of a shock.

I didn't mean to eavesdrop on the phone call either. But Mom is GM's daughter. She's pretty fierce (and loud) when someone does me wrong.

The (one-sided) convo went something like:

Yes, Samantha, I know exactly what time it is in Philadelphia. And since we share such impressive grasps of clocks, I assume we also share a knowledge of calendars. However, I don't really feel like discussing culpability with you. Culpability ... C ... U ... L ... Put Jon on the phone.

I closed my door. Most of the way. And got back in bed.

... this might be the lowest ... Oh, you think? How about her third-grade Christmas pageant ... first Wise Man ... most of the weekends you were supposed to see her ... ninth birthday? ... only freshman to make drama club ... couldn't possibly have waited until the following week? ... Caterers? Caterers? You selfish bas—

You go, Ma.

I put on my headphones.

✦ ✦ ✦

(Seex hours latairr)

Ladies, there is a Part Trois. Who'd'a thunk it? Clouds do occasionally have titanium lining.

3:50 p.m. After way too many hours doing absolutely nothing and a mere ten minutes from flipping the finger at the Fates and slumping out for an extra-large bag of Maltesers (I figured they'd give me a pass for the Dairy Milk, as I didn't buy it):

Ding.

I've got mail. From Will.

I got all tingly. You know, that kinda breathless, giddy feeling you got for the very first time when you unstuck the big construction-paper-heart envelope from the side of your desk in third grade and saw that your crush (Aidan Williams) had given you a Valentine? It didn't matter that it was one of those punch-out ones with a Transformer on it. Or that the girl next to you (Alex) had one, too. He'd signed it. In green crayon.

That's how I felt when I saw will percival@mayfair.eng. No delayed gratification here. No hesitation. I clicko pronto.

Subject: History, Dude

I hear your social calendar suddenly has an opening.

(Do I hate my mother? Don't think I can. Not today. Not even knowing she talked to Will behind my back. Again.)

So, I've been thinking of you lately, Catherine *(yay! yay! yay me! I squeal inwardly),* **and the Katherine of years gone by. I think you need to tread in her footsteps.**

(Oh. Okay. Maybe, thinks moi, he means dancing. Betcha he knows the good clubs. I could try to get Elizabeth to lend me that silver peace shirt. I think she would. And maybe hit Boots for some shimmery eye stuff...)

So I'm issuing you a challenge. Find ten places she mentions in the diary, ten places that still exist in London today, and I'll take you there. Think of it as my birthday gift to you, an excursion into the past. There was a London before Harry Potter and Stella McCartney. -W

Okay. Not dancing after all. But Will. Will who's willing to take me puh-laces. Ten of 'em. Count 'em. Ten. There's gotta be one, I figure, where I can wear a killer silver peace tee. Might have to rethink the eye shadow . . .

29 May

There is a new girl in Town. Her name is Julia Northrop. ~~She looks like the posterior of~~ She is not pretty. She resembles a ginger cat who has eaten a lemon. She behaves like a ginger cat who has eaten a lemon. She was positively beastly to Winnie Stuart at the Ecclestons' tonight, hissing and spitting. Miss Stuart certainly did not mean to spill Miss Northrop's punch all over her dress, but she does have the unfortunate habit of speaking with her hands.

Yes, the dress was white, and yes, the punch was rather pink, but there still was no call for Miss Northrop to use the words "clumsy cow" or "ham-fisted bluestocking." Such unhappy accidents are the stuff of lively parties.

Mr. Eccleston, charming and eager, was there in a moment, offering sympathy and the use of a retiring room. In fact, he had been with us just before the Incident, as had Misters Davison, Tallisker, and McCoy, offering various foodstuffs. They, however, had trotted off in search of sweets, leaving us. They would not have heard Miss Northrup's nasty words. They would only have seen her distress. In the wake of their return, they guided her away, shushing and patting her wrists, and being as foolishly helpless as most young men are.

So off went catty Miss Northrop with her swains. Luisa and I remained with Winnie. As always, Luisa was perfectly kind, insisting it was a sorry mishap (quite true), Miss Northrop is a shameless harpy (true as well), and an epic poem such as <u>Lord of the Isles</u> must certainly, by its very nature, encourage dramatic commentary (perhaps not entirely truthful, but kind and convincing and well aimed). Winnie brightened considerably and said to us:

"I should not have minded at all, really—I *am*, after all, bookish and clumsy—had I not heard her speaking a half hour past with Mr. Baker on the very subject of poetry. I had, of course, thought her to be interested, but now I begin to wonder if perhaps she is truly interested in Mr. Baker, and not in poetry at all."

Winnie is a good sort of girl, but perhaps not the quickest. Although sometimes her insights are sharp as brass tacks.

"I suppose Miss Northrop does not have to be kind," she finished with a sigh. "She is rich."

She is. According to the Misses Quinn, Miss Northrop has ten thousand pounds now, and will almost certainly have that again upon the death of her grandmother. She does not have to be kind. She does not have to be pretty. She does not have to be friends with the other girls in her circle. She is rich. She will be courted by some men, no matter how ill she behaves. And Miss Northrop is not stupid. On the contrary, she is very clever.

As Mama says, One may hide cruel. One may even hide a certain amount of madness. One can never hide stupidity.

The men are flocking to her. I suppose they cannot be blamed for thinking she is a far more pleasant creature than she is. She shows them only her agreeable side. And as Luisa says, if women often consider money when weighing the appeal of a gentleman, shouldn't gentlemen, who are far less influenced by their hearts, be allowed to do the same?

If I were more generous of spirit, perhaps I would agree.

As it is, I am merely reminded of Lord Chilham's odiousness. He does not care a whit for my character; I see it clearly in his eyes. But I am pretty and I am possessed of a decent fortune. And in that lies enough for him.

I am not mistaken. I wish I could be.

I wish, too, that I could be mistaken in Papa's intent. Perhaps I am. Perhaps I am being silly and stupid, seeing things that are not there. Perhaps he does not think it would be a good match (oh, how could <u>anyone</u> but Chilham think it a good match!). Yes, certainly silly.

I do not wish to think of Chilham, not when tonight's party brought such a joyous moment. I have lived and relived it, almost teasing myself into thinking it was not real, that even to write it down would make it not so.

I danced with ~~Mr. Baker~~ Thomas. That, of course, is not <u>The Moment</u>, but it was the beginning. He sought me out not ten minutes after my arrival, and claimed the country dance. How lovely to hold his hand and to have him smile each time we were reunited in the set. As we walked onto the dance floor, he whispered into my ear:

> "Long and empty days may be,
>   with much to weary and naught to please.
> For me, this eve a beacon was,
> A promise of pleasure and of ease . . .

I confess, my heart skipped.

I believe I blushed, too, which would have been mortifying had not he looked softly on my face in that moment, and said, "The dance suits you, Miss Percival."

I suspect that in that instant, I glowed like a star.

Of course, it did not last. How could it for me? As we neared the end of the set, in the final turn, he held my hand tightly and announced, "We shall not meet again for some days."

I could not hide my distress. I was able to make it seem less than it was, certainly. I am not so careless as to show all that I feel. Still, I know I did not appear unconcerned when I asked why.

"A house party in Kent," was his reply. "A tedious engagement, but one I must honour as it was planned some time ago. I would much rather stay."

"How long will you be away?"

"Five days, I expect. Perhaps as much as a sennight. I must, of course, be ruled by the whims of my hosts. I am loath to disappoint them."

("What of me?" I wished I could demand. "Are you not loath to disappoint me? Seven days without you!")

"Of course, I should be loath to disappoint others," he said, almost before the words had left my head, "if I thought . . . there might be cause."

In that moment, he looked hopeful. I do believe he looked hopeful. He certainly looked very, very handsome, gazing down at me from under his bronze curls. I almost could not speak.

"I . . . am certain there . . . is cause," I managed.

"Good," he said, and brightened, like the sun coming from behind a cloud. "Very good." Then, much more blithely: "You will keep note of all that happens in my absence, will you not, kind Miss Percival? And you will share it with me in some long, quiet meeting when I return?"

His alteration from melancholy to pert nearly made me dizzy. Or, rather, I was near giddy with the knowledge that he cares for me. Of course I agreed. As we parted, he gave me the last lines.

>   "Days may pass ere I return,
>   in which a gentleman might yearn."

He returned me to the parlor, where Luisa was chatting with Charles and Nicholas. Charles seemed happy as always; he never seems to mind being in Luisa's company, even if she is merely a friend of his younger sister. Nicholas, as seems to be the way of things since the Bellingham disaster, scowled when he saw me. He grunted a greeting; he would not be so rude as to snub me, not ever-proper Sir Nicholas Everard, scourge of all things impolite. Charles laughed at me.

"You are all pink in the cheeks!" he announced. I wanted to kick him in the shins. "Should I call out Baker for dancing you too briskly?"

Luisa, as always, was perfect. "You do seem overwarm. Shall we fetch ourselves something to drink?" She knew something important had transpired.

As soon as we were in a quiet spot, I told her all, being certain not to leave out so much as a quirk of his eyebrows or pause in his speech. Luisa listened quietly until I was quite done.

"I am happy for your happiness," she told me. "I must say, however, that I shall be even happier when he openly declares himself to you."

Well, of course, so shall I. "<u>I love you, Katherine</u>" is ever so much more promising than "<u>Good</u>", but "<u>Good</u>" will be good enough until I have better.

I shall not sleep tonight, I know. He left me with a poem. I plague myself with questions.

How shall my heart bear such a bursting sensation?

How shall I bear a sennight without him?

31 May

I miss Mr. Baker terribly. It has only been two days, yet it feels an eternity.

I have endeavoured to be home as little as possible. How low I feel, how dishonest. Yet, I cannot stomach the thought of another encounter with Chilham, and as Father remains much in his company, it seems I must also avoid the person I care for most in order to avoid the one I like least. Mama has been of help. She has been quite well enough to escort me during the day. We have been to Bond Street in search of new fashions, to the gardens at Kew for a fashionable picnic in the shade of the Chinese Pagoda, and, despite my reluctance, to the British Museum in search, she says, of something fashionable for the brain.

"Try to see the beauty, Katherine," she snapped more than once as we examined a stone body without a head, or stone head without a body. I could not help giggling each time we passed a marble bottom. I know I should not speak of it, but then, what else are diaries for, but the things we cannot mention in company?

I confess, I found our visit to the Tower most exciting. How many people have walked through those stone ramparts through the centuries, never to walk out? What did Anne Boleyn dream of within those walls? Did she believe, every day, even after her sentence of death, that her husband, King Henry, would relent and come himself to release her from her cold cell?

"Perhaps she thought love would conquer all," I mused as we left the little rooms where she spent her final days.

"Perhaps she should have thought twice before marrying

a man who disposed so handily of his first wife," was Mama's dry retort.

She is not a great lover of King Henry. He was, no doubt, rather hard on his wives. Mama's novel in verse, which she says is nearly complete, is titled <u>The Abandoned Bride</u>. I have not read it. I suspect it is neither sufficiently romantic nor dramatic. The Tower is.

Did the little nephews of cowardly Richard III play within those walls, bouncing balls down the stairs, certain they would soon be free to play on the heath? Do their bones still rest with the walls, near to where they were murdered? Was that a bloodstain there . . . ? No, merely a shadow. There! No, dark lichen. There . . .

"Katherine, you are a ghoul." Mama sighed.

"Perhaps, but I am the ghoul of someone's dreams."

"Oh, Katherine!"

Yet she laughed. And I laughed with her. It was . . . sweet.

Her headache returned as we toured the decidedly smelly menagerie. I would have very much liked to have stayed a bit longer, seen the lion and the monkeys, but though she did not say so, I could see her discomfort in her eyes and in the set of her mouth. I shall certainly return to the Tower someday. Perhaps with my own daughter.

As we turned the corner into our street, I spied Lord Chilham's carriage in front of the house. I confess, I felt ill at the thought of facing him, after such a pleasant afternoon.

Mama saw it, too. "I believe," she announced, "this is the perfect time for a strawberry ice at Gunter's."

She does not care for strawberries. And I know ices make her head hurt. Still we went, and had a long interlude in the tea shop, watching people passing by in the street. We chose for each other items of clothing from the more entertaining ensembles. I decreed Mama must have the bulging brown straw hat with the silk cardinal perched atop it. She graciously gifted me the crocheted shawl that looked as if it had been fashioned from a fishing net. We fought fiercely over the blindingly pink dress with purple bows at the hem. By the time we returned home, the men were gone. We had supper together in the Rose Parlor.

We spoke of small things, of the honeysuckle at Kew, the view of the city from Hampstead Heath, the pretty pearl buttons on the newest gloves. I played the little harpsichord that Papa's grandmother brought with her from France. I even played tolerably.

Mama sat curled in her favourite cushiony chair, feet tucked beneath her. In the moment, with the fire behind her and her face softened by shadow, she was familiar, like a mirror.

"Promise me something, Katherine," she said in a quiet moment.

"If I can."

"Oh, you can. Promise me this: that you will think, in every moment possible, what you want for yourself. And you will stand for yourself, especially in the times when no one seems interested in standing for you."

I did not understand, not really, but I promised nonetheless.

2 June

How very vexing war is. Word has arrived in Town that Napoleon's forces are larger than assumed. They are marching through France. More battles are nearly certain. I do wish they would happen quickly, so our marvelous soldiers could rout him once and for all and end this dismal war. He has eluded defeat far too long.

We would not allow the news to dampen our pleasure in our entertainments. In fact, the Misses Quinn, Luisa, and I all donned our favourite military colours and went to the Cameron dinner dance. It was very merry. As Mr. Tallisker said (he was wearing a wreath of grape leaves on his head and a makeshift toga atop his evening clothes at the time), "When the world is grim, London sets a happy tone." Everyone seems determined to eat, drink, and be merry.

Miss Northrop was not in attendance. It was very pleasant. Of course, all would have been ever so much better had Mr. Baker been present, but I managed to enjoy myself anyway. I danced, I laughed, I found myself the center of a crowd more than once. I felt admired; I felt bold.

Charles and Nicholas were, for a moment, standing with our crowd in the Camerons' drawing room. In truth, it was more that we had enveloped them than that they had joined us, but as they have both served under Wellington on the Continent, they are very popular fellows.

"Are you not frightened to return?" Eleanora Quinn asked Charles.

"Terrified!" He laughed, appearing anything but.

"Is Bonaparte truly the size of a child?" someone else demanded.

"I have not met the man and cannot say, but his opinion of himself is of a giant size."

"Is the wine French?"

"Are there pipers on the field of battle?"

"However does your valet keep your uniform as elegant it should be?"

Charles answered all with patience and humour. Nicholas said very little, but did not seem as stern as he often does. Winnie Stuart stood near him, looking slightly awed and a bit moonstruck. She finds him very handsome and very dashing and has asked me several times, as he is a close friend of the family, how he came to get the scar across his brow. She is not the first to ask, nor to hear that he has never told me. He left for war unblemished and returned as he is. Why people cannot ask him, I do not know. ~~He is rather unapproa~~

Well, why should I not be a leader of my set? It made perfect sense to demand, "Do tell us, Sir Nicholas, how you came to get that scar. We ladies have been ever so curious and are near to wagering on the matter. Was it a Frenchman's rapier? A flashing bayonet? We have come up with the most exciting possibilities and cannot choose among them!"

There. I had done it.

My proud satisfaction lasted precisely two seconds.

"Be so kind as to remove me from your games," Nicholas said sharply, jaw taut and eyes cool. "I am not a suitable subject." He gave a terse bow. "If you would excuse me..." Then, turning on his heel, he stalked away.

There was a long moment of silence.

"Sullen fellow, ain't he?" Mr. Troughton commented at last.

"Oh, but so handsome!"

I do not think Winnie meant to speak aloud. She went crimson with shame, but my friends are not deliberately cruel. Not like <u>he</u> is. The Misses Quinn gamely agreed that he was quite handsome, indeed. Mr. McCoy admitted he wouldn't mind employing Sir Nicholas's tailor. Mr. Davison commented that Nicholas had always been a fine fellow at school, capital on the playing field, and always tolerant of the younger boys. Nicholas was forgiven and Winnie's calf-eyed outburst forgotten.

I knew my own cheeks were burning. It did not help in the least that Charles and Luisa were both looking at me with the same mix of pity and censure.

How could he have been so rude! In front of my friends, no less.

Well, Mama was correct. I must stand for myself, as no one else seemed interested in the task.

The very best, most killing set-downs played through my mind as I went after him. He would cringe. He would cower. He would rue the day he mocked me over that silly charade...

He was standing on the ballroom balcony, silvered by cold moonlight, and he watched me approach with all the warmth of a stone in winter.

"You," I began in my very best Mama voice, "are an ill-mannered boor—"

"Oh, cork it, Katherine!" he snapped. Around us, I saw heads turning. Nicholas must have noticed, too, for he swept his hand in a sharp arc, gesturing me onto the balcony with him. We were in full sight of the ballroom, but could speak without being overheard. I did not particularly want to stand so close. He nearly radiated heat and anger and it was most disturbing.

"I really do not think you should speak to me so," I informed him primly.

He snorted. "On the contrary, I must. No one else seems willing to. For God's sake, enough with the vapidity! It does not suit you in the least."

"Why, you arrogant—"

"Enough. I have had enough. Do you want to know how I got this scar? Well, too bad, infant, for I am not going to tell you. I will, however, tell you something of this war you seem to find so charmingly inconvenient, yet entertaining all the same."

He leaned forward, quite towering over me, and looked very fierce. "War is not romantic, Katherine, or theatrical. It is hell, pure and simple. It is not dinners and shiny uniforms and commandeered French wine. It is week after week of slogging through mud in split boots under enemy fire. It is arriving at your fortress with but half your regiment still alive and all your rations gone, only to find rats in the stores. It is entering a town after it has been under siege for months and seeing more small crosses at the walls than children in the streets! It is surviving and coming home when many, many far better men did not!

"For God's sake, Katherine, think occasionally! With the amount of brain I have seen you using since arriving in Town, you make precisely half of a sensible person. Beauty and liveliness might get you admiration from others, but I cannot imagine that you see much to admire when you look deeply into your mirror!"

He was so angry. The scar, whose origin I still do not know, stood out against his anger-flushed skin. For a moment, I wanted to slap him. He would not strike back. I have known him long enough and well enough to be certain of that. Then, suddenly, I wanted to cry. I had no idea, I realised, if he would comfort me.

I fled, before I could learn that he would not.

Charles was waiting nearby. He handed me his handkerchief and a cup of lemonade, and blocked me from public view until I could compose myself.

"You shouldn't mind him, Kitty," he said at last. "He doesn't like to talk about it, about Vittoria. It was ... frightful, I think."

"I do not mean to be silly," I sniffled. "I do not think I am meant to be."

"Of course you don't. You aren't. You are meant to be luminous."

I blinked at that, pleased. "How poetic of you, Charles."

He smiled and tapped me under the chin. "Wasn't me, old girl. It was Everard." When I started to smile, he shook his head. "Don't get complacent. He said you are meant to be luminous, but seem only to manage shiny."

Well. How frustratingly like him.

"Now promise me you won't keep on pestering the poor fellow. I'll be back on the Continent sooner or later. I'll send you long letters, full of gruesome details."

Luminous. I am meant to be luminous. If Nicholas Everard, boor that he is, sees that, Thomas Baker must certainly as well.

3 June

Our Ackermann's this month is full of dresses simply meant to be worn by a bride. I find my mind filled with pale silk and satin, with delicate net and lace, and sprays of sweet pea. Everywhere there are thoughts of matrimony. Miss Henrietta Quinn has accepted Mr. Troughton. They shall have their wedding in July. Their children shall be very sweet. They will have very pretty blond curls, and no chins whatsoever.

Mama received word yesterday that Miss Cameron is to be married. And to Mr. Piper, the parson! Mama is quite pleased for her. Miss Cameron, with her mousy hair, twitchy fingers, and drab grey dresses. To be Mrs. Piper, with that funny little house that looks green in sunlight and always smells of damp.

Still, I must confess I am pleased for her. Miss Cameron is a good sort of lady. She has always been kind to me, even when I could not be bothered to practice or recite or pay attention, and in those times when I was not very kind to her.

If one squints a bit, Mr. Piper could be found quite handsome. He has always seemed perfectly pleasant, and Mama says he has a gentleman's manners and a sense of humour that most gentlemen do not possess. I do hope he will make Miss Cameron happy. I shall be happy to have her nearby in the parsonage

I do not recall what I'd meant to write about the parsonage. I was interrupted by the arrival of far less happy news than that of Miss Cameron's engagement.

We have just had word that Charles must go, and so much sooner than we could have imagined. Napoleon has taken more of France and will try to take Belgium. Charles's regiment is being sent abroad, to halt the Little General's march. He leaves tomorrow.

I do hope it is not too long before he returns. If all goes as it must, if I am to have an autumn wedding, he must be home by September. I would not care at all to have to be married in the cold dead of winter (or, even worse, have to wait even longer!) because my brother is cavorting with his fellow soldiers in Brussels.

I shall miss him. Frightfully.

I'll Take You There

Okay, so I gotta find ten places ditzy Miss Kitty visited and Will will take me there.

In case I haven't mentioned it already, this is what Katherine does with her life:

1. shops

2. eats

3. dances

4. rhapsodizes about a guy

Don't say it, any of you. I will change the password of this blog and not tell you what the new one is.

I don't dance.

Not here, anyway.

Now, considering that there were no department stores in 1815, restaurants were of the pub-grub-tavern-wench variety, and I don't think the London club scene exactly welcomed nice girls, I'm a tad stumped. And there is no, I repeat *no* way I'm going back to the BM with Will. Once we're old and gray and can laugh about such things, we can go back to the place we met and have a good chuckle. Until such time...

I've been rereading and reskimming. Jeez, enough about Mr. Baker, already. But I did find some possibles among the punch and poetry (which, I feel compelled to agree with that angry Nick dude, still sounds like bad copies of Byron). This is serious, goils. Will has offered me near-total access to him for ten different occasions. Which, even if combined into trips of two, makes for five very nice days.

(He can't mean ten in one day, could he? Or even three? No. No, no, no, no, no. I need to make very sure I choose ten things that require a minimum of five days. Barring Love at First Sight—which was me sailing at him across the BM floor like a baboon on skates—five days should be enough. Right?)

Was Notting Hill a First Date? I can't very well ask, can I? Will's so *British*; I feel intrusive even asking what's on his iPod. "So, BritBoy, are we dating yet?" is beyond contemplation. I mean, Notting Hill kinda fits the criteria: Boy took Girl to Someplace, that someplace being a place he didn't already need to be, and that someplace involved consumption of both food and drink. No sports, education, or group of friends were involved. Definitely Date.

But then there was that impromptu "Mother requested/got some time to kill" thang, too. Definitely Not-Date.

Sadly, I fear, (S)mother trumps Someplace. But I look on this as an opportunity. I have been given the chance to Create-a-Date. Ten, in fact. Yay. The prob? All ten locations have to have been mentioned in a two-hundred-year-old diary, written by Princess Poesy. Bleagh. And Boy might not be thinking Date.

An insurmountable challenge, you say?

Nay.

Never underestimate the power of a good speed-skim and

the Internet. Ladies, I have found my ten places. Each and every one meets Will's criteria *and* mine.

His:

+ mentioned by Katherine
+ still in existence

Mine:

+ no (s)mother
+ no dust
+ no "mates," "blokes," or "posse"
+ requires a minimum of two hours to fully appreciate, as I intend to give Will as much time as possible to fully appreciate me

Drumroll, please.

1. Hampstead Heath
www.flickr.com/groups/hampsteadheath/

Why: Pix, people. Look at the pix. It's one great big, beautiful picnic waiting to happen. I'll pack chicken-and-rocket sandwiches ("rocket," I have since discovered to my great relief and pleasure, is just arugula), fizzy lemonade, salt-and-vinegar crisps, and a big (but not too big—gotta keep close) blanket to sit on. Professor Fungus has one. It's purple plaid. Probably for the bed, but what she don't know won't hoit her. Me n' Will n' hundreds of acres of grass and ponds and sunshine on our shoulders.

Why not: Unless it rains... It won't rain.

I'll wear jeans (don't want to take the pastoral thang too far) and a floaty top. I'll paint my toenails and wear sandals. I'll carefully avoid all goose poop.

2. The Theatre Royal, Haymarket
www.trh.co.uk/

Why: Nighttime. Pretheater dinner. I don't care what's playing. I will be sitting right smack next to Will in semidarkness for two hours. Never mind the hard chair arm between us; if sitting through every Adam Sandler, Sasha Baron Cohen, and Jack Black movie of the last year with Adam the Scum taught me anything, it's that if one person slides their arm forward a little and the other tucks around them, holding hands in the theater is easy peasy lemon squeezy and very nice.

Nighttime.

Should I say it again? Nighttime.

Why not: There goes my allowance for the month, not to mention a chunk of the b-day money I will inevitably get from the grand'rents.

I'll wear a little black dress. H&M is full of them. Only they're red or silver or deep-sea blue. I'll wear one of those. And heels. And just enough Coco Mademoiselle to reach him. Note to self: wash hair late that day, so as to be sweet-smelling just in case that Head-on-Shoulder opportunity arises.

Nighttime. He'll insist on seeing me home. He's that kinda guy. And if there's ever, ever gonna be a first kiss, and it doesn't happen on the velvet heath grass overlooking London Town, this is the time.

Note to self: Altoids.

3. The Tower of London
www.hrp.org.uk/toweroflondon/

Why: Face it, when it comes to doomed queens, we're all ghouls, right, Ghoulfriends?

Why not: Tourists. Lots of them, many American, polyester-clad, wanting to see the ghosts. I don't count as a tourist. I don't. I won't ask about the ghosts. I'll let the tourists do that, then I'll make sure we go where the tour guides tell them to go.

I'll wear whatever makes me look most English. I'll channel Anne Boleyn. From the time before Henry got tired of her, when she was making the most powerful man in the world fall so in love with her that he forsaked (fine, Keri, but you try saying "forsook" with a straight face) his religion.

I don't want Will to forsake his religion. Buddhism, even of the nominal variety, is way cool. I just like that "forsaking all others" idea. You know, the one that comes soon after "Dearly Beloved ..."

4. Hyde Park
www.royalparks.org.uk/parks/hyde_park/

Why: See most of #1. Picnic. Blanket. Sunshine.

They call it "London's Personal Space." Which means, in order to give London its personal space, I must take up as little space as possible, which means being as close to Will as possible. Scientific fact: Two objects cannot occupy the same space at the same time. Cat fact: It sure is fun to try. We'll feed the ducks in the Serpentine. We'll wander aimlessly among the flowers. He'll buy me some. We'll make fun of the rollerbladers in their spandex and kneepads.

Why not: See Why Not #1. This is, after all, London.

I'll wear blue. Like the sky. Like his eyes. Oh, stop with the gagging motions, all of you. Ambience. Y'know?

5. Westminster Abbey
www.westminster-abbey.org/

Why: Byron isn't buried there (Seems like half of English history is buried there. Inside. Which adds a small ick factor, but what the hey), but he has a plaque in Poet's Corner anyway. I've been reading my Byron. I can stand over his (not)grave and recite:

> So we'll go no more a-roving
> So late into the night,
> Though the heart still be as loving,
> And the moon still be as bright.
> For the sword outwears its sheath,
> And the soul outwears the breast,
> And the heart must pause to breathe,
> And love itself have rest.
> Though the night was made for loving,
> And the day returns too soon,
> Yet we'll go no more a-roving
> By the light of the moon.

Pretty, huh? Pretty sad, huh? I can do melancholy. It goes with *my* eyes.

I can say hi to Charles Dickens and Anne of Cleves (a wife Henry VIII *didn't* kill). He can have a mano a mano with Samuel Johnson.

Why not: See aforementioned ick factor. We do not want the boy to think I am a ghoul. But then, I've never met a guy who didn't have some ghoul in him, too. It's a Metrospectral thang.

A combined zillion *Friday the 13ths*, *Chainsaw Massacres*, and *I Know What You Did on Elm Street last Halloween* sez it all.

I'll wear something black. A hat with a veil would be overkill, no? Maybe just my Lucky black hoodie with the wings on the back. Seems right for church, no? With a skirt.

6. Kew Gardens
www.kew.org/

Why: Yeah, yeah, more lawns and plants. And a Chinese Pagoda and a fair amount of fungi. I'll check out Professor Fungus's books and do a little reading up. I'll point out the poisonous 'shrooms. We'll compare lists of who we would feed spore s'mores to (not enough to kill, of course, just enough to induce several days of appropriate digestive distress). We'll relive our slightly-macabre-but-nonetheless-sweet visits to the Tower and Abbey. We'll be cute like Morticia and Gomez Addams.

Why not: See #s 1 and 4. Why not, too: Ya seen two massive urban plant places, ya seen 'em all.

I'll wear a floaty dress. I'll buy a floaty dress. Or maybe Consuelo will lend me one. Yeah, right, like I'm going to fit even half of me into her size-0 Temperleys. But she would let me try. That's what matters.

7. The Royal Academy
www.royalacademy.org.uk/

Why: Everyone needs Art. And after all that fresh air, we'll both be ready for some quiet, informative, inside time. The exhibit now is *Sadanga: Six Limbs of Indian Painting*. Limbs. Indian painting. I envision deep reds and golds and gorgeous gods doing mahvelous things to happy goddesses. I mean, c'mon. *Kama Sutra* under the umbrella of Art. Need I say more?

Why not: Um. Kama Sutra. Y'all know how easily I blush. Need I say more?

I'll wear something . . . modest. Jeans. A tee. Something red. Maybe some gold bangles. Just for ambience. Betcha Elizabeth has some. Betcha Consuelo and Bayard know all about the *Kama Sutra*. I don't think I need to think about that.

8. Covent Garden
www.streamdays.com/camera/view/covent_garden_london

Why: Shops. Street music. Audrey Hepburn in *My Fair Lady*. Brunch, maybe, on a Sunday. *Sex and the City* meets *Bridget Jones*. Wouldn't it be loverly?

Why not: I can't sing. The dog howls when I do.

I'll wear whatever I can that invokes Audrey. Ankle pants, ballet flats. Big black sunglasses and red lips.

9. Bond Street
www.streetsensation.co.uk/

Why. More shops. Nice shops. The sort of shops where you might see the English Kates (MossWinsletBeckinsale). I could channel Audrey again and do *Breakfast at Tiffany's*, London-style. Or maybe just buy something at Zara.

Why not: You're probably more likely to see the Kates' mums than the Kates themselves.

I'll wear Seven jeans, a D&G silk top, strappy Manolos, and my crocodile Birkin.

Yeah, right.

10. Hatchards
www.hatchards.co.uk/

Why: The new Sarah Dessen came out last week. If there's any bookstore in London that will have it, it's Hatchards. Hatchards has everything. Plus, I can let Will talk me into buying some epic, critical, you-absolutely-have-to-have-it-to-call-yourself-Human philosophy tome. I'll let him read key passages to me while lying on a blanket in #1, 4, or 5 with his head in my lap. Maybe I should move Hatchards up the list.

Why not: Give me one example of a movie that had a romantic scene in a bookstore.

Thought not.

I'll wear librarian chic. Little skirt, button-down shirt. Lose the contacts and wear my glasses for the day (he's going to have to see me in them sooner or later). Some sort of bun. Maybe a messy one, anyway. In the philosophy aisle, he'll slip my glasses off, pull the clip from my hair, and gasp, "My goodness, Miss Vernon, you're beautiful!"

And that, ladies, will be that.

(OMG—I almost e-mailed him that whole list, "whys," "why nots," and wardrobe included!! That, ladies, would have been all she wrote. Eesh. Is there such a thing as Chocolate Withdrawal Dementia Syndrome?)

4 June

Charles departed this morning. He will rejoin his regiment in Portsmouth, and go from there to the Continent. I was terribly sad to see him go, but Mama is positively distraught. She truly fears for him, though he has assured her there is no need. He shall be safe in Belgium. It is hardly like last time, when he was forced to advance through terrible mountain terrain in winter. It is nearly summer; Belgium is a civilised place. Nothing untoward will happen to him there.

"Don't rush yourself, Kitty," he told me as he was leaving. "Delight in this time; nothing need come of it but enjoyment." When he embraced me, he added softly, "Do not be too hard on Mother. She understands you more than you might think. And look to Everard if you need anything. He will be here."

Nicholas has been here. He came for luncheon at Mama's request. He seems to comfort her. Heaven knows why. He is such a serious fellow. I prefer fun when I am low. I prefer poetry. I know they were discussing the war before I entered the dining room. The speed with which they stopped speaking told me as much.

I tried not to mind. If they see me as naught but a silly child, there is little I can do to dissuade them. I was determined to be pleasant and cheerful and not let on at all how sad — and lonely — I suddenly find myself in this house with my brother gone. (Papa is scarcely ever here, and I have seen neither hide nor hair of Lord Chilham in days. I know I should be relieved. I am relieved. Yet I cannot be utterly at ease.)

Mama excused herself directly after lunch. She said she was not feeling quite well. I believe she is working on <u>The Abandoned Bride</u>. I wonder if I shall ever read it.

I thought Nicholas would leave, then. After all, he has made it no secret that he finds my company trying. ~~I suppose I wish it were not so, but~~

He did not leave, but followed me into the parlor. I sat and took up my embroidery. I am not proficient at embroidery. I make knots where they are not meant to be and tangles where there are meant to be knots. I would much rather have gone out for a walk, or sat with my copy of <u>Childe Harold's Pilgrimage</u>. It arrived from the binders yesterday and I confess I am finding myself engrossed. I could not have said so to Nicholas of course. He would have mocked me.

Byron's hero had a mother, and a sister whom he loved. He had a life of entertainments and pleasures. Yet he left them, and went off in search of… I do not know just what. I am only through the first canto. Still, for a moment, I thought to ask Nicholas:

What do young men want that we women do not give them? I know there is <u>something.</u>

I blushed at even the thought of asking.

"Katherine?" He was watching me, looking ever so slightly cross. "Are you feeling well?"

"I am fine. I am … Nicholas …"

"Yes?"

He was leaning, that leaning that young men do, against a wall, or, in this case the mantel, to show precisely how tedious the moment is—that their disinterest is such that they cannot even bring their skeletons to support them fully. Nicholas, in a forest green coat much the same colour as his eyes, cravat perfectly starched and white, was every bit the fashionable gentleman, even to the slight lift of his dark brows. If he was in such a hurry to be shot of me, why did he not <u>leave</u>?

Or perhaps I was being unjust. He does not lounge. Not proud, upright Nicholas Everard.

I wondered if perhaps his leg was paining him. How easy it has been to forget that he was badly injured. One cannot ignore the scar; it is there each time he brushes his sable hair from his brow. Yet the other is hidden, unseen, unspoken.

"Well, spit it out, Katherine, whatever it is you wish to say. You look like a fish with a hook in its mouth."

"A <u>fish</u>?"

"Ah, forgive me. An unchivalrously incomplete sentiment. A lovely brook trout, then, lustrous of scale and graceful of fin."

Odious, pompous man. I determined not to give him the satisfaction of mocking me further. I would talk of serious matters.

"I read in the newspaper this morning," I offered— graciously ignoring the further lift of his brow, "that the Duke and Duchess of Richmond have made themselves the center of polite society in Brussels. They will certainly see that the regiments do not lack for entertainment."

"I am certain the regiments are eternally grateful," was his reply. "Heaven forbid they not have a party to attend."

I counted five and tried again. "I have also read that the ladies of Brussels are quite enamoured of the Scots soldiers in their kilts. It is rather like Winnie Stuart and her delight in Walter Scott's Highland warriors."

"Have you read any of Scott's work, Katherine?"

I confessed I had not. "I understand it is very romantic and dramatic."

He all but rolled his eyes. "Just like war, hmm?"

I gave up. What else could I do? "Fine. Fine! I have tried to engage in your sort of conversation, yet you continue to mock me because I choose the wrong words or subject or degree of seriousness. How am I to speak intelligently of current events if no one will discuss them with me?"

"A good question, that. How have you learned in the past?"

"Well, I suppose Miss Cameron chose the materials, as a governess does."

Nicholas shook his head. "Children have governesses, Katherine. Do you not think it is time, perhaps, for you to take responsibility for your own growth? You are eighteen, past time to stop being a child."

I shoved my embroidery from my lap and rose to my feet. It would have been far more satisfying had not the chair tipped first back and then forward into my knees, making me wobble.

"I would rather be eighteen and thought a child than four-and-twenty and regarded as an old man! Is it not exhausting, Sir Nicholas, to be so very <u>impressive</u> at all times?"

I expected him to be angry at that, at least as angry at my insults as I was at his. He was not. He <u>smiled</u>, that lazy smile that so irks me and that silly Winnie finds so dashing.

"I would ask the same of you. Is it not exhausting to always be searching for just the right word or action to make yourself seem fashionable?"

I was speechless. I expect I did resemble a fish, mouth opening and closing, making no sound save a faint popping.

"Poor little Katherine," he said, in a tone so gentle it quite pierced my anger. "You cannot win, can you? Grown-ups will not discuss serious matters with you, yet scold you for twittering."

Sympathy from Nicholas? I confess I was quite uncertain as to what to do with it. I chose to be tart. Otherwise, I feared in the moment, I might cry. I seem to want to cry every time I encounter Nicholas Everard of late. I hate that.

"How kind of you to notice. I am certain, too, you will be so kind as to offer a suggestion as to how I could change that sad circumstance. You always have a suggestion for how I may better myself."

He must have known I was being sarcastic. He would certainly have heard it in my voice. He does, after all, know me rather well.

"I do. Of course I do." His smile turned wry and, although I could be mistaken, self-effacing. He came away from the mantel and stood directly in front of me. "Are you interested in hearing it?"

"Will you go away if I agree?"

"Ah, the Kitty shows claws."

I remembered so many days in years past, when I would pester him and Charles at their play, tagging behind them, mimicking their battle cries until they would chase me off. Or, sometimes, indulge me in a game of chase or hide-and-go-seek, where I would inevitably stand behind a curtain with my feet poking out, or hide behind a pillar not quite wide enough to conceal me. They would pretend not to see but, to my delight, would stumble about in comical haplessness, calling "Here, Kitty, Kitty . . ."

Suddenly I was bone-weary. "I _am_ exhausted, Nicholas," I told him, "by trying to please everyone who cannot be pleased. Papa, Mama, the sticklers in Society, _you_ . . .

"To hell with us," he growled. I gasped when, without warning, he wrapped both hands around my shoulders. They felt very warm and very strong, and I thought how easily he could hurt me. But he was perfectly gentle when he turned me about and guided me to stand before the wall mirror. He stood behind me, tall and serious and, I was reminded by this reflected view of him, only four-and-twenty. So young to be so unyielding.

"This is the view that matters: yours. None of the others. You need to decide what you truly wish to see when you look at yourself, Katherine. I suspect you will be quite splendid when you do. Until then, cease with the twittering. It is wholly unattractive." He dropped his hands and, in a gesture utterly unlike him, thrust them both into his hair, sending it into dark disarray. "Now I will go away."

And he did.

5 June

I do not understand gentlemen at all!

I confess, I was in a Mood after Nicholas left. I sat at my dressing table and glared into the mirror. What did I see?

A lot of dark brown hair that absolutely refuses to do what I wish it to do. I frequently think of cropping it all off.

A pretty face that I do not care to study too long or closely, as I inevitably find a spot in a place not immediately obvious to me, yet visible to everyone else.

Brown eyes. They are a good shape, thickly lashed, bright. I wish they were blue. I am not cruel or stupid. I am not a child,

~~to be humored and molded, seen and not heard. Treated like a pet or worse, a pretty piece of art.~~

I must remember to use Mama's face cream. I am a bit dry around the eyes.

I was not in good cheer as I dressed for the evening. So, of course, I spilled tea on my yellow dress, shouted at Becky when she could not make the pins stay in my hair, and poked so at the spot in the corner of my nose that it grew and turned a brilliant red.

I did apologise to Becky and felt better for it.

It was merely a party. The person I cared most for would not be there to see me not looking my best. So off I went to the Spensers very late and cross in my white dress, with my disastrous hair and mountainous spot. What did I care?

Thomas Baker was standing by the fireplace.

His eyes met mine, he smiled, and I completely forgot the spot.

We reached each other in the centre of the room. "Cruel lady," he scolded, hand over his heart. "I had all but lost hope that you would come."

"As long as you do not lose all hope," I countered, "I do not mind that you have suffered a little. I am not the one who flitted off to the country."

"No, Miss Percival, you are most constant."

We danced. "The weather was appalling," he told me. "Mud everywhere. So I returned."

He did not mention the entertainments or the company. I knew, from Henrietta Quinn, who had been invited but did not attend, that there had been seven ladies and four gentlemen. One of the ladies was Miss Northrop. I was dying of curiosity. Was everyone there very wealthy and fashionable and lively?

Did Miss Northrop play nicely with the others? Did she wear ermine and diamonds to breakfast? Did she flirt with him?

I asked none of it, of course.

After our second dance, when there could be no other without people talking (and really, why should I mind if they linked my name closely with his?), I feared the evening would become dull. Then he asked, quietly. "Shall we stroll in the garden?"

Yes. Oh yes, please.

Being London, the gardens were no more than forty paces square. How I longed for Percy's Vale, with its acres upon acres of Italian terraces and the yew maze and the pine groves. But Thomas tucked my arm in his, and we strolled.

"You promised when last we met to tell me what I missed in my absence."

Emboldened by the feel of his sleeve beneath my hand and his eyes on my face (oh, drat that spot!), I said, "Certain company, I should think, but as I cannot read your mind, I cannot be certain what you missed."

"Ah, so clever." He glanced carefully around the neat paths and ivy-covered walls.

Lady Spenser had filled the garden with lanterns. No less than a half-dozen other couples were among the tidy paths. It was entirely proper, and not in the least private. Until we reached the rose bower. Thomas glanced once, then again over his shoulder. I confess, I did not protest at all when he tugged me inside. Despite the fact that it is only just June and the weather has been cool, there were blooms aplenty, pink and lush and fragrant, brushing against my arms and filling my head with their scent. Nearby, a fountain trickled musically through a mermaid's bronze grasp.

Thomas turned me to face him. It was the second time that day I had had a gentleman's hands on my shoulders. His were not as large as Nicholas's, nor was he as tall. I did not feel quite as ... dwarfed.

Would he kiss me? He should kiss me. I should like it very much if he did. Should I protest the liberty, just a bit? Enough to show him I do not allow just anyone to kiss me, but that he might?

"Mr. Baker—"

"Shh," he whispered. I shushed.

Then I waited. And waited, and panicked just a little. Would I turn my head to the left or the right? What had I eaten for supper? If I closed my eyes and he did not, would he see the spot ...?

"...safe to go."

I had not realised I had closed my eyes until they sprang open. "I beg your pardon?"

"I really do not wish to speak to him."

"Who?"

"Robert Spenser. He has been hounding me all evening." He smiled down at me. "Lovely, amiable Miss Percival. You have spared me a tedious encounter. I am in your debt." Then he took one hand from my shoulder. Now, I thought. 'Twill be now. "Yes, most lovely and most unspoiled. Like this."

He reached past my ear and plucked a rose from the trellis. He tucked it gently into my hair. It promptly sprang free and dropped to the ground.

"Pity," he murmured.

"Yes."

That was all I said, as he tucked my hand again into his arm, as he led me back up the path and up the stairs and into the crowded, brilliantly lit ballroom where he then bent over my hand, let it go, and slipped back into his crowd of lively fellows. I glanced about for Luisa. She was dancing with Mr. Pertwee. I looked for a corner to sit in, a drapery to hide behind.

"Good night, fair ladies!" Mr. Davison was saying. "I fear we must go to places you cannot follow." They laughed, the lot of them, bowing and poking each other in the ribs as they left. Henrietta Quinn rolled her eyes, but did not object to her Mr. Troughton going with them.

"Well, there go the clowns" — she sighed — "leaving us with only this for a circus. "Shall we go watch Miss Spenser? She is going to maul the pianoforte for the next quarter hour or so."

"Yes."

Am I confused?

Yes.

Did I wish for him to kiss me? Yes. Would I have let him? Yes. And yes and yes and yes.

I have a headache. I have too many questions.

Is love meant to make us feel like fools?

Hide and Seek

I'll let you in on a little secret: boys are tricky.

Apparently, all correspondence with Will this week is to be done in text. Which necessitates decoding the subtext. Text Subtext—bane of a girl's existence.

HisText: (in response to my e-mailed Ten Places list): **UR 2 much. So b it.**

Subtext, Option A: *Aren't you just the cleverest thing? I surrender to your desires.*

Subtext, Option B: *Are you f-ing kidding me? I said "excursion," not "seduction." Fine, but I'm onto your game.*

MyText (choosing to ignore even the possibility of Option B): **;-) Glad u like. Heath 2moro?**

HisText: **N. Othr.**

Subtext, Option A: I have a better idea. Trust me, you'll love it.

Subtext, Option B: As if. Your little blanket scenario fools no one.

MyText: **???**

HisText: **W8 > ^ . . ^ <**

Subtext, Option A: It's a surprise.

Subtext, Option B: For God's sake, B, don't push it!

Pause for cuteness sigh. > ^ . . ^ < Cat. *Moi*. Now, considering the fact that it takes a lot less time to type CAT than all those little symbols, I am left with two possibilities.

Possibility A: He is clever, and has seriously dexterous digits.

Possibility B: He cares enough to have created a macro that will give him > ^ . . ^ < with a single key tap. Implying he plans to be tapping that key a lot.

Works for me either way.

Anyway.

HisText: **GTG. CU 2moro. 11 yr place.**

Subtext, Option A: There's a fire in the building ahead. I have doors to kick down, puppies and screaming children to rescue. Much as it pains me, I will have to wait until tomorrow to continue our deep connection.

Subtext, Option B: Enough of this childish chitchat. Better things to do. CU.

Okay. So now I have to go check my list again and plan for any eventuality. Is there a discreet way to pack a picnic, without it being obvious I'd packed a picnic? "Oh, would you look at that! I just happen to have sandwiches and crisps (that's potato chips for you all at home) in my bag, not to mention a purple plaid blanket! What a delightful coincidence!"

Shall I go Morticia chic in the event of Westminster Abbey or the Tower? But then, what if he opts for Hyde Park or Kew Gardens? Black among the blossoms? I don't think so. So maybe I should just go for floaty dress and hope it doesn't read flighty when I should be solemn and serious . . .

I think I can safely rule out the theater. Unless there's a matinee . . .

Merde.

Okay. This isn't brain surgery. It's clothes. Infinitely more chance of humiliating failure than brain surgery. Okay. What would Natalie Portman do? Hey. She would channel Audrey. You can't go wrong with Audrey, right? Phew.

MyText: **CU 2**.

July 16

These Streets

Today was tomorrow.

What Mom said on seeing me in my white button-down, black ankle pants, and mondo shades: "You look like Audrey Hepburn."

What Will said on arriving at the door: "You'll want an umbrella. Looks like rain."

He did say hello first, and looked perfectly happy to be here, so despite the fact that he didn't go google-eyed over my ensemble (and face it, do they ever, unless it's ho chic or lingerie?), I allowed myself to assume he was happy to be here.

I put an umbrella in my bag.

"So where are we going?" I asked as we hit the street. "Or will it remain a mystery?"

"We are going—" He pulled a crumpled printout from his pocket and I recognized my list, "to Numbers Seven, Ten, and Nine, in that order." My heart did that icky little sinking thang. A three-in-one. Leaning heavily toward Not-Date. I tried to remember what Number Seven was. "Honestly, Cat, *Bond* Street?"

"Katherine went to Bond Street!" I shot back.

I thought Bond Street was Nine. So Seven...?

He shook his head, sending a comma of shiny hair into his forehead. *Look. Don't touch. Look. Don't touch.* I really really wanted to touch. "Yah. So, you're planning on looking at overpriced frocks while I ... what?"

Okay, he had me there. "How do you know I don't just want to stroll the hallowed blocks," I countered. "Absorb the ambience of two hundred years of fashionable commerce?"

He was laughing as we ran down the Underground steps to catch the approaching train. He also put his hand on my back as we minded the gap between the platform and the car. "First things first. We're going to the Royal Academy."

Ah, right. Number Seven: *Six Limbs of Indian Painting. Kama Sutra*, here we come...

No *Kama Sutra*.

Still, it was a pretty cool museum. It was a house once, Will told me, belonging to some duke. Some house. Bloody massive, right smack in the middle of London, only set back from the street, so you walk from busy busy into this massive stone courtyard, and it kinda looks like a palace, and kinda feels like a palace, and I gotta say, I felt kinda special walking up the steps with this kinda princely guy.

"I used to come here with my mum," he told me as we followed signs to the Indian exhibit. "She thought it important to balance my father's exterior influence."

I realized how nothing I knew about his family. "Oh. Divorced?"

"Married twenty years and supposedly happy."

"Supposedly?"

"Long time, twenty years." And with that chipper dismissal of

Happily Ever After, Will pushed open the door to a small gallery, and we were alone among the limbs.

I gotta say, it was amazing. The room was full of cases and each case was full of miniature paintings. The biggest was the size of a paperback; some were the size of Triscuits. Each one was of a person or people, head to toe, standing or sitting, alone in the image or in a detailed background. Some were clearly modern (think Picasso with turbans), some were so old that they were faded and creased and torn at the edges.

Not a single one involved heavy breathing. They still took my breath away.

"This was a good choice," Will said softy as we stood, arms pressed against each other's, looking down at a teeny tiny woman floating on a teeny tiny sea. The whole thing was, like, five inches square, but you could see every whorl of every wave, every swirl of the bracelets on each of her (four) arms. "Lakshmi," he explained, "goddess of light, beauty, and wealth. Vishnu's consort." He pointed to the next picture, where the same woman was sitting with a blue guy on a sofa that looked like a coiled snake. Or coiled peacock. Logic aside, it was hard to tell. Vishnu had his (two) blue feet in her lap. Lakshmi had her (four) hands on various polite parts of him.

"So I should pray to her for cash?" I quipped. *Oh, Lakshmi, West End tix are insane and the dollar is crap these days.*

"You can. But be careful just using her for money. She's worth far more than that."

Like Katherine. Well, lookee there, a connection. I told Will. There was a smidgeon of *no, duh* in his smile, but just a little one.

"So, what happened to her, to Katherine?" I asked. "You've gotta know, being a Percival and all that."

"Did you finish the diary?"

Yeah, right.

"Um. No, but I will. I'm at the point where Thomas . . . sorry, Mr. Baker is getting ready to profess undying love or something. Do they live happily ever after?"

"Why don't you just skip to the end?"

I do a pretty good *"what, are you kidding me?"* smile, myself. "Never, never, never. I hate people who read the end first, just to see if they should bother with the middle!"

"Good. I do, too. Do you *really* want a spoiler?"

I sighed. "I guess not."

"Right, then. Ergo, you'll finish the diary."

Well, yes, I will, Will, but I was so temped to whine, *I don't want Charles to die!* Like anyone would—well, except maybe some French soldiers. Like anything could be changed now.

Then there was, "If you, William Percival, are descended from (a) Mary Percival, and (b) at least one Lord Chilham, it really doesn't look good for Katherine and Thomas."

Both revelations would be spoilers in a big way, several ways. Ergo. I guess I'm gonna finish the diary.

Will and I wandered through the rest of the exhibit. Here's what I learned:

✦ He took a train through India on his way to Tibet.

✦ It's hard to see past the poverty, but when you do, the beauty is indescribable.

✦ The fact that he did it alone (the friend he'd been traveling with went in another direction) made it all the more powerful.

✦ Lakshmi is his fave goddess, in small part (he admitted with appropriate shame) because she spends a lot of time rubbing her hubby's feet.

- I look absolutely nothing like Lakshmi (he didn't say so, but a thousand years of paintings don't lie).

- The Six Limbs are Head, Torso, Arms, and Legs.

- In art, they are Form, Line, Proportion, Color, Beauty, and Feeling.

- They figure prominently in the Kama Sutra.

- Just not in the Royal Academy.

- If one is missing, everything else is going to be outta whack.

It was raining when we walked out. Of course Will didn't have an umbrella. What is it about guys and umbrellas? Of course, he'd told me to bring one. Now, the sort of umbrella that fits into a Betsey Johnson bag is not the sort that opens to epic proportions. In fact, it pretty much just covers one person. So, when Will ducked under with me, it was totally necessary to have his arm around my shoulders, mine around his waist, and our hips pressed together.

"The Twelve Limbs of Us," Will said as we headed for our next destination.

Be still, my Torso.

As it turns out, Number Ten (curse it), was right across the street. Number Ten, of course, was Hatchards. Think Borders, but all dark shiny wood, brass, and thick carpeting. The pair of Geek Chic-alikes behind the register desk looked posh, bored, and faintly suspicious that I was going to grab a copy of *The History of Cheese in Three Volumes* and make a run for it.

THERE WILL BE NO COMICS OR FILM NOVELIZATIONS SOLD HERE is almost written over the door. It is the Buckingham Palace of bookstores. There are actually all these painted coat-of-arms-looking things behind the cash registers. According to Will, they're kinda like royal monograms. If the Royals like a store, they literally give it their seal of approval.

I didn't see Prince William's. I wasn't about to ask, not with princely William right next to me. Next to. No longer entwined with. Sigh. He gestured me up the curving stairs.

We went to Religion. Sarah D. would have to wait.

Will made a beeline for the top shelf and pulled down a paperback. He tossed it to me with slightly less reverence than most books in the section probably get. At least I didn't drop it. The cover looked liked one of the paintings we'd just seen, lots of incredibly detailed people. But this was a battle scene. "*Bhaghavad Gita*," I read the title.

"Do you have it already?" he asked.

To my credit, O my friends, I didn't laugh.

"Don't laugh!" he scolded. *Oops*. "This is probably the most important book about choices and eternal consequences ever written."

"I thought that was *The Nanny Diaries*."

"Har har." He poked at one of the figures on the cover. "The prince Arjuna has to decide whether to wage war on his own family. The god Krishna, in the form of his chariot driver, gets him thinking about doing the *right* thing instead of the obvious one or the easy one."

"And I should be interested because . . . ?"

"It's our challenge, isn't it—everyone's—deciding whether what we're fighting for in life is the right thing? Whether we're motivated by duty or lust or greed? C'mon, Cat. It's the Great Why."

Why, I always want to ask, *do the clever boys go for philosophy?*

The Great Whys either give me a headache, or make me feel kinda guilty . . .

Oh, great. "Is this about America fighting in the Middle East?" I asked, getting ready to get defensive and a little pissy. I'm becoming a tad tired of taking flak for decisions made by a bunch of people (who, I would venture to guess, have never read the *Baghavad Gita*, either) I wouldn't vote for—even when I can actually vote.

"Absolutely." Will shoved a hand into his hair, making it stand up in three different directions before flopping back into place. Okay, so clever boys can be awfully cute when they're being philosophical and earnest. "Iraq. Afghanistan. Pakistan. And Napoleon and the Duke of Wellington and Hiroshima and celebrating life and deciding between Prada and H&M."

Hmm. "Well . . ."

"Critical matter, Cat. It's about seeing beyond the heavy stuff that comes at us in everyday life to the bigger picture. You find the same philosophies in Jeremy Bentham and Utilitarianism, Cicero, Karl Marx . . ." He must have noticed my eyes crossing then. "Fine. Fine. Even J. K. Rowling. I bet she's read the Gita."

Boys and their obsessions. If it ain't Eastern philosophy, it's baseball. Or PlayStation. Or Bulgarian punk bands. At least Will knows when he's Ranting Obsessed. He paid for the book. And grabbed a copy of *Hitchhiker's Guide to the Galaxy* for me, too. "At least this one will give you a laugh."

I found what I was looking for in the basement, where Hatchards hides the less lofty stuff. I snagged my Sarah Dessen and, for His Highness, *Angus, Thongs, and Full-Frontal Snogging*.

"*This*," sez I, "is the ultimate book of choice and eternal consequence."

As we left, I looked up Piccadilly and realized how close we were to the West End. *Nothing ventured, nothing gained*. "The Theatre Royal's thataway. Number Two? Let's go get tickets to something."

"Not next on the schedule (*shejule*), I'm afraid," was his response. "Come on. Let's get some lunch."

We went to a nearby pub. It was crowded and sticky and full of twentysomethings in business suits. A couple of them checked me out approvingly. Apparently *they* appreciate Audrey. I perched on one of the low padded stools that masquerade as seats, and tried to look more like Heidi Klum—or even Seal—than a wet seal on a greased beach ball. While Will ordered BLTs and Cokes (from a modern-day tavern wench who, judging from the pout and boobs-in-his-face lean, obviously appreciated floppy aristocrat), I had to wonder: Is he ever going to ask me out after the sun goes down?

Whaddaya think, my Philly Greek Chorus? Is he just not that into me? Or, even worse, is there something else he does at night that might make me very unhappy? (Sophie, if you so much as dare to mention yearning, saintly bloodsuckers, I will scream. There will be no vampires here.) I hate not knowing, and can't even begin to imagine how to ask.

So how does Girl suggest to Boy that she is available at night and very curious as to whether he is, too, without making it obvious? Well, she steers the conversation toward nightly subjects, of course.

What I made sure Will learned about me in the following thirty minutes:

✦ I like stargazing.

✦ I like sunsets.

- ✦ I think it's destiny that I'm named Cat. Cats are night creatures.

- ✦ I'm a night owl. I hate early mornings.

- ✦ I am frequently late to my first class.

Don't worry. I was subtle.

He:

- ✦ Used to play cloud games with his younger sister, until he hit puberty and everything started looking like a nude Kylie Minogue.

- ✦ Was blown away by sunrises in the Himalayas.

- ✦ Was named after eight other William Percivals, the fourth of whom would have been as famous as Francis Drake had he not pissed off Queen Elizabeth right when she was going to fund his exploratory journey, and hence spent the following four years in the Tower.

- ✦ Wasn't in bed until nearly four the night before, and up again at nine. Sorry 'bout the yawning.

- ✦ Is hoping not to have morning classes when he starts at St. Andrew's.

When we left the pub, Will squinted toward the West End. *Yes, yes, yes. Theater tix. I'll buy.* "Stars, huh? I think the Adam Sandler film about the astrologer is playing in Leicester Square. I'll buy."

It was not what I had in mind.

There was a guy busking on a street corner. He had a fire-engine red Mohawk and a shirt that told me THE TRUTH IS OUT THERE. He was singing "Shut Up and Let Me Go." Slow, acoustic version. It was surprisingly melodic. It's a sign.

I must have said that out loud.

"What's a sign?" Will asked.

I pointed to Red, who winked and did a little hip-thrusting turn. The back of his shirt said RUN!

"A sign of what?" he pressed.

"Um..." *Think fast, Sherlock.* "Rock-and-roll is dead? Long live rock?"

"No." Will jerked his chin toward a spackled-white, black-lipped, chain-dripping trio of . . . well, gender probably didn't matter...doing a jerky *Psycho*-knife dance to "Someday My Prince Will Come." "*That* is a sign."

He was right, of course.

Something else I know about him now:

✦ He is very discreet, but as the check-your-phone-in-class-discreetly diva, I see all. He checked his phone. Several times.

As far as I am concerned, *that* begs asking the Great *"Why?"*

Beautiful Girls

I am turning into a nervous wreck. Okay, Ditzy Miss Kitty, you've started asking some good questions. (Is love meant to make us feel like fools? you ask. Probably not, sez I. But by all science decrees, bumblebees shouldn't be able to fly, either.)

My questions:

Knowing all we do about the Male of the Species (i.e., they are happy with two pairs of shoes, they frequently smell funny—and don't seem to care, they actually believe the Five-Second Rule, and they think asking for directions is infinitely more humiliating than being seen in the parking lot of a Hooters ...), we still want 'em more than Marc Jacobs on tap?

Do I ask too much? Have I? Of my dad, of Adam, now of Will? I don't think so. But then, what do I know...?

I know one thing for shore:

When the thang with the boy ain't happening, there ain't nothang like a girl thang.

Consuelo's house is a mere ten blocks and an entire world away from the flat. It takes up a quarter of the block, has double front doors, and doorknobs the size of grapefruits. It's on a square that has its own little park in the middle. The park is locked. Only residents get keys.

So there we were, Elizabeth, Consuelo, and I, sitting on the grass in the park, despite the fact that it's nine o'clock at night and only about 50 degrees. Imogen was on a date, with an Italian race-car driver she met at a club last weekend. He arrived to pick her up in a Maserati. She texted Elizabeth forty minutes later. Marco was taking her to dinner in Brighton—fifty miles from London. They were there already, in a restaurant that looked out over the sea, with a bottle of Moët on ice, and a blazing fire nearby.

The three of us dateless losers (Bayard is off sailing or skydiving or shooting at things in Scotland for the week) were huddled in Consuelo's park with a massive bottle of cheap wine Consuelo nicked from her brother and four tins of Pringles. We were in the park because Elizabeth says the family's butler makes her twitchy.

"He's always around, isn't he?" she complained, struggling with the bottle cap. "Skulking about, making sure I don't run off with the family jewels."

I would have snickered at the term "family jewels," only Consuelo's house is actually full of fancy silver and gold stuff, lots of which has glittery stones on it. I'm pretty sure they're real.

I like Consuelo's butler. His name is Huggins and he brings Diet Coke and Pringles to whichever of the thirty rooms we're hanging out in.

The conversation started with my day with Will (the movie was funny; Will having me home by 4 p.m., not so much).

Consuelo: "Of course he fancies you! He bought you a sexy book, didn't he?"

Elizabeth: "That's the *Kama Sutra*, darling cow. What he bought Cat was a treatise on finding enlightenment, not the sweet spot. Sorry, Yank, doesn't look good."

It moved naturally to Would You Rather . . .

Elizabeth:" . . . publish your diary—that would be your private little blog, Yank—or have a film made of your most humiliating dating moment?"

I went for the dating moment. Throwing up in the middle of *Year One* was almost appropriate, after all. Consuelo opted for the diary ("Well, someone's making an absolute mint off that *Secret*

Diary of a Call Girl, aren't they?"). She doesn't keep a diary.

And inexorably (ooh, ooh, SAT word!) on to the fact that I am still a virgin, with no prospects in sight. I'm really really afraid Philly boys just aren't going to look the same after a summer in London with Will Percival.

Consuelo: "Bayard and I planned for months. Where? When? Who would brave the Boots for condoms? Silly git, he bought glow-in-the-dark."

"How old were you?" I asked.

"Fifteenth birthday," she said cheerfully. At my expression, she shrugged. "We've been together since junior school. What else were we waiting for?" She took a swig of the wine and shuddered. "It was disastrous. Hayloft over our stables. Horribly prickly. I had a rash for days after."

"But let me guess," Elizabeth said drily. "Bayard had a grand old time."

Consuelo laughed. "Of course he did. Do note, he has improved tremendously since."

I looked at Elizabeth. "Last summer," she admitted. "South African law student I met at a world debt rally. Disgusting student digs in Brixton, but God, he was gorgeous." She sighed.

Consuelo sighed with her. "He was. He really was."

"What happened with him? Why aren't you seeing him now?"

Elizabeth shrugged, or tried to. She'd borrowed one of Consuelo's dad's oilskin Barbour coats and it weighed a ton. I knew because I was wearing another one. "He went off to Harvard last September. Doubt I'll ever see him again, but I think of him fondly every time I see peaches." She passed me the bottle. "Haven't done it yet, have you?"

"Is it that obvious?"

"Only to the brilliant and ultraperceptive." Elizabeth can be kind(ish) sometimes, too.

So I told them about Adam and the uncertainty and the wrestling (me moving his hand out of my bra, him putting it between my legs, me moving it, him slinging a leg over my lap, me moving . . . all while trying to have a nice deep kiss . . . *exhausting*) at his house, at my house, in every movie theater in Philadelphia. "I just couldn't picture it, my first time. With him. All I could imagine was his skinny bare butt and those foul silver Nikes. In bed."

Elizabeth: "Good for you! No way a bloke who wears silver shoes would be good in bed."

Consuelo: "You were absolutely right. First time's too important. Well . . . sometimes . . . No, no . . . too important . . ."

Elizabeth: "If I had it to do again, I'd go for a weekend at the Ritz. Room service."

Consuelo: "Rose petals and candles."

Elizabeth: "A copy of *The Joy of Sex.*"

Consuelo: "Oh, well, we did have one of those. Maybe a *newer* edition . . ."

By the time the wine was gone, we were feeling plenty warm, and had come up with this:

The Top Ten Things Every Girl Should Have the First Time

1. A real bed. With clean sheets (Elizabeth's addition).

2. Condoms. And not XL ones because, honestly, *none* of them really are. (Consuelo's addition. She has three brothers and eight male cousins.)

3. A clear head.

4. A girlfriend on duty at home, just in case you have to tell *someone*.

5. A guy who realizes it's a big deal for you, this time.

6. A guy who understands that it's a big deal every time.

7. A guy who tries to make it special. Every time.

8. A guy who uses your name, not "babe" or "God" or, God forbid, "Delilah."

9. A guy who sends a poem after.

10. A guy who says "I love you" before.

And this:

The Top One Thing Every Girl Should Have. Period.

1. Good girlfriends. As many as possible.

How lucky am I?

The tricky boy texted as I was making my slightly wobbly way into bed.

HisText: **U up 4 c-ing ded ppl?**

MyText: **A-B? Y. 2moro?**

HisText: **N. Fri.**

MyText: **OK.**

HisText. **Gr8. GTG. Nite.**

MyText: Will?

HisText: ?

MyText: Fave poem?

HisText: P.I.M.P. by 50¢.

MyText: :P

HisText: OK. No Second Troy. Yeats. Y u ask?

MyText: Tale 4 othr time. Nite.

HisText: Dream > ^ . . ^ <

Oh, I will, Will.

Westminster Abbey, day after 2moro.

Just how bad will it be for me to walk among the dead, imagining doing very live things with Will? I guess we'll stay away from Queen Victoria's tomb. She would not be amused.

I think Byron, on the other hand, would approve.

Sad Story

He canceled on me.

Unlike my father, at least he had the decency to do it over the phone. Well, he talked to my voice mail, but that's not his fault. My phone was in fridge. Don't ask; I have no idea.

Cat. I'm so sorry. I'm not going to be able to see you tomorrow. I have to drive down to Kent and . . . anyway, ring me. We'll arrange another day.

No biggie, right? I mean, I think there's a cricket test match on the telly.

Sigh.

I even had my Byron ready. *So, we'll go no more a-roving . . .* Prophetic? Or just pathetic?

GTG.

6 June

So today my breakfast tray arrived with a note from Papa. "We shall drive in the Park at four o'clock. Do not make me wait."

I did not. I was carefully dressed and ready and waiting in the hall by ten minutes to, as nervous as if it were my court bow to the King and Queen. My shoes were polished, my fingernails impeccable. He has been known to check.

One goes to Hyde Park in the afternoon to see and be seen. The footpaths are filled, the roads clogged with fashionable carriages full of fashionable people. Sitting beside stern, silent Papa, I realised how I have liked coming to the Park with Mama. She laughs with me about the ridiculous hats on the silliest ladies, about the foppish young gentlemen whose cravats are so starched that they must keep their chins in the air, about the carriages full of laughing girls my age and their single, bored chaperones whose primary task is to keep their charges from tumbling excitedly into the road and being run over by an oncoming carriage full of laughing girls.

Papa nodded to several acquaintances of his. They were all older and overly done up. The ladies were rouged and held rheumy-eyed pugs on their laps, the gentlemen in fancy coats and, I suspect, corsets. I knew them a little: all wealthy, all titled, all foolish. Then I spied Mr. Eccleston walking with his sweet younger sister and waved happily. "Do not make a spectacle of yourself, Katherine," Papa growled.

"Yes, Papa." I stopped waving.

"And do not sit on your hands! You are not a child."

I had not realised that I'd shoved my hands under my legs at his first command. It was habit. When I was first allowed at the adult supper table, he scolded me so for waving my hands about as I spoke that it became nature to slip them beneath me at the first sign of disapproval. I had just done it again. For a moment I thought of Winnie Stuart, and that she must have enjoyed family meals in a way I have never, all the Stuarts discussing <u>Waverley</u> and events of the world and arguing happily, inadvertently flinging bits of food at the footmen with their waving forks.

Beside me, Papa cleared his throat. "I have come to a decision, miss, about your future. I have decided it is high time for you to be married."

Why do ideas that sound so marvelous in our voices suddenly sound so disagreeable in a parent's? "But I am . . . I do not . . . I am only eighteen."

"More than old enough. You are finished with the schoolroom. I trust you are as capable of butchering Mozart sonatas and sewing nothing of usefulness as any girl of our class. What else is there for you to do? To be? A husband will give you value."

In that moment, everything surrounding me took on a startling clarity. I could hear each clap of the horses' hooves against the hard path. We passed a young couple in the road. She had a mole on her chin. His heavy eyebrows met in the middle. There was sunlight glinting on the Serpentine, little diamonds that vanished into glassy ripples with the slice of a punter's oar. Papa's hands, where they crossed atop the gold lion's-head crown of his walking stick, were pale and slack. He was utterly unconcerned with my thoughts on any of this.

"I take it you have someone in mind," I heard myself say dully.

"I might, perhaps. And should I present you with a man I deem worthy, you will accept him."

I thought of Chilham and shuddered. "I will not."

His hands tightened then on his stick. I could not look at his face. "And I will pretend I did not just hear those words from you. Shall we try this again? When I decide to hand over responsibility for you, you will go, miss, and you will do so with a curtsey and respectful farewell!"

"But I am to marry Thomas Baker!"

Oh, the mortification! I had not meant to say the words aloud and would have given the world to take them back.

"That ridiculous young fop? All hair and hot air. My daughter, married to a poet? I should sooner see you wed a pig farmer. The product is the same."

"But, Papa—"

"Preposterous. God, how like your mother you are, surrounding yourself with poets and painters, and persons of no consequence whatsoever!"

"He has consequence! He is clever and charming and—"

Papa snorted. Then demanded harshly, "Has he declared himself to you?"

"He will."

Something in my face made Papa smile slightly. "So that is how it is. He has not. And he will not. Stupid, stupid girl. Now heed me well, Katherine. If I hear you are making a spectacle of yourself with this poet, or with any other worthless young man, for that matter, you will have cause to regret it. I will have you out of London and back at Percy's Vale before you can say 'rusticate.' Have I made myself clear?" When I merely gaped at him, he snapped, "Have I made myself <u>clear</u>?"

This time, I nodded, thinking, for the very first time in my life, that I hated him.

He said not another word to me on the drive home. Nor did he help me from the carriage. He waited, cold and silent, looking straight ahead, while the footman did. I was scarcely on the ground before he commanded, "White's!" to the driver, and they rolled away.

I stood in the street, watching as they turned the corner and disappeared. I will leave, I thought. I will run somewhere until I can run no more. I will go to Luisa. She will shelter me until I can send a message to Thomas. I will . . .

I will do no such thing. I have a fortune men would marry me for, yet not a crown in my pockets. I could get to Luisa, but what then? I could just as easily send a message to Thomas from home. Saying . . . what? He has <u>not</u> declared himself.

He will. Certainly he will.

He must.

I thought of Charles, so far away. I do not know what he could do, but it would be something. He always does. Or Nicholas. He would come, if only because he had promised Charles he would. I could summon Nicholas and tell him that I do not <u>want</u> to be an adult, if this is what it means. Tell him that I want to go back to the days at Percy's Vale when it was enough to be pert and pretty, and when I informed everyone that I would marry a prince, they laughed, but not unkindly because, after all, it was vaguely possible . . .

~~Poor~~ Stupid girl, indeed. Stupid, stupid girl.

Lord Chilham, with his pudding head and spider legs? I will drown myself in the Serpentine first!

I did not see Mama standing on the stairs when I entered the house. I could not see much of anything through my hated, angry tears.

"Katherine?"

She was there before I could say anything, arms around me, guiding me into the sitting room. She sat with me on the settee while I cried until I could cry no more. When she tried to move, I clung to her as I have not done in so very long.

"I think he means for me to marry Lord Chilham" was all I could manage.

"Yes, he probably does, the selfish wretch."

I have seen Mama bitter and cold and furious. I have seen her rail at Papa; I have seen her throw books and cushions, and even once a crystal decanter. I still do not know what he did to anger her so, but I do know he laughed at her when she missed by a yard. I have seen her turn pale and silent in his presence. I have never seen her go so completely, quietly hard.

She cupped her hands around my face, heedless of the tears and blotches and of my dripping nose. "Look at me, Katherine. Look at me. I promise you, as long as there is breath in my body," she said fiercely, "that will not happen. Your father cannot force you to marry someone he chooses, just as he cannot stop you from someday marrying whom _you_ choose. Not Chilham. Of course not Chilham."

Suddenly I felt just that little bit better.

"No, but you cannot—" I hiccuped loudly. "You cannot stop Papa from wishing it, and from thinking so terribly ill of me!"

"That is something lacking in him, the fool. Not in you. As for what he wishes . . ." She smiled slightly, but it was a hard smile. "He has long wished for a yacht, but he does not have one, does he?"

"Well, no."

"Nor have I stopped writing."

I felt badly for wanting that, too. She must have seen it in my face. She laughed. "Not even for you, my darling. Like the tiara. You spent fifteen years wishing for a diamond tiara. Do you have one?"

"No." I actually laughed with her, and hiccuped again, remembering many arguments and several notable tantrums over the subject. "I do not."

"Then trust me, my dearest, my beloved girl, when I say there will be no marriage to Lord Chilham."

I believed her. I <u>believe</u> her.

Cannonball

How it began, yesterday:

> HisText: **2moro ok 4u?**
>
> MyText: **Y**
>
> HisText: **H-Park?**
>
> MyText: **Y**

Yes. Yes. Yes.

> HisText: **Gr8. 11. Boathouse?**
>
> MyText: **CU**

Hyde Park. Yay. And at lunchtime, no less. Pick-a-Nick. I couldn't quite manage the how of taking an entire three-course meal, including the proverbial loaf of bread and bottle of wine, in any of my bags. So I settled for one of Professor Fungus's plastic tablecloths and a chocolate orange. They (the oranges) break into little sections—how cute is that?—just the right size for slipping into someone else's mouth while they recline on the grass in the middle of Hyde Park. Nice prelude to a kiss, no?

How it is, today:

Nice day. I mean *nice day*. Birds singing in the trees, roses blooming, even the traffic seems pleasant. A taxi actually *stops* to let me cross into the park. London is in a splendid mood.

I stop to let a chain of little kids bounce by on their ponies. Kids. Ponies. Little black velvet hats (on the kids), ribbons (on the ponies), Mary Poppins in jodhpurs on a white horse trotting along behind them. I check one of the Park's excellent map boards. X ← tells me I am **here**; the boathouse is **there**.

Then, I'm heading down one of the wide roads toward the lake and the boathouse and it hits me: this has to be the road Katherine drove down with her father on the day he told her she had to marry someone he chose. The same road. I confess, I shivered. But in a good way. Like, she was here. X ←.

And, man, did she get a losing ticket when it came to the dad lottery. The saddest thing—after the fact that she might actually have to marry the creepy cousin—is that she's figuring it out. The Bad Dad thing. Wising up, and I can actually feel how she's feeling.

Kinda, anyway. Maybe the fact that Dad bailed on me wasn't exactly a shocker, but yeah, Alex (and don't you dare feel smug; you all know me better than I know me), it hurt. It hurts. But hey, at least he isn't trying to hand me off to the overdressed, dumb-as-a-post, marry-for-the-money earthworm. Oh, wait. He's doing that to himself. Har har.

I can still laugh. It just kinda stings a little. Me and my *merde*-y luck with men . . .

But that's getting ahead of myself.

The Park is hoppin'. Duh. Beautiful summer day, lunchtime. Other than the requisite dazed-looking tourists, the place is full of rollerbladers and business types with BlackBerries in one hand and sandwiches in the other. Texting with one thumb, all of them. I could never get the hang of that. Then there are all the happy couples. Walking and holding hands. Sitting on the grass, holding hands. Young, old, really old, and I'm thinking about being a hundred and two and walking here with some guy. Okay, Will. And don't you dare laugh, any of you, because you know you do the same thing after the first date, if you wait that long.

As I get closer to the big part of the lake, I see couples in the water in rented boats, and even they're holding hands. The ones with the foot-paddle-boats, anyway. Although there's one pair of cute guys rowing together, one tucked with his back against the other's chest, literally holding each other's hand as they row. I sigh at them, too. Boy Love and Oldsters. Neither is me.

And then I see Will. He's leaning against a bike rack, looking totally hot in jeans and a T-shirt with a Buddha hand symbol on it. His hair is lifting in the breeze and he's smiling, laughing. Wait wait. Laughing and smiling at this tall girl in a tiny, sheer dress who's leaning next to him. And he's not, like, "Oh, hey, how cool is it to run into you here, of all places? Me? Oh, I'm waiting for the love of my life to arrive." Nope. This was, "I wanna hold your hand."

She says something. I can hear his laugh from a hundred yards away. Have I mentioned he has a killer laugh? It reaches me in deep places. Except this time it makes me feel kinda sick inside.

He sees me, then. And waves. She looks up, sees me, and waves. She freakin' *waves*. I don't know her. I've never *seen* her before. She's waving at me like we're freakin' BFFs.

Will starts talking before I've even reached them. He's introducing me to this other girl while I'm still across the path from them. Can't even wait for me to get within handshaking distance. Like I wanna touch her. "Bella, *this* is Cat. Cat, this is Bella."

Yes, she is. Very *bella*. Yards of red-gold hair, yards of leg, lots of skin that looks like cream. I always thought that was just an expression they use in romances. Creamy skin. And I know, no question, that Will has firsthand knowledge of it. He's had sex with this girl. Lots of it.

"Cat. It's really good to meet you. Will's been telling me about your travels together." To top it off, she's as posh as he is. It's probably Lady Bella. But of course, she would never let on. Because girls like that don't have to.

And of course, there's me, "I ... er ... yeah ..."

"He's a wonderful guide, isn't he? Insufferable know-it-all, but manages to be completely adorable at the same time."

"Oh, um. Absolutely." Me again.

There's Will, looking back and forth between us, looking almost-but-not-quite awkward, which for him is a major event. Will doesn't do awkward, even almost. He's smooth as silk. As cream. I don't really want to look at him at that moment, but I *really* don't want to have her imprinted on my brain any longer. My self-esteem can't take it.

I concentrate on her left ear. It sticks out. I feel marginally better. Until I focus on the pea-size emerald stud which just oh-so-perfectly matches her eyes.

"I hope you don't mind, Cat," Bella trills, "that I invited myself along. As soon as Will said Hyde Park, I thought Apsley House, and I've never been there, if you can believe that. Well, to the museum anyway. I've been to the duke's house, to the odd garden party. But I have *got* to see the Napoleon statue. I had a great-great-grandsomething at Waterloo. Well, we all did, didn't we?" The aristo inside joke. She laughs up at Will.

No, actually, I wanna say, *we didn't. We had great-great-grandsomethings who cleaned out stables in Philadelphia, then took their pitchforks and kicked your great-great-somethings' posh English asses off the continent.* Like she cares.

"They all died, of course," she says cheerfully, "there on that

Belgian field. So terribly sad. Anyway, I'm dying for a coffee, but then let's go!"

Will, to his credit, asks me, "Coffee, Cat? Or tea? Maybe a kugel?" Our own little inside joke.

"Absolutely," I manage. "Coffee. No kugel."

So we sit at a table overlooking the lake and the happy boaters and have coffee, which burns its way down my throat and sits, bubbling in my stomach like acid. Bella talks. Will shakes his head a lot. Only I think it's kinda fond-and-lovingly-exasperated boyfriend head shaking, instead of implying that she's full of *merde*.

They traveled together. I got Hatchards and an exhibit of Indian paintings. She got India. Didn't go to Tibet with him ("All those monks!"). Only got back to London last week, after eight weeks in Greece ("Our friends"—obvious meaning hers and Will's, not hers and her posh and permissive parents—"had this completely amazing villa on Kefalonia. My balcony literally jutted out over the Aegean . . . "). She'll be at Cambridge in the fall ("Can you imagine, Cat, wanting to spend winters in *Scotland*? What *was* our lad here thinking?"), studying comparative literature.

Whatever that is.

On this side of the table, ladies and gentlemen, we have English. Note the long vowels, the backstory, the titles, the wealth of descriptive experience. The experience. Ahem. Well. Think Shakespeare, Donne, Austen. And on this side, American. No history to speak of, no subtle theme or elegant verbiage. Cuteness, some charm, but still . . . Think Seuss . . .

Then she touches the back of Will's neck. She doesn't leave her hand there. She doesn't have to. Just a quick, soft pet, familiar and thoughtless (yeah, right) and possessive. Like peeing on things.

And I just can't do it. I can't go anywhere with them, can't walk back across the Park to the museum. Because even if they don't hold hands, like all the other lovers around, I will be waiting for them to, walking a couple of paces behind them, so I will see it happen. I can't.

I can, however, be sneaky when I have to be.

I pull my phone from my bag, as if it had vibrated, and flip it open. "Sorry," I mutter, interrupting *bella* Bella as she starts a story about a punnet of strawberries on the banks of the Cherwell. "So rude. Sorry. But I have to answer this. Excuse me."

Then I walk away from all the tables, turn my back on them, and press the phone to my ear. I don't pretend to talk; they can't hear anything over the chattering tourists and happy punters anyway.

My chest feels tight, like I can't draw a full breath without it hurting. And the light around me seems extra white. I notice too many details (there's a guy wearing acid-wash jeans and red-and-white suede Adidas at a table nearby, one of the ducks begging for food at the edge of the lake has a bent tail feather, the air smells like hot dogs) for being almost completely numb.

I think of Adam and the out-of-the-blue e-mail that, maybe, shouldn't have been so out of the blue. I think I'm a smart girl in so many ways. I think I should have seen this coming. The phone calls when Will was with me. The "friend" he traveled with. The simple, shoulda-said-it-all fact that I never saw him at night.

He's no vampire. He's taken. I'm an idiot.

I take a deep breath. It hurts. I go back. I have to go.

"I'm really, really sorry," I tell Bella with my best frozen smile. I hate her. But I'm a good actor. Remember? The only freshman to make drama club? "I can't do the museum with you. My friend needs me. She and her boyfriend . . ." I shrug and manage a face.

You know. Let them pick a friend-boyfriend scenario to suit them.

"Oh, what a shame," she purrs. I hate her. But I can't blame her. She didn't set this up. She didn't make me fall a little bit in love with Will. He did that. He never mentioned the gorgeous girlfriend in Greece. Can't blame her for coming home. "Not here a month and already on call. You *are* good at making . . . friends."

"Always thought so," I shoot back. Hate her. I still can't look at Will.

"Anyone we know?" she asks. Again with that plural. *Yeah, yeah. Message received,* I think dully. I think I need to go. Now. But I can't resist.

"You must know Consuelo Spenser," I say. I figure everyone knows of Consuelo. Now that I know Consuelo, I realize I've seen her in the society pages of *Tatler*. And British *Vogue*. "Or, I'm sure you know *of* her. She's always in *Tatler*. And British *Vogue*."

Ah, finally, a smidgen of respect. I silently apologize to Consuelo, Bayard, and the panda. They'll understand.

"Nice meeting you, Bella," I say, fumbling with my phone, my bag, my pockets. I am Cool. I am Gracious. I would rather tickle a tarantula than shake her hand. "Gotta go."

And I go.

I manage to get all the way to the bottom of the Park without looking back. Then I need to sit down. I'm shaking a little. I perch on the edge of a bench. At the other end, a Nanny McPhee–alike (the wart and snaggletooth and unibrow Nanny McPhee) is shoving a crying baby back and forth in a space-age pram. Between us, a girl who looks my age but is wearing a suit is thumbing her BlackBerry and eating an apple.

You know how you felt when you were three or four, the first time you looked up in Macy's and your mom wasn't there? That's me. As lost as is remotely possible, considering I have a pretty damn good idea exactly where I am. Panicking. *I will never get back to where I was. I will be lost forever.* I think of Mom, of what she told me when she found me that day, probably only about three minutes later, sobbing under a rack of Day-Glo clearance parkas with fake-fur-trimmed hoods.

"If you get lost, stay where you are, my little Cat, and call for help. I will always find you."

I could call Mom. She would understand. She would even come get me in a cab. But what would I say? *He has a girlfriend, Mommy. He never said he didn't, but he never said he did, and I liked him sooooo much...*

I did the only sensible thing I could think of. I called Elizabeth.

She picked up just when I was sure I was going to get her voice mail. "Yah?"

"He has a girlfriend!" I wailed, earning me a glare from the nanny and a sympathetic half smile from Apple Girl. "I came all the way to bloody Hyde Park to meet him"—another glare—"and he shows up with his girlfriend! And she's goo-oor-geous." I was already starting to hiccup. Bad sign.

There was a long pause. Then, "Cat?"

Oh, crap. *"Imogen?"*

"Yah. Sorry. Elizabeth left her mobile in my car. Where are you?"

Uh, duh. "Hyde Park."

"Yah. *Where?* It's a big place, Cat. What's the nearest gate?"

Oh, yeah. I felt the first snuffle coming on. I shuffled across the path and looked at the map board. I am here. X ←. "Albert."

"Good. Walk out and stand in front of the Sloane Street side of Harvey Nicks. Can you do that?" She took my next snuffle as an affirmative. "I'll be there in ten minutes. I'll find you."

It was closer to twenty, but who's counting? She screamed up in a dented little vintage convertible, top down. She was wearing huge shades, a scarf over her hair, and a stripy French shirt. She looked like a black Jackie O. "Get in!" she called over the noisy rumble of the engine.

For a second, I debated just not doing it. I mean, I'd just been skewered in the back by Cupid, followed by a sad sad twenty minutes snuffling in front of London's most chichi department store, watching women who looked a lot more like Bella than like me going in and out, bearing bags full of things I would probably have died for, and looking at me like they were wondering if they should give me loose change. One actually tried. Beyond that, Imogen still scared me. I wasn't sure I was going to be able to stand her utterly cool perfection, not to mention her pity.

I got in. I was too battered not to.

She thrust a wad of paper napkins into my lap, gave my hand a quick, firm squeeze, then veered back into traffic, narrowly missing being squashed by a red double-decker bus.

I didn't know what to say. Turns out I didn't have to. She tapped a tiny, Swarovski crystal-encrusted earbud into her ear, pressed something on her similarly embellished iPhone, and handled everything.

"Lizbeth," she yelled. "I've got Cat with me. Meet me at Consuelo's in a half hour." There was a pause. "I don't care, do I? This is important. Saving the rain forest can wait. Trust me, I've been. Good. Now listen, bring loads of Häagen-Dazs. Hang on. I'll ask. Cat? Häagen-Dazs choice?"

"Vanilla Swiss Almond," I mumbled into my scrunched napkin.

She understood. I guess it's that way with Häagen-Dazs. And Imogen. "Vanilla Swiss Almond. And Dulce de Leche. And that vile Chocolate Peanut Butter that Swell likes. Okay? Yah," she said, reaching out and squeezing my hand quickly again. "She'll be fine."

I don't know how she did it, driving a stick shift, poking the right phone buttons, making sure I didn't literally fall to pieces in the old leather seat. She did it. We zoomed around Buckingham Palace (she waved), up several wide streets and countless small ones. She tapped again. "Swell. Where are you? Mmm-hmm. That was TMI, darling. Now listen. Get your things together and go home. I've got Cat in my car and we need your bed. Yah. Lizbeth's bringing ice cream. Yah, of course I told her to get yours. You'll stop at the vid? Get *Eternal Sunshine, High Fidelity* . . . oh, fine, *Chasing Amy*, and something bloody . . . *Terminator 2*? Kiss Bay for me. No, not there."

Then she made a last call. I don't know who to. It was brief. "Can't make it today. Oh, stop. Something *very* important. I'll ring you tomorrow."

We careened around one last corner, nearly taking out an old lady and her pug. I recognized Consuelo's private park first, then her house. Imogen turned down a narrow, cobblestoned lane and bumped to a stop in front of a large garage.

"Come on, then," she coaxed as she came around to my side of the car. "Out you go."

She looped one arm around my shoulders and guided me through a little gate and into the gardens. The only other time I'd been in them, I'd been pretty awed. I mean, they're not huge, but, in the middle of London, still pretty impressive. Any other day, I would have wanted to dip my toes in the mermaid-centered fountain. I think Imogen saw mermacidal intent in my eyes, 'cause she hurried me along the gravel path. She didn't knock; she walked right into the house. Huggins met us in the hall.

"We'll be in Consuelo's room," Imogen told him.

He nodded. "Shall I bring up refreshments?"

"Spoons. Lots of spoons." Imogen was already leading me toward the stairs. "And tea, please."

I wasn't going to protest. I read Jane Austen and Marian Keyes. Apparently sweet tea cures all ills short of decapitation. I'd give it a shot. I did, however, add a very quiet, "Pringles?"

Huggins nodded solemnly, as if I'd just requested boiling water and a scalpel. "Certainly, miss. Pringles it is."

Imogen got me into Consuelo's room (rooms, actually; she has her own little living room along with the palatial bedroom and bathroom), got my shoes off, and sent me into the bathroom to wash the mascara off the better part of my face. "I would have taken you to my house," she told me as she handed over the thickest, softest towel I'd ever held, "but I thought circumstances called for Swell's."

I washed my face, dried it on my shirt, then climbed with my teddy towel into the huge marble bath. It was big enough for two people, easy. I started to sniffle again.

Eventually, I heard Elizabeth come in, and soon after, Consuelo. There was a short bout of whispering, then a tap on the door. "Cat?" It was Elizabeth. "Come out or I'm coming in."

I came out. They were all there, in a line, three Furies. Not as good as you, my Fab Furies, especially when Adam the Scum sent that e-mail, but pretty damned Fab nonetheless. I wanted to sic them on Will. I wanted to thank them for all of this. I wanted to crawl under Consuelo's king-size bed with my towel and stay there.

"Talk now or later?" Imogen asked.

"Later," I said.

We did talk later, and they slagged off Will just exactly the right amount to make me feel just the right amount better. But for most of the day, we all squashed into the bed, eating ice cream and Pringles and watching Sarah Connor kick butt.

We all shared the chocolate orange. Elizabeth showed me the right way to break it into its little segments. You bang it against a hard surface. Worked for me. It was delicious.

I was almost human when Imogen dropped me at the flat at nine.

Turns out she's not so scary after all.

8 June

This arrived for me this morning, amid a bouquet of roses. There was no name attached, but I think there is little doubt who the sender is.

In Naturalness
For the eyes of Miss Percival alone.

So light of step, so bright of eye,
Draped in gossamer, pearled with dew,
This woodland creature that I spy;
Of you I yearn, I beg, I sigh:
Tread careful, lest you rend me in two
And leave me on the field to die.
Heed me, Nymph, and be not cruel
When bold I come into your bower;
In Nature's crown, you are the jewel,
The gentlest breeze, the sweetest flower,
The softest earth, the deepest pool,
The prize at end of darkling hour.
How blest the man who meets such grace
Of mannerism, warmth of heart,
To know the beauty of her face
Owes more to nature than to art;
He must tread careful through her place,
And give to her his eager heart.

If I had any question of his regard, I do not now.

I shall carry it upon my person always. I shall show it to Luisa. I know he wishes it to be for my eyes alone, but she is my dearest friend and can be counted upon to keep my secret. Yet how I hope it need not be secret for long. I want to cry to the rafters, to Society, and to Papa that Mr. Thomas Baker is composing such verse to me. To me!

Oh, what a splendid life I shall have, after all!

I have just come from Luisa's house.

She said the poem was very nicely rhymed, quite perfect in that regard. She agreed it was certainly most gratifying in its declarations, and most romantic in its pastoral tone.

I could see the corners of her mouth twitching all the while. Finally, I could stand it no longer.

"What? What is it?" I demanded.

She began to laugh then, in fact laughed so hard that tears streamed down her cheeks. "Oh, I am sorry, Kitty!" she gasped, most sincere, yet still laughing. "It is a lovely poem, but does it not put you just a bit in mind . . . With all that earth and field and 'tread careful' . . . Does it not . . . Does it not just make you think of treading in cowpats?"

~~Well, now it~~ Of course it does not. Luisa really has the lowest of humour sometimes!

Last Words

Thanks, goils, for the video message. Never was Gloria Gaynor channeled with such style. Yes, I will survive. I'm just gonna wallow for a day or two. Maybe three. See pic, and if you laugh, I will hear you from across the Pond and I will cry. (I would threaten violence, but who has the energy?) Apparently "washes out in one shampoo" is intended for those who wash with Clairol Carbolic. I look like one of Adam the Scum's anime girls, which would be all well and good if I had eyes like blank CDs and any breasts whatsoever.

I appreciate the list du jour (and yes, I think it probably is illegal to try to get the *bella* B. inducted into the Marines). Youse are da bomb.

Top Ten Things I Wish Weren't True

1. Chocolate is not as healthy a food as, say, brussels sprouts.
2. My grandmother won't live forever.
3. There's no such thing as Santa Claus.
4. Bees are disappearing all over the world.
5. You can never take back hurtful words or violent actions.
6. Catered canapés are higher on my father's priority list than I am.
7. There will not be another Harry Potter book or Heath Ledger movie.

8. The polar ice caps are melting; polar bears are drowning (okay, that's two, but they go together).
9. Will loves Bella.
10. I had to find out the way I did.

10 June

I do not know what this evening has meant, but I am feeling most anxious suddenly.

I have been so confident of Thomas's feelings for me, most certainly after the arrival of the verse (the Cowpat Poem, Luisa calls it). And when I spied him across the room tonight, I felt as if I were walking on air (oh, bother Luisa; now all I can think of is brisk country air and wet grass and treading in ~~animal~~ ... oh, bother!).

I waited all evening for a quiet interlude with him, like the one we had in the Spensers' garden. I fully believe Papa will send me back to Percy's Vale if he hears my name connected with Thomas's, and I do not know how even Mama could stop him. Yet if Thomas does not declare himself soon, I fear worse from my father than banishment to the country.

So I kept my distance and hoped desperately for a stolen moment. The opportunity did not arise. We were separated by our friends in the party crush, then separated by a table at dinner. I found myself seated beside Mr. Tallisker, who had already clearly consumed too much drink and wished only to speak of pheasant hunting. Thomas was seated beside Miss Northrop. He caught my eye several times, and smiled. He even once gave me the smallest of winks while Miss Northrop prattled away at his side.

I cannot imagine how Mr. Tallisker spied that small gesture, yet he did. "Looks like something's brewing here!" He chuckled, bumping my arm with his. Really, he can be quite a boor when drunk.

I blushed and lowered my face. It would not do at all to let our attachment be known before we have properly defined it ourselves.

I confess, I would not object to a bit of impropriety.

When I looked up again, Thomas had turned back to his conversation. Julia Northrop laughs like a horse.

Mr. Tallisker leaned in, assaulting my nose with wine fumes. "So, old Baker's on the path to the altar, eh, Miss Percival?"

"I really could not say, sir!" I replied as primly as I could manage, yet I silently cheered. If a careless sot such as Tallisker sees it, everyone must!

After supper, as always, the dancing began. The idea of dancing with anyone but Thomas was not appealing. I wished to be by his side alone, or to be alone. Yet alone is not a popular place to be during a party. So Luisa kindly sat with me in a corner of the room, two wallflowers for an evening. She was not, however, particularly kind about Thomas's attentions to Miss Northrop.

"I do not care if this is his method of discretion," she announced tartly. "It is discreet to the point of disrespect."

Across the room, he was partnering Eleanor Quinn in a quadrille. Miss Northrop and Mr. Tallisker were in the same set. "She has not had a poem from him," was my smug reply.

"So far as you know."

True enough, but I did not think it terribly kind of her to remind me.

"I do not mean to be unkind," she went on, reading my

mind as usual, "merely pragmatic. You are open with your heart. I do not wish to see it broken. You know I wish you only the greatest of happiness."

I am not open with my heart. Now she was being kind. It is she who is affectionate and easy in her manners. I am merely loud, I fear, and not skilled at hiding my emotions.

"We cannot all be as reserved as you, Miss Luisa," I said, rather more sourly than she deserved.

For the last several weeks, she has taken no notice whatsoever of the young men who vie for her attention. Not that she ever did, really, but she has become most disinterested. I know there is someone who has captured her fancy, if not her heart. I have quizzed her on the matter several times, but she denies all.

"Do not tease me, please, Kitty. I beg you. There is nothing to tell. When I have anything at all to speak of, it shall be to you. I promise."

I do not believe her that there is nothing to tell, but she is my good and true friend. I will not press her, no matter how curious I might be. She has done so much for me. I can do this for her.

So, as I watched Thomas with one eye as he stepped and twirled, I kept the other open for a man who might be enthralling my friend. Mr. McCoy? Charming, but not nearly clever enough for Luisa. Mr. Pertwee? No, she would never accept a gentleman who wears a corset. Mr. Eccleston? Too pert.

My eye fell upon Nicholas.

Could it be Nicholas? He is handsome, certainly, and clever. A bit starchy, perhaps, but I do not believe she would mind that overmuch. She would certainly appeal to him. She is pretty, intelligent, and disinclined to prattle. She is also wealthy. Not that money matters in the least to Nicholas; he has plenty of his own, but it certainly would not hurt any romance to have a fortune thrown in.

Still, I do not think them a good match after all. She is far too sharp of tongue. He does enjoy a good debate, but not more than occasionally. And he, he is too tall for her. And too used to having his own way in all matters. No, they would not suit at all.

I was just realizing how unsuitable they were when suddenly Thomas was there, standing over us. My heart thumped and my palms grew moist. I wondered if I could discreetly wipe them on my dress before taking his hand.

He did not offer it to me, but to Luisa. "Would you do me the honour, Miss Hartnell?"

For an instant, Luisa looked as if he had offered her a snake. Her eyes widened, then slewed to me. I confess, I, too, was startled. Was he not perhaps taking discretion a step too far, especially as I have not so much as hinted at my father's threats?

Or was it all a very clever ploy on his part?

I could only give Luisa a faint nod. She hesitated a moment, then rested her hand on his arm—she did not take his hand—and allowed him to escort her onto the dance floor. It was hardly her fault, but there I was, suddenly alone almost in the middle of the party, feeling confused and completely foolish, and looking, I am sure, even worse than that.

"I am sorry, Miss Percival. Thank you for waiting for me. Shall we?"

There was Nicholas, hand extended. I hesitated a mere second before taking it. As we followed Thomas and Luisa, I lifted my chin and managed a smile.

"Good girl," Nicholas murmured, and guided me into the dance.

He does not care to dance. I do not believe he minded so very much before he went to war, but I know the constant twists and turns are difficult for him, with his barely healed leg. So for him to step and spin this way and that—and with me, no less, in whom he finds so much fault and tedium, was notable. And people noted. They always pay attention to young Sir Nicholas Everard. When he attends a party, one hears whispers of a future in Parliament, of high expectations for a brilliant career, marriage, dynasty.

I have been amused by this attention to the Nicholas I have known since he and Charles collected frog spawn in their hats. If only the whisperers knew, I have thought time and again, that he becomes seasick just stepping in a puddle, and is not at all fond of spiders.

This time, I was grateful for the fact that people watch him. His choosing to dance with me made me, for the moment, notable, too. As Thomas had ignored me, Nicholas paid court. He watched me as we moved upward through the set, smiling when our eyes met, and when the steps brought us together.

"This is not your best face, Katherine," he said into my ear. "More snapping turtle than fish, perhaps, but still watery."

"Oh, so witty," I whispered back. "Be careful you do not impress yourself too much. Hats can only be made to fit so swelled a head." He laughed aloud, as if that had been the wittiest reply ever heard.

"I always know that if I wait long enough, I will see the sweet, malleable girl whose only desire is to attend to my pride."

"I would sooner attend to your feet!" I retorted, but by now I was smiling, too.

He laughed again, only this time it was his familiar, deep chuckle. People turned to watch him, to watch us. I saw several faces break into their own grins. I had forgotten that his laugh has that power. I have heard it so seldom this Season. I felt my spirits lift. He had done me a very good turn, Sir Nicholas Everard. I liked him very well indeed, as much as I ever have, through all these many years that I have admired him.

After the dance, he found me a seat, and another for Luisa. He fetched punch, stayed with us while we drank it, and pretended, bless him, to be having the most lively time possible. When Mr. Davison came to request a dance from me, Nicholas did the same for Luisa.

"Thank you," I said quietly as we all walked onto the floor. "You have been very kind."

"It was nothing." He shrugged. "A promise to your brother that I would look after you should you need it."

I cannot decide, as if I should care one way or the other, if those words were gallant—or quite the opposite.

Not that it mattered at all, in the end. Luisa grew tired soon after and, as I required her escort home, we prepared to leave. Luisa went in search of her mother.

Thomas was waiting for me just outside the hall door.

"Are you forsaking me, Katherine?"

I could not help it; at the sound of my name on his lips and the sight of his questioning eyes, I forgave him the pangs of uncertainty he had caused me. There could be no question but that he desired my favour now.

"I am leaving," I told him—a bit sharply, I must admit. I did not object to him suffering, just a little. "It is not the same thing."

"Stay," he coaxed.

"Why? So I might sit and not dance for another hour or more?"

"You danced. You danced with Davison. You danced with Everard."

I liked very much that he had noticed. "Still." I did not say it, but "Not with you" hung between us.

"Stay," he commanded again.

"I will not."

He shook his head, making his bronze curls wave and glint in the candlelight. "Cruel Nymph."

"Yes, I am," I agreed, just as Luisa and Lady Hartnell appeared at the end of the hall. "Good night . . . Thomas."

All the way home, I held his words close. Cowpats, pah!

11 June

I am having my portrait done. Mama and I traveled to the artist's studio in Harley Street for the sitting. It is not so very far from the Spensers' grand house, but seems still a world away. The painter, Mr. Turner, is an odd man, perhaps the same age as Mama, but unmarried and assisted in his studio by his own father. He is not handsome; he has a great deal of nose, eyebrows, and chin, but very little light in his countenance or vitality in his mien. This is most curious, because each and every canvas in his studio (and there are dozens, one stacked against the next on the floor, piled on every table, stuck haphazardly to the walls) is a riot of colour and motion. There are crashing waves illuminated by lightning, rolling fields enflamed by the blaze of sunset, snowcapped peaks turned silver and black by a nighttime blizzard.

It scarcely makes sense for Mr. Turner to be painting me. He is talented, certainly, and well known. He is a member of the Royal Academy, and exhibits there every year. He creates these roiling landscapes that almost frighten me. What he does not do is portraits. Yet he painted the little watercolour of Mama which hangs above her dressing table. In it, she appears as if she has just come in from one of the long walks she used to take at Percy's Vale. She looks slightly flushed and very lovely.

Mine is to be larger and done in oils. So I sat on a lumpy chaise just so, shawl draped over my arm just so, and tried not to move. Just so.

Mama and Mr. Turner chatted while he sketched, in low voices so I could not hear many of their words. I daresay he wishes her patronage. She, always so pleasant to her motley collection of painters and philosophers, did not appear to be discouraging him. I do wish she would not giggle and blush so. She is far too old.

Mr. Turner said little to me during the sitting, not much above "Lift your chin" or "Be still, for pity's sake!" Yet in the end, as we were leaving, he asked quietly, "I am curious, Miss Percival. What future are you seeing with that faraway gaze?"

Somehow it did not seem as impertinent a question as it might have. I certainly was not so impertinent as to inform him that my distant gaze had far more to do with boredom than prophecy. Yet I was most glib when I replied, "I see stormy seas and battles waging." I had spent the afternoon staring at several of his paintings on those very subjects.

I rather think he knew exactly what I was doing, and was amused by it. "Ah. You are to be our next Helen of Troy, perhaps?"

"Oh, Katherine fully intends to inspire epic verse," Mama teased.

"Rather than write it, certainly," I replied with a smile. "I have no talents or aspirations there."

"Aspire for love and glory, then," Mr. Turner advised me in like spirit. "You could do far worse. I could do far worse in my own endeavours."

I liked him, odd as he was. I only hope I like my painting just as well. How dismal it would be to look upon a rendition of myself, and find the sight distasteful.

Viva Forever (Radio Edit)

Mom was interviewed for BBC Radio today. Radio Four, to be exact, the one where they put all the book-y stuff. They're doing a Regency literature month, all stuff from those few years around 1815 when King George went so mental that they had to put him in a rubber room and his son had to rule for him as Regent. Not a great time for British royalty, but pretty damned impressive for literature. Byron, Blake, Austen, Keats . . .

The guy who was supposed to come talk about Mary Shelley (she wrote *Frankenstein*, lest you've forgotten) had an unfortunate encounter with an electrical current. How freakily appropriate is that? I ask you. Apparently he'll be fine, but they needed a sub, and fast. A few phone calls later and presto whammo, the (s)mother and I were sitting in the studio (she's in the inner; I'm in the outer, still feeling heartbroken-sorry-for-myself and not really having anything better to do than be there), and the interviewer was pretending to be fascinated with Mary Percival. Shelley—Percival, what's the diff?

(Fame, fortune, many movies, and a gazillion printings, but who's counting?)

It was live, but you'll be able to listen as soon as they upload it, whenever that is. www.bbc.co.uk/bbcfour/

So Mom was in this room with typical radio equipment, and

an interviewer who looked like she reads doorstopper books about the inner lives of famous Victorian women. Or, maybe, stuff like Mary Percival's unfamous books about Regency women. She had short gray hair that stuck out in all directions, red-framed glasses, and a sweatshirt with roses on it.

Intros over, she jumped right in. "So, Polly," she asked in a surprisingly Cockney voice (c'mon, you expect plummy posh on English radio, don't you?), "what's the biggest difference, as you see it, between English and American literature?"

"Other than the language?" Mom quipped. Her fave joke. But she has a good voice for radio, smooth and kinda deep, and she made the comment sound cool and funny. The interviewer laughed, a real laugh, said something about how there isn't a Brit alive who can do Edgar Allan Poe or Eminem justice, and I decided I liked her and the whole thing was going to go just fine.

Just then the production assistant came back into my space. His name was Luke and he'd made sure I was extra comfy when we arrived. He clearly thought I was a bit of all right. He wasn't bad, himself, with his spiky yellow hair and nerdy-cool specs. He plunked down next to me with a sigh, then took a huge gulp of his drink and promptly started to choke and splutter. I thumped him on the back a few times. It felt like twigs under a tarp. How is it that English guys can do weedy-skinny and kinda-sexy at the same time?

"Cheers," he thanked me when he was able to breathe again. "You'd think I'd learn not to inhale Coke. This kind of Coke." He rattled the ice in his cup, as if he really needed to clarify. "Not the other. So, enjoying yourself? You must be chuffed to see your mum in there."

I opted for honesty. "Better than the dusty depths of the BM, sure."

Inside, they were still talking about the difference between American and English. Yawn. I spied a MacBook just like mine on a desk nearby. There was something I'd been meaning to do for days. I just hadn't felt up to it. Now, with weedy-but-cute Luke making eyes at me, I felt ready.

"Wireless access?" I asked, pointing to the Mac.

"Yeah." He almost tripped over himself in his eagerness to get the thing open and in front of me. "No porno, huh? Don't want the tech lads doing the nudge-nudge-wink-wink for the next six months." He gave a *"just kidding"* grin. Nudge-nudge-wink-wink.

I went straight for Google. I had it up on the screen in less that ten seconds: *"No Second Troy"* by William Butler Yeats.

> *Why should I blame her that she filled my days*
> *With misery, or that she would of late*
> *Have taught to ignorant men most violent ways,*
> *Or hurled the little streets upon the great,*
> *Had they but courage equal to desire?*
> *What could have made her peaceful with a mind*
> *That nobleness made simple as a fire,*
> *With beauty like a tightened bow, a kind*
> *That is not natural in an age like this,*
> *Being high and solitary and most stern?*
> *Why, what could she have done, being what she is?*
> *Was there another Troy for her to burn?*

"Wow" was about all I could manage after reading through it. Wow, Will.

Luke nudged his way in. "Ah. One of his finest moments."

"You understand this?"

"Oh, yeah. I studied literature at Durham. Critical Theory 1850 to 1950. Believe me, they serve you Yeats with a trowel."

"So explain it to me in twenty words or less."

I could almost see him counting. "Nope, can't be done. But in a nutshell: it's about a wild gorgeous Irishwoman Yeats was in love with, Maud Gonne. Like crazy in love. She didn't feel the same way. In the poem, he doesn't hold it against her, but can't stop loving her. Some people think the poem is mostly about that, about his massive passion for this woman. Others think it's more about the Irish war for independence. She was a nationalist, a rabid one. Didn't think England had any right to be in Ireland and needed to be gotten out, whatever it took. Hence the teaching common men to fight, with sticks if they didn't have guns."

He paused to catch his breath. "Personally, I lean toward the love thang. Yeah, it's about war, but it's more about the fact that everyone wants this incredible woman, who can't be tamed or blamed or controlled, enough to follow her into hell or battle. Enough to commit violent acts because of her. Like Menelaus did, attacking Troy to get his Helen back. Man"—Luke sighed—"how sick, how flippin' unreal would it feel to be in love with someone like that? To even *know* someone like that?"

Pretty unreal indeed.

The perfect time, I thought, to turn my attention back to the (s)mother and her moment in the proverbial spotlight. She was reading from the battered old brown book that I knew was her first-edition copy of Mary Percival's *The Abandoned Bride*. Not that there was a second edition. She complains about that every time she can get someone to listen.

> *"In later years, though few remained,*
> *Her mind oft turned to what was gained*
> *And lost upon that sacred altar*
> *When his tongue amid the vows did falter.*

When second sight is diamond clear,
When looking back costs the heart dear,
'Tis harder to pretend all's well
Or that heaven cannot turn to hell.
Our dreams: familiar, ordinary—
Whom to be, to follow, to marry?—
So quickly turn to nightmare stuff
When we realize love is not enough."

"Autobiographical?" the interviewer asked.

"Almost certainly," Mom answered. "And prophetic. Her marriage, by all accounts, was a love match originally that soured within a few years. Her husband was a womanizer and a gambler who loathed intellectual women."

"Why did she marry him?"

Mom laughed a little, and rolled her eyes. "Why do any of us pick the wrong guy? She was young; he was good-looking and probably very charming. Everyone pretty much spends the first few months of a relationship pretending to be perfect, right?" That got her chuckles from around the studio. "At the turn of the nineteenth century, when Mary was young, you were already married by the time you stopped being perfect and figured out he wasn't, either."

"So she had an unhappy life?"

"Not at all. I think for the most part, she was probably very content. Her essays and first two novels were published to general critical success. She had a wide circle of fascinating acquaintances, including Turner, Byron, and Scott, among other writers and artists. She probably had affairs with one or more of them, although there's no way to be certain. Unfortunate marriage aside, I think she loved well. She certainly adored her children."

"You used the word 'prophetic.' How so?"

"Mary Percival died in February 1816, four months short of her forty-fifth birthday and less than a year after completing this work. She was living separately from her husband at the time."

"Hmm. Young." The interviewer sighed. "How did she die?"

"Well, as with her contemporary, Jane Austen, we can't be entirely certain. Medicine at the time was far less advanced than people even imagine. Her letters and her daughter's diary mention a long illness, with symptoms like frequent headaches, nausea, and fatigue. Just from basic research I've done, I suspect it might have been kidney disease. Again, like Austen. It was sadly common."

I felt cold suddenly. Katherine's diary was from the summer of 1815. That meant her mother was going to die in less than ten months. I watched Mom carefully turn a few pages, finding the next excerpt. I didn't hear what it was she read. All I could think was, *She's almost 45, exactly Mary's age. She could die and then she would be gone and I really really don't know what I would do without her...*

And I felt absolutely sick—real sick, not slangy—that I knew now what Katherine didn't then, that she was going to lose her mom just when she was kind of finding her. It was two hundred years in the past, but still in the future. Bizarre.

Is that what happened? Did Mary die, and without her, Katherine couldn't fight off her father and Lord Chilham? How could she have, really? Especially if Charles wasn't around, either. I wanted to rush back to the flat to read the rest of the diary. At the same time I kinda never wanted to touch it again.

"Hey. You okay?" I came out of my freaky funk to find Luke looking at me like I'd sprouted horns. "Can I . . . er . . . get you something? Tissue? Er . . ." He rattled his ice again. "Coke? This kind, I mean?"

"No, thanks." I realized I was crying. Okay, so I cry at Hallmark commercials, but it's definitely been a rocky few days, emotions-wise. "Well, maybe a tissue." I really should start carrying Kleenex, if I'm going to be leaking all over the place.

The interview wrapped up soon after that. Mom stayed in the booth for a few minutes chatting with the interviewer. When she came out, she was all chipper and smiley. I caught Luke giving her the once-over. Horn dog. But she did look pretty great. Even I thought so.

"C'mon." She slung a arm around my shoulders. "Let's go have a carb fest. Fish n' chips?" I wrinkled my nose. "Chip n' chips?"

"Tea," I said. She stopped walking and slapped her free hand to my forehead. "Very funny. I mean a real English Afternoon Tea. Sandwiches and scones and cakes."

"What a fabulous idea." We headed out of the studio. I waved over my shoulder to Luke. He waved back, but his eyes were focused on my butt. Or Mom's. I didn't really wanna know. "By the way, Astrid gave me a few suggestions for your birthday dinner."

"Astrid?"

"The woman who just interviewed me." Mom rolled her eyes and sighed. "You didn't listen to any of it, did you?"

"I listened to *most* of it," I informed her huffily. "It was sad. People are really named Astrid?" I thought of the hair, sweatshirt, and lack of any makeup whatsoever. "Lemme guess, Vegan Garbanzo Palace?"

"Not even close. Apparently there's a new Kashmiri restaurant in Bloomsbury that's so hot they turned away Victoria Beckham last week. Astrid said to let her know if we were interested; she'd get us reservations."

I snorted. "Yeah, right. How gullible are you, Ma?"

"Nice, Catherine. Very nice. Do explain."

"First of all, *no place* in London would turn away Victoria Beckham. Tabloid suicide. Hole One in Astrid's brief tale. Plus, Victoria Beckham doesn't eat, hence no turning and Hole Two. Finally, no offense to Astrid—she seemed okay—but did you *look* at her, Mom? Astrid and 'hot' are totally oxymoronic."

Mom's not a smirker, but she was definitely smirking as she waved for a taxi. The driver waved back in a very friendly and appreciative manner. As did the older man we hadn't seen sitting in the back. "Not to blast your powers of insight or deduction, Sherlock, but it just so happens that Astrid is married to Russell Tarrant."

"No."

"Yup."

Russell Tarrant who won the Best Actor Oscar this year for playing Count Dracula. Russell Tarrant who you, Kell, called "smokin' even if he is fifty." Russell Tarrant who happens to be on the cover of British *GQ* this month. Wow.

"Kashmiri sounds good," I told her.

"Smart girl." An empty cab pulled up and we got in. "The Dorchester, please," Mom told the driver, and off we went. "When Mary Percival was alive, there was a tea shop in Berkeley Square that was famous for its sweets—"

"Gunther's . . . Gunter's?"

She looked at me, stunned. "How . . . ?"

"Katherine's diary. Her mother took her there one day." My turn to smirk. "I do pay attention."

Mom put her arm around me again. "I would have loved to have taken you."

"Yeah," I agreed. "That would've been cool."

12 June

It seems we shall communicate through puzzles now. A wink, a brush of arm against arm, a riddle. This arrived not amid flowers in a florid hand, but in bold printing, tucked into a book, fresh from the binders. It is Mr. Scott's <u>Waverley</u>, very fetchingly bound in red leather, with a tartan ribbon sewn in to mark my page. I never thought the gift of a book would make me so happy, but I have wanted to read this one, and the knowledge that Thomas, who so scorns novels, has given me one because I might like it, brings flutters to my core.

I have not yet solved the riddle. I will. I will <u>not</u> show it to Nicholas this time. He would comprehend it in a minute, and would goad me to try harder. Mama and Miss Cameron have always said that I am an intelligent girl, but that England is fortunate that it is not I who has the crucial task of decoding enemy communiqués. They are absolutely right.

<u>A Riddle for Miss Percival, by An Admirer</u>

My first is in the Lanes but not the Plants.
My second is in the Song and in the Dance.
My third you'll find at Court but not at Home.
My fourth comes when you Walk but do not Roam.
My fifth is in the Skies and in the Rain.
My six begins not Bliss, yet ends the Pain.
My seventh is in Whole but not in Part.

My eighth is in your Head but not your Heart.
When joined together, you shall surely see
Our lives have always been; So shall we be?

     I believe I shall take <u>Waverley</u> with me to the Quinns' house party tomorrow. I do not think there will be much time for reading; we will be much occupied in celebrating Henrietta's engagement, and there is to be quite a large crowd. Still, I wish Thomas to see that his unsigned gift has been met with delight.

     I must decide what to pack for my two days in Surrey. My pink dress with the roses, certainly. Any memories of its sole wearing, to Vauxhall, must be exorcised. The gold will do for the second night. Then I must take two white day dresses, my green walking dress, the yellow-sprigged muslin in case we have a garden party, two hats, and sufficient shoes to cover any occasion and weather. A spencer or perhaps two, should the days be cool, and my softest Kashmir shawl. Nights in the country are often chilly, and if Thomas and I can steal even one moonlight stroll, it shall be soft beneath his hands.

Lev Din Liv

My last day to be sixteen. I don't feel especially sweet.

Will has been texting.

HisText#1 (the Day After the Horror in the Park): **Ur friend OK?**

HisText#2 (the day after that): **U OK?**

HisText#3 (eight hours later): **> ^ . . ^ < ?**

At that point, I figured I needed to respond. I mean, after all, I am not a sad sad girl who, feeling desperately sorry for herself, spent several days in orange pajamas on an orange sofa, drowning her sorrows in Club Orange, *Eastenders*, and *Hello!* (helloooo— no matter how bad things seem, there's always Jennifer Aniston's love life to make you feel better about yours; I mean if *Jen* is having a hard time finding It . . .) Nope, that's not me. I am out and about, Girl About Town, happy as a clam.

MyText: **Sorry! Will call, Will. Crazy bizy x 2. :-)**

Did you know that if you drop potato chips into a glass of Club Orange, they dissolve in, like, a second? This stuff is the piranha of drinks.

That London pigeons come in no less than seventeen color variations?

Or, that if you stay in front of the telly long enough, you can actually plot the downward spiral of *Friends*?

I fear I have regressed somewhat. I would hit Mom up for fifty quid and hit H&M, but I just don't feel like shopping.

Woo-ahhh, woo-ahhh.

That's the sound of an English ambulance. I seem to have fallen into a ridiculous funk, and I can't get up.

I haven't seen the girls in a couple of days. Elizabeth has been crashing an EU conference on human rights. She knows one of the Slovenian aides from school. She says the food is great, but she hasn't been able to get into any of the really interesting talks. Security's too tight. She tried blending in with the Spaniards, but apparently their junior attendees all just want to party. Consuelo is in Ireland; Bayard is doing a Bike-and-Pub around the Ring of Kerry. Imogen met a member of the Norwegian royal family the night of my meltdown (he'd just stepped in dog poop on his way to a party in her neighborhood; she gave him a roll of toilet paper . . . excuse me, *loo roll*, and a cup of tea) and is trying to decide whether she should abandon Oxford for Helsinki Tech.

One of them has called me every day. Chocolate-Overdose-Watch in rota. Elizabeth will be back at the shop tomorrow. Consuelo gets back the next day. I've been looking up key phrases in Norwegian for Imogen. Just in case.

Unnskyld meg, men jeg er en prinsesse. Excuse me, but I am a princess.

Kommer dette i en størrelse §? Does this come in a size 6?

Har du en bror for min Amerikansk venn her? Do you have a brother for my American friend here?

Det er et reinsdyr i min sjokolade. There is a reindeer in my chocolate.

Chocolate. As soon as *Eastenders* is over, I'm heading out for my daily fix. I've gone every day this week at this time. Yesterday, Mr. Sadiq called, "Hullo, Catherine!" as I walked in. Only notable when I mention that he was sorting tea boxes in the back and couldn't see me. So I'm becoming predictable. So what.

Today, I think . . . Curly Wurly. I'm in a caramel state of mind.

(later)

They were lying in wait for me.

I got to the shop, exchanged my pleasantries with Mr. Sadiq, and was just heading for the candy shelf when they came tumbling out of the back: Elizabeth, Imogen, Consuelo, even Joanna and Sarah.

"God, I thought you'd never get here!" Elizabeth complained. "Smells like feet back there!"

"It's Consuelo," Imogen informed her.

"Well, I'm sorry," Consuelo shot back, "but I *have* been traveling with a group of disgustingly sweaty boys, and you didn't give me a chance to go home and have a bath."

She got up at five this morning in order to make it back from the west west of the west of Ireland for me. Imogen turned down an invitation to an England-Australia test match in Birmingham. Apparently Ragnar-Haakon Ludvig-Knute is a cricket fan. Elizabeth missed a luncheon for Eastern European delegates to which her Slovenian actually had tickets.

"No big deal," she told me with a shrug. "Really. The menu was going to be beet-heavy, anyway, and I can't understand a word the Croats say."

"Honestly, Cat, as if I wanted to go to *Birmingham*," Imogen drawled.

"I smell like feet" was Consuelo's addition. "Need I say more?"

Joanna and Sarah hadn't given anything up; they came because they didn't have anything better to do.

It was the best prebirthday party I've ever had.

We improvised on the refreshments. Apparently the bakery where Imogen ordered the cake last week was a front for a counterfeiting operation and got raided by the police early this morning. Imogen said she could *see* the cake in the case. They'd baked it. But she couldn't get the constable inside to open the door and give it to her. "I already paid for it!" she muttered. "It's not like I was going to ask him to give me potential evidence as change for a fifty-pound note."

Fortunately, we were in the right place for improv. Everyone chose something from the shelves. I can't say I loved the Roast-Beef-and-Mustard flavored crisps (Joanna), but I quite enjoyed the Cheese-and-Onion Hula Hoops (Consuelo). Elizabeth tried to stick candles in the Hobnobs (Imogen), but they kept breaking apart.

I chose Curly Wurlys. In celebration, Mr. Sadiq gave one to everyone who came into the shop while we were there.

There were presents, too. Elizabeth gave me a black tee with a sequined Union Jack across the front. "Don't kid yourself," she said affectionately. "Peace isn't really your thing. Besides, you're always going on about your boobs. This will make them look bigger." I put it on. She was right. Something to do with the horizontal and diagonal stripe combo, I guess.

Imogen gave me an all-in-one makeup kit from Space-NK Apothecary. It's the size of a paperback and has *everything*—including sparkly eye shadow. Most cool.

But I gotta say I liked Consuelo's best. It's a digital subscription to *Hello!* For the next year, all I gotta do is click a button every week, and I get the entire edition online. How perfect. The other two agreed ("Fab, Swell!"), although Elizabeth still thinks I should be reading the *Guardian*. I made sure to point out that Keira Knightley has been featured there, too.

Mr. Sadiq gave me a CD ("What? You expected chocolate?") of Iraqi hip-hop. He obviously was tickled by the idea. Sarah rolled her eyes. "I wanted to give you Lily Allen," she told me.

"Thanks," I said to both of them. I really meant it.

In the middle of it all, Will texted.

HisText: **Ur B-Day 2moro. 2 Bizy? Or can I C U 4 it?**

"Maybe you should try to forgive him," Consuelo suggested quietly. "He's certainly trying. Seems like he really wants to see you."

"Seems like he's a complete tosser," Imogen disagreed, "springing the girlfriend on Cat like he did."

I've been thinking about it a lot. I think maybe he's just clueless. That maybe he had no freakin' idea how much I liked him.

"Rubbish!" Imogen snapped when I offered that possibility.

"Not bloody likely" was Elizabeth's addition. Consuelo didn't say anything.

"We are frequently clueless, just so." Mr. Sadiq stood behind the counter. He looked embarrassed. "I am sorry. You probably do not wish to hear anything from me on this matter."

Well, yes, actually, I would rather have discussed my love life with Bayard's entire crew, the men fixing the street outside, and the tweedy old guy in frayed corduroys at the crisps display, before discussing it with a friend's dad. But I couldn't really say so, could I? I managed a weak smile.

"He's right, love," the tweedy old guy said to me, bringing his salt-and-vinegars to the counter. He extracted a twenty-pound note from a wad in a shiny silver money clip. "Thick as bricks, we are, until you spell things out."

"But damned if we don't feel like the king of the world when you finally do. Eh, lads?" This one had a shaved head, tattoos up his neck, and wanted a pack of unfiltered cigarettes. He and the old guy and Mr. Sadiq grinned at each other like complete idiots.

Consuelo tugged on my ponytail. "So, Cat Cat, here's one for you: Would you rather have him in your life as a friend, or not at all?"

That's a good one.

"How would you answer if it were Bayard?"

She laughed. "Don't be daft. Bayard's not my friend; he's my lobster *("lobstah"—it is easy to occasionally forget how posh and clever Swell is, especially when she smells like socks or is dipping Pringles in chocolate syrup)* and is complete crap in the Häagen-Dazs moments. You girls *("gels")* are my friends."

Hmm. Häagen-Dazs for thought.

MyText: **Bizy 2moro. Friday?**

HisText: **Y. M glad.**

We always think that they know, right? That they know we're making sure to be walking near their lockers right when they're getting out of class. That they know we're writing their names on the back of our notebooks, but without ink, so you have to look really closely to see the indentations in the cardboard. That they know, and are either being conceited or shy or are pretending not to know because they're really just not that into us and would rather it be über-popular Francesca Newberg or Molly Perry hanging out by their lockers ...

I'm beginning to wonder.

So here's one for you, my Yank posse: Would you rather that every guy walked around with a cartoon thought balloon over his head, or a keyboard that allowed us to put the words in his mouth?

July 30

Happy Birthday

Happy Birthday to me. Happy Birthday to Me. Happy Birthday to Meeeeeee. Happy Birthday to Me. The H&M gift cert came through, O Goddesses of Friendship. I adore it. I adore you. I should shop. I will shop. When "upright" once again refers to both my morals and physical state.

It's nearly noon. I feel like I swallowed a cat. Well, maybe only a kitten now. It was Garfield when I woke up. Elizabeth and Imogen and Consuelo took me to a club last night. Of course, they're over eighteen and are legal. I think Consuelo paid off the bouncer.

The club was good. Really good. Loud, packed, hot as hell. Literally. And we danced so much that I single-bodily raised the temp at least another ten degrees (Celsius). I wore my new shirt and slap. I looked pretty great.

There were boys. Of course, they were three-deep around Imogen, but the rest of us did just fine. I danced and danced and downed the faintly green drinks that seem to be the thang, then made one false-alarm rush to the ladies', and danced some more.

At one point, I found myself wedged between a table and a three-hundred-pound guy in a white-suit-black-shiny-shirt combo while his much smaller and slightly better dressed friend (no suit jacket anyway) told me about his SUV.

"Brill," he gushed. "Flippin' brill. Come up fast behind those poncey little Smart Cars on the M1 and they get out of the way right sharpish!"

He had long blond hair that he kept flippin' around while he talked. I looked around for any sign of the Girls.

"D'ya know ya look just like that bird in the American telly program?" he asked. "Ya know. The one with all the talking. What's it called again?"

"*My So-Called Life?* Claire Danes?"

"Who? Nah, the one who's married to that actor bloke. Tom Cruise."

Ah. Suddenly he seemed almost cute.

"Katie Holmes. *Dawson's Creek.*"

"Right," he said. "That's it. Brill. Wanna go someplace private?"

Oh. Suddenly Imogen and Elizabeth were there. Imogen steered me one way; Elizabeth and my new friend went the other. "All right, Cat, no more mojitos for you. What *were* you thinking?" Imogen demanded.

"He's not so bad!"

"He's over thirty," she shot back, "and looks like Draco Malfoy's squib uncle."

She was right, I fear. I have no idea what Elizabeth said to the Malfoy, but I didn't see him again.

I am slightly embarrassed to admit the evening ended a little earlier than expected. That's what happens when you have several mojitos on top of Vietnamese pho and then bounce around under strobe lights. Believe me, you don't want the details. Suffice it to say there was no false alarm the second time, and there will be no more alcohol, lime juice, or bean sprouts in my foreseeable future.

They got me back to the flat and into bed. It's all a little hazy at that point. But when I got up this morning and staggered into the bathroom to see if there really was fur growing on my tongue, I found *Happy Birthday, Yank* written across my forehead (backward, no less, so I could read it in the mirror) in black eyeliner pencil.

I love them. Mojitos, not so much, but these three English girls, I love.

Mom offered to stay home from the BM and spend the day with me. Didn't want her to. I had other plans, and she's taking me out to dinner tonight anyway. The Kashmiri place.

I don't know how much of my return she heard last night. Enough, probably. I remember Consuelo singing "Live Your Life" (that's "Lev Din Liv" in Norwegian, in case you missed that) on the way out of the club, in the taxi, and in front of the flat. Mom didn't come out of her room. I'm guessing she'll have something lengthy to say on the subject. But after my b-day is over. The note she left propped in front of the king-size glass of orange juice this morning said only: *Happy Birthday, C—I know this is your day, but I just have to tell you—it's my favorite day of the year, every year, for the last eighteen and the next fifty. Love you.—Mom*

I think there's the iPod of my dreams in that box. I'll open it when she gets home. I opened everything else as it arrived. I am not good at delayed gratification. GM gave me a whopping eBay gift card. And another one for Fourbucks. She likes to stick it to Mom every once in a while. Now who's the child in that scenario?

Dad and Samantha sent a card. There's a pair of fuzzy ducklings wearing party hats on the front. Inside it says, *Quacking Great*

Birthday Wishes from Both of Us. She signs her name in pink ink with little hearts after it. She's twenty-seven. My father is marrying a woman almost twenty years younger than he is, who signs her name with hearts. There is so much wrong with that that I can't even be bothered to list it.

I looked twice, even shook the envelope, just in case, but there was nothing else there. I gave him a birthday present, a thumb drive with his name engraved on it. So who's the child in this scenario? I know if I remind him, he'll take me shopping for a guilt gift. It's happened before. So here's the question of the (b-)day, My Beloveds: What's worth more, a pair of expensive jeans or my pride?

Anyway.

What I did on my seventeenth birthday day: I went to Hampstead Heath. I took the plaid blanket, a little one-person picnic, and Mary Percival's book, and sat overlooking London until I needed to come back and get ready for dinner.

It's a pretty short book. It's a pretty sad book.

In a nutshell: Girl, Susannah, meets boy, George. Parents object (George has no money and not a particularly good rep). But Susannah won't listen. After a hundred-odd pages of secret meetings and coded messages, she climbs out a window and they run away together. For another hundred-odd pages, they make a run for Scotland, her father hot on their heels. They get there. A blacksmith marries them.

Yep, a blacksmith. Apparently they were allowed.

By the time her father catches them, it's too late. They're married and have spent a night together. Daddy disowns Susannah on the spot. She knows he won't change his mind.

The lines my mother read in the radio interview were from almost the very end. That was it; that was the story. George abandons Susannah as soon as there's no chance of getting her inheritance. She spends the rest of her life living alone in a tiny stone cottage, surviving by embroidering tablecloths and cushion covers and whatever she can sell.

There's a river near the cottage where Susannah walks, each time picking up a stone and putting it in her cloak pocket. She leaves them there, adding one each time. Mary doesn't tell us what happens. This is how it ends.

> How sad, how sorry to have lost
> a lover and at such a cost,
> but the crime she never could condone
> was giving up a soul—her own.

I think maybe I'm ready to go back to Katherine's diary. Soon.

(Late. Not soon.)

At the moment, I'm digesting. Food, yeah, the food was fab. Ambience, sure. The place looked like every good Indian restaurant in West Philly. Dark red tablecloths, elephant candleholders, big-ass Shiva statue inside the door. All perfectly lovely. Mom and I ordered everything Russell Tarrant suggested. I spilled saffron rice everywhere. We ate too much and I tried to undo the top button of my jeans while the cute guy from *Coronation Street* and the toupeed presenter from one of the BBC morning shows pretended not to be looking, Celebs shelebs. Yawn.

And then.

Orlando Bloom came in just as our last plate came out. Phool-Gobi Rogan-Josh. Seriously. Phool-Gobi . . . No, no. Orlando. And nobody seemed to care. Or everyone was doing a really good job at pretending not to care. He was with three other guys, all pretty unattractive, and four gorgeous girls. They looked like Bella: yards of shiny hair, big white English teeth. Actually, I amend that. Three of the girls were gorgeous. The fourth was . . . well, average. Curly blond hair, big nose, upper arms that were substantially bigger around than the toothpicks of the other three. She had a really great laugh. So does Orlando Bloom. They laughed together a lot. I wish I knew what they were saying.

I was so busy trying to listen and watch without looking like I was watching and listening that I wasn't listening to Mom. So all I caught was:

"You okay with that?"

Orlando said something to the girl. She playfully tugged at his hair (yes, he really does have hair as gorgeous as it looks on-screen; *he's* as gorgeous as he looks on-screen).

"Mmm-hmm. Yeah, sure, Mom."

". . . you and Will."

Okay, that succeeded in getting my attention. A little more of it anyway. "What about Will?"

She sighed. "You haven't been listening to a thing I've been saying, have—" She followed my lustful gaze then. "Oh."

"Yeah."

"Isn't that . . . ?"

"Yeah."

"Wow."

"Yeah."

"No, no, I mean it. *Wow.*

"Okay, Ma, stop drooling. He's half your age."

"He is not. He is, however, twice yours."

"He is n—" I did the math. "Oh."

"Yeah," she said. "Now about going to Percy's Vale . . ."

Apparently Will's parents have invited Mom to visit Mary

Percival's house. They live there. Will had never mentioned that. Either bit.

"No," I said flatly when I got the info I'd missed first round.

Mom didn't snap back. Instead, she rested her elbows on the table, propped her chin on her hands, and studied me over the confetti remains of cauliflower, lotus root, and basmati rice. "I was right. Something *did* happen between you and Will."

"Did not."

"Oh, Cat. Please. I have been your human lie detector since the moment you were old enough to deny having just pooped in the closet."

"Mom!" My head slewed around. No one, most especially Orlando, was paying any attention to us.

"I'm just saying. So . . . ?"

"Nothing happened."

"'Nothing,' as in, 'Everything is just peachy keen between Will and me, nothing wrong at all'? Or 'nothing,' as in, 'You are old, intrusive, clueless, and occasionally evil, and I will share nothing with you'?"

"'Peachy keen,' Ma? Old and clueless as you may be, even you postdate 'peachy keen.'"

"You are not the only one to have watched *Scooby-Doo* as a child, smart-ass. Now answer the question."

And, much to my surprise, I did. "Nothing happened. Like really nothing. No snogging, no smooching, no *ing* whatsoever. But I liked him. I really liked him. And I kinda maybe thought . . ."

"He liked you, too. As well he should." Sometimes having one's (s)mother as your Number One Fan isn't all bad. "And? But?"

"But. He has a girlfriend. She's gorgeous."

"You're gorgeous!"

"Mom."

"Well, you are"—she sighed—"but I get it. So you don't want to come with me to Percy's Vale?"

"No, I don't think I do."

She nodded. "Okay. I need to go. Mary's letters from the last year of her life aren't at the BM; I'm hoping they're in Somerset. You don't have to come."

"Thanks, Ma."

We sat in companionable silence for a minute. Almost not staring at the demigod nearby. Then: "You know," Mom said thoughtfully, "I bet if I told the waiter that it's your birthday, everyone would sing. Including Tall, Dark, and Mind-numbingly Handsome over there—"

"*Mom!*"

She laughed. Then I laughed. I couldn't help it. Across the room, Orlando Bloom looked over at us and grinned.

Wow.

13 June

Mama was not well enough to come with me to the Quinns' country house party. It does not matter. Lady Hartnell is keeping an eagle eye on me as well as on Luisa. For two days, I shall have another mother. I do not mind; she is sweet and cheerful, and lent me her beautiful garnet chain to wear with my dress tonight.

It is a pleasant party thus far. We all arrived this afternoon and had tea on the lawns. There were archery targets set up on the hill below. What fun! I do not think it was entirely fair of Nicholas to scold me as he did. My loose arrow came nowhere near him.

I do not know why he is even here. I suppose he and Frederick Quinn are friends; they are of an age and were at school together, with Charles, but still. I suppose, too, Nicholas is considered a rather eligible fellow, a good catch. Both Mrs. Quinn and Mrs. Hartnell seem altogether too pleased with him. For Luisa's sake, I hope her mother does not imply anything foolish. I really cannot imagine he would even think twice of Luisa, no matter how beautiful and clever and sweet she might be. Why would he?

Thomas is to come tomorrow.

I should very much have rather he came today. I was joined in performing charades with Eleanor Quinn, her brother, and Mr. Davison. We were given "A ~~Midsummer's Night~~ Midsummer

Night's Dream." Mr. Davison would insist on lying in the centre of the floor, pretending to snore. It was a dismally insufficient clue! I was gratified to see that Miss Northrop (why must she be invited <u>everywhere</u> these days?) fared no better with Henrietta and her brother and Winnie Stuart. They had to enact "A School for Scandal," and Winnie, while certainly dramatic, was not a convincing student, nor Henrietta a pupil. I thought it far less scandalous of Miss Northrop to display much of her silk stockings than merely crass.

Nicholas, Luisa, Lady Victoria West, and Mr. Troughton trounced us all soundly. It was not at all fair. Their charade was far easier than ours. It involved the ladies stealing the gentlemen's dice from their gaming table and hiding them. The men proceeded to bumble about in hapless search while Lady Victoria followed them around the room, making mocking faces behind their backs. Luisa laughed so hard, she could barely choke out "Paradise Lost!"

Lady Victoria is a widow. She is very elegant; she stands and sits so very prettily, and when she moves from one resting place to the next, one cannot help but notice her fine figure and manners. I wish I had such ease and unaffected grace. She is the daughter of a duke, and cannot be more than six-and-twenty. Her husband fell from his yacht last year while sailing around Ireland and succumbed to a chill. I overheard Mrs. Quinn telling Lady Hartnell that it was not a happy marriage. He was fond of sporting, whisky, and ladies not his wife, in that order.

How sad it must be to have made such a poor match, and then to find oneself alone at such a young age! I believe I shall make an effort to befriend Lady Victoria tomorrow. She seems a lively, amiable, delightful creature, and I'm sure would be glad of the camaraderie.

Luisa is yawning and grumbling at me to extinguish the candle. I am happy enough to bring an end to the day. After all, Thomas is to come tomorrow. Papa cannot know that, and there is no one who would spy upon me for him.

I cannot help but think that whatever happens in the next two days shall tell a great deal about the rest of my life.

14 June

The Fates are against me. One of them, I fear, is named Mrs. Quinn. Another is called Weather. The third is my Luck.

It has rained since morning. Even now, past midnight, it patters and splashes against the windows, mocking me relentlessly. It was a very long day. Thomas did not come. The rain, I am certain, made travel too arduous, even only twenty miles from Town.

We had a long breakfast, hoping the storm might cease and we should at least be able to walk the grounds, or perhaps take carriages and explore some castle ruins. I ate too much. I do not believe I shall be having scrambled eggs or mushrooms for a while, and there is little I care to say about cold toast.

When it became clear that there would be no morning out-of-doors, Mrs. Quinn arranged a scavenger hunt throughout the house. Now, had I been partnered with Thomas, or even Luisa for that matter, I should have been perfectly content. But there was no Thomas, and Luisa went off happily with Freddie Quinn. Mrs. Quinn had me paired with Winnie. I suppose it might have been Julia Northrop. Or Nicholas, who went on his way with Lady Victoria on his arm.

To be fair, Winnie is a good partner. She adores such

entertainments. I suppose there is not a great deal to do in Scotland, especially in inclement weather. She made quick work of the first three clues, finding them in a sideboard, a suit of armor, and within the fronds of a potted plant. I followed along, helping very little and saying less. Puzzles, after all, are not my forte.

"'Mrs. Quinn has but one place,'" Winnie read the card attached to a ribbon around the plant. "'Mr. Quinn has three. Though her presence is much stronger, his has been here longer.' I suppose it might mean chairs, perhaps in a drawing room. Or perhaps it refers to sets of china. After all, this is his family's ancestral home . . ."

We had left the senior Quinns in the dining room with each other and a great deal of hot chocolate. They seem equally content in large groups and alone. I rather think they are in love. There are certainly enough junior Quinns running about. Freddie is the oldest. The youngest are still in the schoolroom. We encountered them while struggling with the suit of armor's visor. They thought it most amusing and I suspect they might have had a hand in the difficulty.

I think I should like to have a house full of lively children.

"Of course! It must be a portrait. How silly of me not to have gotten that sooner." Winnie huffed and pulled my arm. "Well, come along. I believe the long gallery is this way. At this rate, we shall not be the first there."

It was, and we were not. Nicholas and Lady Victoria were ahead of us. We entered the gallery just in time to see them tucking a paper back into a gilded frame. "Sluggards!" she called over her shoulder. She was still clinging to Nicholas's arm. "Do not think you can defeat two intellects such as ours!"

We could hear her laughing all the way down the hall.

"I do not care for her," Winnie said simply as she reached for the puzzle card. "She twitters."

In the end, we did indeed come second to Lady Victoria and Nicholas. The prize was a box of Turkish Delight. I rather hoped it would stick her teeth together. I have decided I do not care for her, either.

After luncheon, the first moment they possibly could, the gentlemen closeted themselves in the billiards room, where even Lady Victoria did not venture. We ladies settled ourselves in the drawing room with our books or embroidery or quiet thoughts. Miss Northrop plunked herself down and played loudly and not terribly well on Mrs. Quinn's piano. Waverley lay unopened in my lap. I had a very good view of the drive from my window and watched it for a long time, willing a carriage to appear.

Nothing did, but rain and more rain.

Lady Victoria continued to twitter throughout the afternoon and evening. When she was not twittering, she was posing. Draping herself over one settee, perching upon the arm of another. It was all very practised and contrived. In deference to my wits, I did not watch her before, during, or after supper. The men, of course, did.

When supper ended, the familiar pattern began. The gentlemen prepared to go off—again—to drink and smoke and whatever else they do; the ladies would retire to the drawing room to stare at each other until the gentlemen were finished drinking and smoking and whatever else they do. I did not think I could bear it, another hour of watching Lady V. arrange herself on furniture to the accompaniment of Miss Northrop's plinking. I was on the verge of pleading a headache when a flustered maid rushed into the room and whispered to Mrs. Quinn.

It transpired that the youngest Quinns, while playing at siege in the drawing room, had built themselves a model catapult. With which they launched a real lead ball through the largest window. As the only tuned instrument was there, we would have no dancing.

Not that it mattered overmuch. Without Thomas, I did not much care to dance. Still, we were a subdued group as we filed from the room. I wandered wearily over to the farthest window and waited to be told where to go. Nicholas stopped beside me on his way to his manly entertainments. "Are you sulking over the rain or absence of poetic swain?"

I was in no mood for his amusement or his mock sympathy. I was cross. No Thomas, no moonlight walk, and no indication that either was forthcoming.

"Save your appalling poetry for her," I muttered.

"Her?"

"Oh, please. Should you not be by her side? Two intellects such as yours could not have much to say to us sluggards."

He stared down at me, blinking lazily. Rather like a lizard. "Mmm. Lady Victoria is rather perfect, isn't she?"

"Oh, certainly," I countered, "if one does not mind vapidity."

"A decent word, 'vapidity.' Did Miss Cameron teach it to you, or was it your putative poet?"

"Putative? Putative? How dare you call him such a name? Why when compared to that ... common ... creature, Mr. Baker is positively ..."

I confess it is most difficult to find a contrasting word to "putative" when you are not entirely certain what it means.

Nicholas continued making his lizard eyes at me. "You know, Katherine," he drawled, "you really ought to be careful making comments about my tastes, lest I soundly prove you wrong."

Oh, the thought of him marrying that creature—of having to endure her drapey presence at countless dinners and parties, and all those occasions when his position as Charles's closest friend would make it a certainty—it was just too distressing to contemplate. Sadly, my vocabulary was not what it might be, and I struggled for any clever, stinging, perfect retort.

I am sorry to say I resorted to sticking my tongue out at him and flouncing a few feet away to the next window.

And there I was still when the butler appeared in the doorway, cleared his throat, and intoned the ~~two~~ three sweetest words in the English language. In any language. "Mr. Thomas Baker!"

There he was, finally, my Thomas. Hair damp with rain, eyes alight, smiling at the company and looking like heaven itself. He started into the room, toward the assembled party, toward me.

"Oh, splendid!" Mrs. Quinn cried, appearing in the doorway behind him. "Now we have an even number. Come along, Mr. Baker, all the young gentlemen, follow me now. Ladies, you will wait five minutes, then come into the grand parlor."

We were to have dancing after all!

We did not. We arrived to find all of the furniture pushed back against the walls. There was a chair for each lady, set before a makeshift screen—a sheet held up tightly by two household servants. Behind each sheet sat a gentleman we could see only in profile, a shadow, a silhouette. I was not surprised to find several sheets of heavy black paper and a small pair of sharp scissors on the chair to which Mrs. Quinn waved me.

"Ladies, cut out your gentleman's silhouette. When you all are done, we shall move you to a different seat. Gentlemen, you will then cut a silhouette of the lady at your screen. At the end of the evening, we shall arrange all finished images on a table. Only I shall know which is of whom. You shall write down who you believe each is. The person with the most correct shall have a prize."

It took me a single glance around the room to see the outline of Thomas's curls against Miss Northrop's screen. It took even less time than that, a single sharp glance, to recognise the profile in front of me. It was more than familiar. Oh, perverse Fates: Mrs. Quinn for her game, the rain for spoiling the day and delaying Thomas's arrival, and my Luck for placing me before the one person I wanted least to reproduce.

"Resist the urge to give me horns, if you please."

How had he known? Not only that it was me, but precisely what I was thinking. Against all desire, I found myself smiling. It has always been this way, as long as I can remember. The first gentle tease from Nicholas and I am hard put to stay angry.

"I shall be as faithful as my meager talent allows, although I daresay none shall know you in the absence of your scowl and scar—" I had not meant to mention the scar. In fact, I had quite given up ever learning the truth of it. "I am sorry, Nicholas, I did not mean to be indelicate."

From behind the screen came a snort, but not a harsh one. "You never do."

"Be kind. I shall promise not to speak of parties or Belgian chocolate or war . . . only . . ."

"Yes?"

I do not know why it happened then. Perhaps it was the

dubious divider of the screen separating us, or the gentle candlelight flickering, but I heard myself asking, just once more, "Will you tell me, please? I so very much wish to know . . ."

"What happened to turn me into such an ugly creature?"

"What utter rot, Nicholas! You know perfectly well how handsome—" I sniffed. "Vain creature!"

He chuckled. "And you such a gullible one." Then, far more seriously, he said, "Give me one reason I should satisfy your lurid curiosity."

"Because," I replied without thinking, "I cannot help but believe that if I am able to understand how you have come to be who you are, I will understand why you find me so lacking in who I have become."

There was a long silence. Then he sighed. "Ah, Katherine. You really do understand nothing at all." But before I could get huffy, he sighed again. "Very well. It was almost exactly three years ago, and we had been fighting for weeks. The French had been holding the walled city of San Sebastián, and Wellington was determined to take it . . ."

He told the story quickly, sharply, only pausing to scold me when my hands stilled. "Keep cutting, Katherine. That is your part of this bargain."

Oh, Nicholas.

His regiment was among the first to reach the walls. But it was not a French cannon that fired the fateful blast; it was English, his own country mistakenly shooting her own soldiers. Large segments of the wall fell on him, breaking his leg in two places and pinning him to the hard earth. He stayed there while the battle raged over him, expecting every minute to die, to see a massive stone falling, or a French sword or bayonet stabbing down to where he lay helpless. None came. And eventually, the screaming and the thundering and the booming stopped. Still, no one came.

He lay there for two days, trapped beneath the rubble, listening to the moans of the wounded and dying, smelling the stench of blood and gunpowder. He listened while the lowest of British soldiers ran wild through the city, destroying and pillaging and looting. He lay there, silent, knowing that a call for help was as likely to bring death as aid. He waited to die, waited for a French soldier or one of the thieves who rob battlefields to find him and finish him off.

By the time he was discovered by one of Wellington's aides, he was nearly dead, his leg crushed, his face in tatters, and the city was burning.

"They did not support the French, the people of San Sebastián. They were not the enemy. They lost everything because they lived in a place two warring countries desired. That, Katherine, is why I don't speak of it. That is what war is to me."

I had not realised I was crying. The little maid who was holding half of the sheet screen silently handed me a corner of it to wipe my eyes. She was crying, too.

I was poor company indeed for Mr. Troughton while he attempted my silhouette, although he did not object. On the contrary, he praised me for my stillness. When all were done, I did not recognise my image (I later discovered it was the one that resembled a ferret in a bonnet), but nearly everyone recognised the one I did of Nicholas. Henrietta won the prize, correctly identifying seven silhouettes, but Mrs. Quinn declared mine the very truest and promised Nicholas that he would have it at the end of the party.

I did not exchange more than a dozen words with Thomas

before the clock chimed one and Lady Hartnell hustled us off to bed.

"Your presence was missed," I managed as we stood examining one of the lumpish silhouettes.

"By the important parties, I trust" was his rejoinder.

"I should like—" I began.

"I believe it is time—" He stopped. "Please."

"No, you continue." In truth, I did not know what I wished to say.

"I believe it is time for us to speak in private, Miss Percival."

And there it was. At last. I know I would have felt that long-awaited, that eagerly anticipated thrill of victory, of joy, the certainty that <u>no one</u> could force me to marry a man I did not love. But I was still haunted by Nicholas's tale.

"Yes," I did answer. "Yes."

"Soon" was his promise, just as Miss Northrop arrived and tugged him away, giggling and chattering that he simply <u>must</u> see her creation.

I ~~felt~~ feel a new certainty

Wait. I believe I hear steps in the hall. Thomas?

I have returned. It was not Thomas, come to speak to me. A good thing, too, I must say. I could not have had him in my chamber, most especially not with Luisa asleep in the bed. How scandalous, too, would it have been to be creeping about with him, seeking a place for our conversation. To receive a proposal in a dark hallway, or even worse, a linen cupboard!

It is all a moot point. I did see something, a gentleman's leg and foot, I believe, disappearing through the door of a chamber near the far end of the hall. Whose, I do not know. I believe at least two gentlemen have a room there, as do Lady Victoria, Lady Hartnell, and Miss Northrop. The hall is quite long and very dark. The leg and foot might have belonged to any of the men, although considering the amount of leg I did see, I suppose he must be rather tall.

Oh, I have a headache.

I am tired. Luisa snores.

15 June

By the time I arose in the morning, the gentlemen were all gone, on their way back to London. I returned home to discover Mama much recovered and well amused. I have received a voucher to attend Almack's. Lady Sefton, always lauded as the sweetest of the Patronesses, was kind enough to see to it. What a pity I no longer care overmuch. What is a night of dancing when one cannot count upon the right man to be there as a partner?

· ·

You Can't Always Get What You Want

Will was waiting for me in front of Apsley House, thankfully alone, and holding the gaudiest gift bag I have ever seen. Purple and green metallic striped, blindingly adorned with gold glitter, scads of corkscrew ribbon spilling over the top. He left a little trail behind him when he walked up to meet me.

"Happy Birthday, Cat."

I eyed the bag. "You shouldn't have. Really."

"Oh, this? This isn't for you. It's my laundry."

"Har har." I reached for it, glitter and all. He pulled it out of my reach.

"First things first. History lesson, then laundry."

We walked up the stairs and into the museum. I expected the guard to promptly seize the bag and rush it into some nether region where a bomb squad would drop it into a vat of disabling goop. The guy just nodded us in.

"I wasn't sure you would come," Will announced as we rounded a corner.

"I . . . Oh." There it was, the huge statue of Napoleon. A naked Napoleon. Well, he is wearing a fig leaf, but for all intents and purposes . . . I seriously doubt the runty little guy we learned about in European History had that bod. I don't think Orlando Bloom even has that bod. I lost my train of thought for a sec. "Ah...um... Oh, yeah. Why?"

Will gave the statue a dismissive once-over. "Doubt Napoleon had those biceps. I, however..." He grinned and did a decent flex. I saw a muscle or two. "You tore off so fast last time."

I didn't wanna go there. I so didn't wanna go there.

I shrugged. "You know us girls. When someone we care about calls..."

"I get it. But let me apologize anyway. I shouldn't have brought Bella along without checking first. Not on our time. It's just that she's been in Greece for much of the summer, and . . . well. You understand. When someone you care about calls..."

Now you tell me; what was I supposed to say to that? Huh? "No prob," sez I. Then exactly what I *shouldn't* have said, for my peace of mind, anyway, came tripping merrily out of my mouth. "She's really pretty."

"Yeah. She is."

Oh, *stop* me, someone! "You've been together a long time."

"Three years."

Three years. *Three years.* Like he was ever going to jeopardize three years of *bella* Bella for a couple of weeks with me. No wonder he likes that Helen of Troy poem. He's got his very own personal Helen. Because she is, ya know, much as I hate to admit it. Beautiful, careless, confident enough to ask for what she wants and to expect to get it.

Me? I think Adam the Scum once wrote me into one of his god-awful rap songs. In the first line, he described me as "my itch." The next one rhymed. He thought it was flattering.

I made another deliberate, deliberately weak grab for the gift bag.

"Uh-uh." Will shook his head. His hair still smells like ginger ale. "Come on, then. See the rest."

The rest, I gotta say, was a little like upstairs at Tiffany. Silver, silver, china, and more china. But with the silver and china is some stuff you don't see over breakfast.

"The sword Wellington carried at Waterloo," Will informed me. Unnecessarily. I can read the display cards. I figured it would be too snarky of me to mention that. "And Napoleon's." Shore 'nuff.

I thought of Charles Percival and wondered if he'd been at Waterloo. He'd certainly been in Belgium at the time. Katherine's diary was about the spring of 1815. The Battle of Waterloo, the display card told me, was June 18, 1815.

I haven't gotten back to the diary. After Mary's über-depressing (not to mention rhyming) *Abandoned Bride*, I needed something less incredibly heavy. The new Sarah Dessen, this seems a good time to mention, is really good.

As we wandered, I read some of the info on Waterloo. One card made me stop and reread. "Is this right?"

Will leaned in. "I'm sure it is."

"No way. Twenty-two *thousand* soldiers died? In one *day*?"

"Or were wounded. And it's closer to fifty if you count both sides."

I looked at the lists of the regiments. Foot Guard, 70% of the company lost that day. Dragoons, 45% percent lost that day. 61% lost. 93 . . .

As it turns out, it all happened in about twelve hours. A crazy, furious twelve-hour battle that ended a long, ugly war. Go read about it. www.bbc.co.uk/history/british/empire_seapower. I don't feel like writing down details. They're too sad. Or gross. Or both.

I really didn't feel like looking at more plates. "Let's go," I begged after about half an hour. I even tugged at Will's arm. I needed out.

"It's really not that big a deal." He thought I was going for the bag again. I let him.

We wandered into the Park. I didn't care that the last time I was there was the fateful Bella fiasco. It's a big place. It's an amazing place. I was sad and hungry and tired of everything. I flumped down on the first bench that was free of tourists, nannies, or pigeons. Will sat next to me and stretched out his long long legs. He was either wearing the same jeans as the day we went to Notting Hill, or he has more than one pair with those soft creases at the tops of his thighs.

His mobile rang. He ignored it.

"Here." He handed me the bag. Inside, nestled in tissue paper, was a little plastic model of a satellite (see pic below; isn't it wonderful?). "You told me, at the caff that day, that you wanted your own satellite. So . . ."

You can't really see it in the picture, but there's a little blue button under the wing-y, mirror-y thing. When you press it, a voice says "Aim for the Stars!"

I started crying. Yeah, again.

Over the silly, wonderful present.

Over the fact that he *remembered* the satellite thang.

Over the lost chance that he might be Mr. Maybe.

Over Charles and Nicholas and all the young guys who died in that stupid war.

Over any war.

After a minute, Will got up and walked away. *Great*, I thought as I tried to snorfle my way to calm. *Typical. Is there one guy out there who doesn't go all skittery at the sight of tears?*

And then he was back.

He sat down and handed me a bunch of paper napkins. My English Kleenex. "Thanks," I hiccuped, and blew my nose.

"Not at all. You carry on with what you're doing."

Actually, it didn't take long. He waited until I was down to a hiccup-snuffle every ten seconds or so. Then he bumped me with his elbow. "I can take the satellite back, you know."

That got him a watery giggle. "It's not the satellite. I love the satellite. It's brilliant. It's . . ."

What? The fact that, my luck with men (and I am including Prince William, Orlando Bloom, Philly tossers with silver shoes, and even ones to whom I am related) is something less than stellar? That at this rate, the only guys I'll be able to actually *comprehend* are the ones behind the counter at the video store? The ones with Doritos crumbs in their wispy little beards. Eww. But hey, we'll be able to talk *Lost*, *Lord of the Rings* (me: movie, them: books, but I assume that's like Portuguese-Portuguese versus Brazilian—enough commonalities for comprehension) and the current incarnation of Doctor Who. And it will almost make sense.

I contemplated an idiot-smack to my forehead, but didn't wanna look any more insane to Will than I already did.

"It's this war thing. All these guys our age dying. It gets to me," I finished. Lame-o but true.

"Sure. I—" His mobile went again. He ignored it again. "Try to look at it this way. Napoleon was trying to swallow Europe whole. Without Waterloo, we couldn't possibly be friends. I would speak French with a bloody snooty accent, would wear ridiculous hats, and wouldn't even *consider* eating one of these. *Que Dieu m'en préserve!*"

I hadn't noticed the carry box at his side. The napkins made sense. I accepted a hot dog. There were even fries. My dream picnic it was not, but I'm not complaining. I did have a momentary silent grumble over the absence of ketchup. Vinegar just ain't the same. Still, you can't have everything. I just wish he didn't sound so *très très bon* speaking French.

"I know how you feel, about the war thing." He tossed a french fry to a hopeful-looking pigeon. Almost immediately, there were ten more. Of course, being English Hyde Park pigeons (think of them as the dirty doves they are), they were almost polite, refraining from clawing and flapping over our feet. Had they been Philly pigeons, they would have been on our heads by then. "No matter how it ends, it ends badly for most everyone involved."

One pigeon edged forward. It was noisily chastised by the others and crept back, clearly ashamed of itself.

Will polished off his hot dog and eyed mine. I bared my teeth. He laughed. This time, when his phone trilled, he pulled it out of his pocket. "Sorry. It's Bella." Like I wouldn't have guessed. At least he didn't answer it. He even turned it off. What a guy. "So, what's next on the agenda, *mademoiselle*?"

"Bond Street?" I said hopefully. Dirty doves got nuthin' on me. My shopping jones is edging back. Hallelujah.

"Not a chance. I thought we could catch a play at the Royal, but then it occurred to me: What's a place Katherine visited when compared to the place she lived? I promised Mum I would drive you and yours down for the weekend." I turned all my attention to the delicious, fascinating, rapidly congealing hot dog. Will leaned over to look into my (no doubt blotchy) face. "You are coming, aren't you? To Percy's Vale?"

Nope. No way. Not if the London sewers burst their pipes and carry off bella Bella in a flood of disfiguring muck. "Sure," I heard slip out of my mouth. "I'm coming."

"Good." He reached out a hand toward my face. It hovered near my cheek. "Um, Cat?"

"Yes?" *Yes. Absolutely. Go right ahead.*

"You have mustard. There."

"Oh. Right. Absolutely. Go ahead."

He wiped it off, then flopped back against the bench and tossed another fry to his adoring flock. It was gone in a momentary flurry of beaks and feathers.

I had a thought, O my friends, while I sat there next to him. A thought about boys. A good one is kinda like a hot dog dropped in Rittenhouse Square. We are the pigeons.

16 June

We have received a letter from Charles, at last! How quickly it arrived, just five days after its dispatch.

> Brussels, June 11
>
> My Dearest Family,
>
> How odd it might seem for me to be here, waiting for battle, and having nothing to write of save pleasures. I cannot even speculate as to when I might be called to action, or called home. Everything we hear is rumour; we know not what is fact until after it occurs. There is rumour that the enemy is as near as Cambrai. Perhaps they are not so close, yet perhaps they are closer. Each day we wait for news that we are to move. I am restless. There will certainly be a battle, either here in Belgium, or nearby in France. The wait is interminable.
>
> You will be happy to hear, Kitty, that we are not lacking for marvelous entertainment. There is much more talk of social balls than cannonballs among our ranks. Why, not three nights past, I attended a most lavish ball given by Sir Charles Stuart. It was all very lively and very English. Even the Belgian ladies in attendance sported much British decoration. Sir Charles is a single fellow, disposed to be sociable and much inclined to do things

on a grand scale. I daresay he is a career Diplomat in the making, destined to a life of politics and luxury in foreign climes. If he were but a few years younger, and I did not so despise the idea of you living abroad, Kitty, he might do for you. As it is, he filled his house with the best and brightest of the city. There was a splendid feast upstairs, dancing down. Wellington himself was there, kitted out with gold embroidery and all the trappings of a general.

Yesterday, a group of us rode into the countryside, where we availed ourselves of the hospitality of a Monsieur Legrand and his family. He is a wealthy merchant who has made himself a fortune in carpets and lace. I shall try to send some back for you. His wife and daughters treated us as if we were royalty. I must say, women here are as charming and cultured as any I have met, and quite lovely, but I shall always prefer a good English rose. We had far too much roast and beer and rolled and groaned our way back to our billet. I confess I have developed a notable fondness for Belgian beer and chocolates.

As soon as I have reliable news as to the Regiment's movements, I shall write again. Until such time, be assured that I am merry and well fed and entertained.

Yours ever,
Charles

He seems cheerful enough. I do not care for his certainty that there will be a battle, and soon. I shall have to hope for the best, that the French shall be stopped before they get any closer. It has happened before; Napoleon has been defeated. I can think of no reason it will not be the same now. Perhaps he is already so, the enemy all surrendered. I shall eagerly await the newspaper this afternoon and tomorrow morning. Perhaps I shall even encourage Mama to invite Nicholas for supper. He receives word from sources we do not possess and might know what even the newspapers do not.

Yes, I believe I shall go and suggest it now.

August 5

Falling Slowly

Tweets.

catTcat: Will drives like maniac. Land Rovers wobble on curves. English country roads not good 4 girl w/inner-ear issues. Darkness does not help.

catTcat: Between (s)mother and ride (didja know that means hottie-object-of-desire over here?), didn't get going till after dinner.

catTcat: Listened to Beatles whole way down, 2+ hours in wobbly car. Only thing Will, (s)mother, & I could agree on. Used 2 luv John.

catTcat: Will sings. Not well but with enthusiasm. Shoot me, plz—(s)mother sang with him. Used 2 luv "8 Days a Week."

catTcat: Will brakes for anything in road. Am composing my obit in my head. "Bloved friend. Gr8 taste in shoes&shades; fatal at luv."

catTcat: Question for peanut gallery: Where does nausea become noble suffering become martyrdom?

✦ ✦ ✦

I'm practicing Twittering for the future: no London, no love, no need for long blog entries, right? It's kinda like the haikus Mr. Djanikian had us writing, only it doesn't have to be poetic. Just 140 characters or less.

Wonder if there's a site for haiku tweets.

catTcat: Driving through the dark—heading for Will's distant home—really gotta pee.

or

catTcat: Deep in countryside. Percy's Vale is really old. Wireless access?

or

catTcat: First view of the house—fifty windows full of light—Kitty, are you here?

Even in the dark, Percy's Vale is beautiful (will send pix tomorrow). All honey-colored stone and mullioned windows and marble steps that have been so hollowed out by centuries of climbing feet that Will says you sometimes find tadpoles in them. I think he's kidding. Maybe not.

Will's parents are pretty great. His mom is about six feet tall, and looks like a Swedish movie star. She sounds just like Consuelo. She wears black cashmere, even in July (not to complain, but it's slightly glacial inside the house), covered with dog hair. Fortunately, the dogs are a quintet of black Labs, so the hair is not obvious unless you're really close. Unfortunately, they slobber for five. Dog slobber on black. Not pretty. Dog slobber on my jeans. Not much prettier. Mrs. Percival ("Oh, don't be ridiculous—call me Bronwen.")

writes books about sixteenth-century architecture. She met Mr. Percival ("HAL!" he bellowed when Will introduced us; apparently he's both effusive and a little bit deaf from a lifetime of shooting big guns) when she was working on her master's thesis and came to see Percy's Vale. She and Mom hit it off within five minutes. They're both fascinated by things old, obscure, and dusty.

Mr. Percival...HAL!...works with Prince Charles on promoting organic farming. It occurred to me that he could probably get me somewhere where Prince William is likely to be. I'm still thinking about whether to pursue that. He looks like a slightly shorter, slightly wider version of Will. He wears orange Crocs and smells (not ickily, surprisingly) of compost.

Will's sister, Caroline, is a copy of their mother, minus the dog hair. She's thirteen. She seems friendly enough, in a thirteen-year-old sort of way. Meaning she stopped texting long enough to give my jeans and T-shirt the (approving—thanks, H&M&Elizabeth) once-over, ask if I've ever been to a Jonas Brothers concert, then disappeared back into her room.

I give them all props for being sociable at ten o'clock. They even tried to feed us. Will's dad disappeared for ten minutes, then came back with this massive tray full of cheese-and-pickle sandwiches, curry-flavored crisps, and pink-topped cupcakes. HAL! plunked down the tray, plunked himself down, and sat smiling at us like the entire measure of his life's success depended on our enjoying his colorful offering. I tried. Really, I did. Fortunately, Will ate three sandwiches and most of the cupcakes. My picking was enough.

"I'm afraid there isn't much of Mary left here," HAL! told Mom as soon as he was satisfied we were eating and could turn his attention to other matters. "You're welcome to dig around, but I did have a look. Found a few books, but sod-all else. Everything went to the BM when my grandfather died."

Seems the old guy had a hard time letting go of anything. On top of several centuries of family papers, he left behind fifteen hundred issues of the *Times*, ninety-nine broken flowerpots (he was an avid gardener; his wife managed to get a groundskeeper into the greenhouse every five years or so to dispose of empty seed packets, out-of-date almanacs, and whatever pots had broken during that period), and his own university wardrobe.

"He left Oxford in 1910," Bronwen announced. "Half of the tweed suits had knickers." Her own legs go on forever, and I'm pretty sure her black wool pants cost more than my entire wardrobe put together. "Everything weighed an absolute ton."

"It was all from Savile Row," HAL! informed us a little sadly. "Lasts forever." I get the sense he's a bit of a hoarder himself. There is a dramatic number of out-of-date ecology magazines and single wellies around the house.

While the 'rents discussed the future of England's past, Will and I took the dirty dishes into the big, modern kitchen and loaded them into the big, modern dishwasher. The dogs wriggled and rolled and thwapped us with their tails until we gave them the last sandwiches. They are truly appreciative of HAL!'s cooking. Will told me there's a cook who comes in daily. She comes before lunch and leaves after dinner. Bronwen, apparently, burns water. Leaving it to HAL! to happily feed whatever hapless persons arrive during off-hours.

"So, want a tour?" Will asked. Finally. Despite the fact that it was pushing eleven. "I'll show you the best parts of the house."

"Got any secret passages?" I joked.

"Absolutely. Dungeon, too."

"Are you kidding? You're kidding."

He wasn't kidding. "Old house. Illustrious ancestors." He grabbed a flashlight ('scuse me: *"torch"* as in *"carrying a torch for you"*) and led the way to a narrow flight of stairs that stretched up and down endlessly, very dark, most creepy.

He flicked a switch. There was flowered wallpaper lining the stairwell in both directions.

We didn't end up in either a secret passage or a dungeon. We ended up going up and out a third-floor dormer window onto the roof.

Big roof. Big. Long way down. "Mind the shiny bits," Will told me. "They can be slick." I looked around frantically for shiny bits, but all roofs look pretty much the same to me late at night, fifty feet in the air. Will clambered between the oxidized copper panels like a deranged orangutan. "Here. Give me your hand."

I might have enjoyed that little bit of hand-holding ("I wanna hold your ha-a-a-a-and . . .") had I not been a tad concerned with going over the edge. Which, I gotta be truthful here, was a good ten feet away. Finally, we reached a little alcove. Will sat down and pulled me with him.

"My favorite place in the house."

It was pretty amazing. Even in the dark, you can see plenty. Like car headlights shining along the twisting roads, houses with one or two windows lit, houses with ten or twenty. And overhead, a gazillion stars.

O, my urban cohorts—I always forget what it's like to be outside, outside the city, until I'm actually there. I scanned the sky for anything I recognized from those (in)formative summers at Camp Dark Waters. (Remember the mosquitoes, Djenan? The archery? The archery-teaching counselor??? So hot.) "I think that's Pegasus." I pointed. All us girls at camp learned that one. Must've had something to do with twelve-year-old pony obsessions. "And Capricorn. And, hey—that really bright one might be Venus."

"Ah, I think that might be an aeroplane, actually."

"Smart-ass." But yeah, Venus was moving at a pretty impressive clip for a planet.

There is *nada* whatsoever like the night sky to make a girl feel small. I shivered.

"Cold?" Will asked.

To be completely honest—no. I swear it's ten degrees warmer outside the house than in. "A little," I said. 'Cause I had a suspicion that good things might come of a little white lie. And one did. Maybe not the *best* good thing, but not bad. Will whipped off his sweater and helped me into it. Like scrunched it up so I could get it over my head, then pulled it down when I had my arms in. It was warm from his body and smelled like his hair.

I snuggled in. In the distance, I could just see a red-orange glow. "What's that?"

"Bonfire. Happens a lot in the summer."

I thought of PBS shows about earnest people in big hooded cloaks, dancing around fires and chanting about earth goddesses and phases of the moon. "Wiccans? Druids?"

"Nah. Most people vote Conservative 'round here. This lot is more likely to be in chain mail and helmets. It's an Iron Age hill fort. Legend has it, King Arthur had his court there."

"Wait, wait. That's Camelot? You live near *Camelot*?"

"Entirely possible. The era's right, and that's the River Cam there. But no one actually calls it Camelot."

"What, then?"

He was kinda leaning against me now, his shoulder against mine. I couldn't help it; I kinda tilted my head until I felt his jaw bump against the top of it. I could feel my hair catching just a little in the sandpapery shadow of whiskers that guys have late at night. *I could get used to this. I could so get used to this—*

"It's Cadbury Castle. Our village is South Cadbury."

And there it was. Cadbury. My chocolate. Will's village. Camelot and knights and Once Upon a Time. I wanted it. To sling my bag into the back of Will's Land Rover and come down for the weekend. Most weekends. To be welcomed so warmly by the effortlessly cool mom and the funny, contented dad. Like I belonged. Like I'm sure Bella has been for three years. I wanted all of it. I mean, who wouldn't? And Will. Oh, Will . . .

I jerked away so fast I almost gave myself whiplash. What was I thinking? I mean, could I *be* any more pathetic than to melt like cheesy cheese over a guy who, while always incredibly *nice* to me, is givin' the goods to someone else?

"Cat? You all right?"

Oh, yeah. Peachy, thanks. "Fine," I told him (I'm sure a little shrilly). "Thought I was going to sneeze."

And so it is, O my friends, that I have ended up in this amazing house, with this amazing guy, near *bleeping bleeping CADBURY Castle*. There should be neon going off everywhere: SignSignSign. Only. It's. Not. And I don't get to keep *any* of it.

To add insult to injury, Will produced a Cadbury Dairy Milk bar from somewhere and gave me the bigger half.

We stayed out for another hour. Here's what we talked about:

✦ He actually knows most of the constellations. Charterhouse had a midnight astronomy class for seniors. Just like Hogwarts.

✦ He's read all seven Harry Potter books (fave is *Azkaban*), but he was a late bloomer, not even reading the first one until two years ago when he and Bella and a group of friends went skiing and he sprained his ankle on the second day. He finished the last one in a sleeper car on the Edinburgh

Sleeper train, speeding from London to Scotland through the night. He was sure he saw J. K. Rowling at a café later the next day, but readily admits that, considering his complete lack of sleep the night before, it might just as easily have been a local barrister or meter reader on her lunch break.

✦ His grandfather is called Harry, but it's short for Harold (as is HAL!). There have been a good dozen Harold Percivals in the family's written history, as well as nine Williams and at least fifteen Charleses. Seven of whom lived between 1760 and 1860, fathers and sons and uncles and cousins.

✦ Hence he has no idea whether Katherine's brother survived Waterloo.

✦ He doesn't know what happened to Katherine after the diary days, either.

✦ He's game to search the house tomorrow for clues, Scooby-Doo.

✦ There are forty-six rooms in the house.

✦ I waited at Head House Books for three hours with the posse to make sure we got copies of *Deathly Hallows* before 12:05 a.m. Cried so hard during the last few chapters that when I went to reread it last summer, a bunch of the pages were wrinkly and stuck together.

✦ My fave Scottish writer is still James Herriot.

✦ One of my first memories is watching *Dr. No* with my dad, who will turn violent at the suggestion there is any James Bond other than Sean Connery.

- He wanted to name me Honor after Honor Blackman, who played a character named Pussy Galore, and it had absolutely nothing to do with pornography.

- That, apparently, caused the first of several parental near divorces before the real thing occurred.

- I'm named after my great-great-grandmother, who was thrown in jail not once, not twice, but six times for marching for women's right to vote.

- Despite Kelly and Jen's best efforts, the only protest I've ever really been involved in (the D.C. wandering-among-PO'd-librarians doesn't really count) was a petition to keep Diet Coke in the vending machines at school.

- I'm embarrassed by that.

- I'm kinda afraid my photocopy of Katherine's diary got recycled along with two weeks' worth of the *Times*, *Hello!*, *Okay*, and the *Guardian*. The last time I saw it, it was on the brown sitting-room carpet.

And what we didn't:

- I am a sad but decent liar. As in "Oh, yeah, I'm tired, too. Absolutely, we should go inside."

- I am a shameless thief, too. I'm still wearing his sweater. I plan on sleeping in it.

And some more Twee-kus to shut off the computer by:

catTcat: When going off roofs—the very best way to fall—is slowly slowly.

catTcat: Yes, I can do this. Be chipper gal pal he wants. It's only two days.

catTcat: How he said good night: "Have sweet dreams, Moneypenny." Just like Connery.

catTcat: Damndamndamndamndamn. I'm not over him at all. Damndamndamndamndamn.

18 June

I woke to see a lone magpie in the tree outside my window. Mama and I used to sing the Magpie Rhyme as we looked for the second bird. We always sang; we always found a second magpie, or more.

> One for sorrow, two for joy
> Three for a girl, four for a boy
> Five for silver, six for gold
> Seven for secrets never told.

Today I did not sing. Why would I? Of course, I searched the garden for a second, but not with any true effort. I could not be bothered. I wonder, if I had . . . But no, things would be just as they are.

Supper is being served in the dining room. I am not hungry. I cannot imagine when next I shall be so.

Luisa has gone home, taking her comforting presence with her, but leaving the unhappy news with which she came. Thomas Baker is to marry Julia Northrop. The ceremony is to be in four weeks' time at her family estate in Northumberland. There is to be an engagement dinner at the Northrops' next week. I assume I shall be invited; it would be just like her to do so. I do not think I shall attend.

Mama has just tapped on my door yet again. I do not wish to talk to her. I do not wish to talk to anyone. I wish to stay right where I am, thank you very much, perhaps until the Season is over and I may go home to Percy's Vale.

Luisa does not think He loves Her. Luisa thinks he is badly in debt to a number of persons, and desperate to find a way out of it. Luisa knows he owes Robert Spenser a great deal of money, an amount Mr. Spenser is too polite to allow to be known, but Mr. McCoy has hinted it is above five hundred pounds.

I do not care. I do not care if it is ten times that. What is money in the face of affection?

Then, again, what is affection in the face of want of money?

I am too sad to write. I believe I shall go to bed.

20 June

There are so few pages left in this diary. I suppose I should purchase another soon. Only I do not much feel like writing.

Luisa has just left again. She has been worried for me. She arrived with a box of Irish linen handkerchiefs embroidered with various handheld weapons (I have no idea how she managed to have that done so quickly, but how they made me smile—I especially like the dagger), far too many Gunter's chocolates, and Nicholas. He did not come into my bedchamber, of course, but stayed with Mama in the drawing room.

Luisa says she encountered him outside the house, pacing back and forth, uncertain as to whether he ought to come in. Poor fellow. Nicholas is scarcely ever at a loss for words, but I daresay this might flummox him. He has heard. I am certain all of Mayfair has heard. I am not to have Thomas Baker; petty, rich Miss Northrop is. It does not matter that I did not make my expectations widely known. I am the heartsick foolish girl nonetheless.

I do not want anyone's pitying glances. I do not want Nicholas's sympathy. It would be hard to bear. Even if there were not a touch of "Did I Not Tell You?," and I expect he could control any such impulse, I am not ready to face him or any of my friends just yet.

I cannot even begin to think of the audience I shall have with Papa. The very idea makes me feel cold.

Luisa asked me no questions, for which I am grateful. Mama, too, has refrained. I have no answers, only questions of my own.

Did he ever care for me? I was so <u>certain</u>, even if only for a short time.

Had it all been decided already when we met at the Quinns? Before, on the night when he danced with everyone except me?

Was it a jest with him, a challenge to make me fall a little bit in love with him, a game?

Am I not pretty enough for him?

More to the point, am I not <u>rich</u> enough for him?

I do not care for the way I feel. I detest the way I feel. So foolish, ~~so foolish and sad~~ angry, and . . . I have never imagined heartbreak to be so angry. Miss Austen has not, I think, taught us much about anger. I had always imagined I should feel as Marianne Dashwood (oh, that I have had a Willoughby! how galling!) does: ill and weary and possessed of a sorrow that turns a girl's visage pale and lovely. I am blotchy and red-eyed and my hair, very much in need of washing, resembles a rat's nest.

I find I do not wish to cry. I wish to yell. And should people not stop scratching at my door when I wish to be alo

I yelled. Mama yelled. Papa yelled, but only briefly, before the two of us quite shouted him down. He has stormed from the house with his portmanteau and though, for a moment, I almost went after him to beg him to return and not be angry with me, I did not try to stop him. Mama certainly did not.

I will <u>not</u> marry Lord Chilham. I do not care in the least that he wants me. It does not matter, although I suspect I will come to care a great deal later, that father so wished him to have me.

"I would sooner wed a pig farmer!" I yelled. "Far sooner, as a farmer has an honourable profession, and produces a great deal more than hot air! Give me a ditchdigger. An undertaker. A beggar! In fact, I could easily spend the rest of my <u>life</u> composing a list of the men I would sooner marry."

Father was holding a brandy glass, now empty, so tightly that I feared he would snap it in two. "A life you might damn well spend alone! Do you think there will be another offer for you, miss?" he bellowed, going so red in the face that I scarcely knew him. "I hear your poet fellow did not want you. If a stupid, penniless scribbler does not wish to marry you, tell me who will!"

I admit, that quite knocked the wind from me. That was when Mama began shouting. "And you, you selfish, arrogant beast! Just because *I* was stupid enough to marry a man clearly my inferior in all ways, do not think for a moment I will allow my daughter to be pushed into doing the same! Thank God Chilham does not have a pretty face or clever tongue to hide behind. The toad one sees is the toad one gets!"

There was a harsh crash as Papa slammed the glass against

the mantel. It shattered, leaving him brandishing the base and jagged stem. I am certain he did not intend to threaten us with it, but in a motion, Mama and I stepped in to stand shoulder to shoulder, the two of us an indestructible wall against him.

He sputtered for a moment, then cursed and flung the remains of the glass into the fireplace. It broke in two, but lacked all of the drama of the first shattering.

"I am leaving. And do not think I will return!" With that, he stormed from the room, slamming the door so loudly behind him that it banged open again and thudded against the wall.

I stood, mouth open, staring at the spot he had just been, and felt tears welling, tears I had not shed in the two days prior. I would perhaps have bawled, would perhaps even be standing there still, caterwauling like an angry tabby, had not Mama suddenly slumped against me.

I helped her to a chair, and offered to call for the doctor. She waved off the suggestion, and my concern. "No, no. I shall be fine. I rather believe we all had that coming sooner or later, and I have merely staggered when relieved of the weight of it. God, what a pitiful exit. I could have written him an infinitely better one."

Suddenly she was laughing and crying at the same time, and I was laughing and crying with her. It did not last long. Soon enough, we were sitting with tea (Mama did have a good amount of Papa's brandy with hers), Luisa's chocolates, and a house to ourselves. Until Charles comes home, I believe we shall have everything very much to ourselves.

I am calmer now, several hours later. I am clearer in my own mind. In truth, life shall be much as it was before we came to London. I shall be Miss Percival of Percy's Vale, an important house in our little part of England. I shall be expected to marry well—when I choose to marry. Chilham will wed some other poor girl. He will produce toadlike children, hence depriving Papa of both the title and the possibility of being grandsire to future Lord Chilhams. I do not care if I ever see the baron again. I do not know when I shall see Papa. Eventually, I am certain, but perhaps not soon. Mama does not believe he will go to Percy's Vale. He has never been happy there. I expect he will stay here in London, with his pompous, overdressed friends and stuffy gentlemen's clubs.

We shall go back to Somerset when the Season is over. I shall forget Thomas Baker. At least, I trust I shall forget how very miserable he made me and how foolish that made me feel. I hope I shall not forget how nice it was to be part of our lively little group. I shall certainly not forget Luisa. She has promised to come to Percy's Vale later in summer. And I expect we shall all meet again at the occasion of Henrietta Quinn's marriage to Mr. Troughton. I think perhaps Mr. Baker and Miss Northrop, who should by then be Mrs. Baker, will <u>not</u> be there. Luisa has heard they will be rusticating on the Isle of Man at least until autumn. Perhaps by then I shall feel gracious enough to wish them well and mean it.

I have received a note from Nicholas. His handwriting is very difficult to read. I do wish he had printed the missive. I cannot make heads nor tails of several words.

Katherine,

Your mother has informed me that you have (I do not suppose he can have written "slimily deceived") a voucher for Almack's. Although I still believe it to be ("a <u>machine</u>"??), it would be my pleasure to escort the two of you there Tuesday next. I shall even wear (I would not even hazard a guess as to what he has written there). You have only to inform me of your desires.

Most sincerely yours,
Everard

I sent a reply: "Yes, thank you."

I believe I shall be saying a good deal less in general in coming days. Shakespeare himself has said that brevity is the soul of wit. Miss Cameron was very fond of Shakespeare.

21 June

Although it is nearly midnight, we have had another note from Nicholas. He could not deliver it himself. He has gone to Whitehall to gather any further news.

Word has arrived from the Continent. There has been a Battle, near a village called Waterloo, some ten miles south of Brussels. Reports of casualties are severe. I shall return when I have further information to give you.

N.E.

Oh, dear heaven. Oh, Charles.

I'm Yours

The Top Ten Things I Have Learned from Jane Austen (in our relatively brief and limited acquaintance)

1. There are a lot less rich, handsome, decent guys than there are pretty, terrific girls who should have one. Meaning, we are all Elizabeth Bennets, but the guy sitting next to us in Biology ain't no Mr. Darcy.

2. Getting a guy really shouldn't be Everything, but somehow, still, it is. Even though Jane herself didn't in the end.

3. The Competition is always prettier, smarter, richer, nicer, or meaner. Or a frightening, insurmountable combination thereof.

4. Silly (s)mothers will do more to damage a potential relationship than chronic halitosis; good mothers are the Altoids of the parenting realm.

5. The good guys don't want stupid girlfriends.

6. Being clever, erudite, and slightly enigmatic helps. But . . .

7. Guys generally need us to come with subtitles, cue cards, and liability waivers.

8. Second loves are often the Real Thing.
9. It's really hard to look good in really hot weather.
10. Guys whose names start with W (Willoughby, Wentworth, Wickham . . .) will always break your heart at least once.

I woke up the morning after the night on the roof feeling slightly less than fine. Here I was, on the verge of having a full 24 hours with Will, and I had a stomachache. Okay, not stomach, actually, A little higher. Like my entire rib cage hurt. I guess this is it; this is why it's called heartbreak.

Outside, it was pouring rain. Great.

I had a shower, remembered to put a sweater (not Will's alas—I'm not *that* pitiful) on over my shirt, and slumped down to breakfast. The Percivals actually put maps of the house in the guest rooms. I still got lost, and ended up in the mudroom instead of the breakfast room. They have a breakfast room. A room just for breakfast. I found it eventually by following one of the dogs. HAL! was the only one there. He looked up from his coffee and pile of newspapers and grinned, obviously delighted to see me. The dimple, apparently, is a Percival family trait. This morning, he was wearing what I was pretty sure was an Edun sweatshirt with his threadbare cords and Crocs. I figure he probably knows Bono, who owns Edun and is a green god, too.

"CATHERINE!" he bellowed. "Sit down! Let me get you some breakfast!"

I had images of him whipping up some green eggs and ham. But no, there was an array of cereals on the sideboard, and a funny little toaster that would have looked antique had it not had twelve buttons and three digital displays. The coffeemaker looked like its evil twin.

"Cook's off today," HAL! told me as he shoved bread into the toaster. "Breakfast is DIY. Cereal? Everything's organic and whole grain."

Sure enough, the cereal boxes all displayed photos of bumpy brown flakes, krisps, or twigs. "Oh, no, thanks. Toast will be great." Oddly, it was. Must've had something to do with the butter, which was like no butter I have ever had in the U.S. Yum.

Anyway. Three pieces of toast and cup of coffee later ("Hope you're all right without orange juice," HAL! said apologetically. "We're having free trade issues with Brazil."), I felt human enough to ask if we were the first up.

He laughed. "We won't see Caroline for another hour, but everyone else has been and gone. Your mum's off somewhere with Bronwen, delving into history. Here." He whipped an iPhone out of his pocket and tapped furiously for a second. "Ah. Will's in the office. Fiddling with the routers, no doubt. Can't convince him that this *is* high speed for Somerset . . . Now, you just go out the door here, turn left, and go down the hallway until you reach the main hall. Go right across and through the third door . . ."

I did fine until I got to the main hall. I assumed it was the front of the house, the main entrance. We'd come through a nice, welcoming little ivy-covered courtyard the night before. This was all twenty-foot ceilings and marble floors and a big sweeping staircase going up two ways, with crested banners along the sides. There was even a pair of standing suits of armor flanking the bottom steps. *Très* creepy, the way they look at you with those eyeholes. Every time I have ever seen one in a museum, I've wanted to lift the visor and peek inside. So I did.

"Unhand me, demoiselle!"

I jumped a foot, let go of the visor, and squeaked when it snapped down on my finger. I hadn't seen Will standing in a doorway off to the side. "Well, that's ten years of my life I won't get back."

"Couldn't resist it." He grinned (floppy hair, dimple . . . gonna kill me faster than fright) and levered himself away from the door frame. "You looked so . . ."

"Furtive?" I offered.

"Excellent word."

Ah, SATs. I rested one arm across the armored shoulders and gestured around the hall with the other. "This is all very . . ." No SAT word came to mind.

"Pretentious?" Will suggested. "Pompous? OTT? Doesn't usually look like this. The place is usually full of boxes of pamphlets and bins of onions. But Dad's group had a herd of potential investors here last week from Texas. They like the naff English trappings." He patted the second suit of armor on top of its helmet. "These are from my grandfather's house. He decks them out in Portsmouth colors, despite the fact that the club hasn't won the division title in sixty years."

"There's a red something hanging inside the helmet. Looks like a scarf."

"Sock. So, on this beautiful day, in or out?"

I looked through the window at the deluge and pointed. *"Out?"*

He pointed, too. *"England."*

"Right."

"So?"

"Out."

"Brilliant."

I had already been in the mudroom that morning. It was delightfully familiar. Will sorted among the countless Barbour coats and wellies until he found some for me and we made a dash for his

Land Rover. A few minutes later, we were bumping and squelching our way down the long drive and away from the house. I turned in my seat to watch it get smaller in the back window. I can't say I'd felt much of Katherine, or anything other than the current Percivals' cheerful presence. But it had only been twelve hours.

As Will showed me his hood, I kept my face to the window. It helped not to look at him. I was afraid that if I did, I might climb over the gearshift and into his lap. I was afraid, if I did, I might cry. So I swallowed the sadness and watched the English landscape slide by.

It's awfully pretty, even in the rain. There was the big house on the hill where Will's best friend, Sam Goodwin, lived, the village of South Cadbury that I pretty much missed because I was trying to clear the condensation from the window, the modern local school that Will attended when he was very small, and finally, Cadbury Castle. Or, at least, a small sign, a big hill, and some trees. It was all very, very green.

"That's it?" I demanded, peering through the water rivulets that were cascading down the window, looking for stone walls or anything resembling a castle fort. "There's nothing there."

Will stopped the car and leaned over to look. "You think you're going to look like much after fifteen hundred years? It's a pretty spectacular view from the top. Wanna try?"

I could see small rivers running down the hill. "Umm ..."

"How about elevenses, then?"

We ended up at a half-full half pub, half teashop nearby. (See pix; yes, that is a real, stuffed dormouse in that teapot—very Mad Hatter's tea party). The woman running the place greeted Will by name, asked after his family, and passed on a message for his grandfather. Apparently bookies are giving 179–1 odds against Portsmouth winning next year, either.

Will thanked her, greeted the dormouse ("Gordon") like an old friend, then settled us in a corner with our coffee and cakes. "I thought we'd have a look 'round the house this afternoon, see if there's anything there about Katherine."

He downed half his coffee, then turned the mug back and forth, back and forth between his palms. Truth be told, he was looking a little rough. Gorgeous but rough. Why oh why does my brain not have a torture-prevention switch? All I could think of was him whispering till the wee hours over the phone with Bella. Who, no doubt, was stretched out in La Perla'd splendor in London, longing for him. I felt no pity.

"So, Catherine."

"So, William."

"There's something I've been meaning to ask you."

Oh, the possibilities. "Shoot."

"Why did you ask me about my favorite poem?"

Allow me to refresh your memories. *#9* on the list of things a girl should get from a guy the first time: *Sends a poem after.*

I blew on my coffee, added another sugar, gazed around the room (must've missed the stuffed cuckoo coming out of a clock— at least I assume it was a cuckoo—not sure I've ever seen a cuckoo, but enjoy using the word). Stalled. Had a stroke. Of genius.

"Why did you pick '*No Second Troy*'?" Gracefully deflecting the question.

"That's dodging the question. But I'll humor you. First year at Charterhouse, my Housemaster's wife was a mind-bogglingly gorgeous woman from Galway. She liked Yeats. Every boy in the house learned some Yeats that year. That one made sense to my hormones then. Now"—he shrugged—"I like all of it: the imagery, the symbolism, the idea that love and war are so close." He did the one-eyebrow thing. "Doesn't hurt that it reminds me of Mrs. Fahey."

Not Bella at all. He hadn't chosen a poem about the most irresistible woman in the world because of irresistible Bella. He liked it because he's Will and he'd been awed by the power of the words. He'd chosen it because of an adolescent crush on a hot older woman from Galway. I let my fingers do a quick, cheerful little Irish step dance on the lace tablecloth.

"Now tell me why you asked," he commanded.

"I was drunk," I said. "It's a good drunk question."

He didn't look entirely convinced. No dummy, Will Percival. But just as much to his credit, he's not a pest, either. "Fair enough. Your poem?"

"I'm still working on that one," I admitted, "but lately it's 'She Walks in Beauty.'"

"Ah. Byron." Will snagged a piece of my cherry scone. "Good choice, although I'm a 'So We'll Go No More A-Roving' man, myself. No one does breakup songs quite like he does."

Twee-ku:
catTcat: Do I deserve this? Add insult to injury: the boy knows Byron.

After eating, we decided it was high time to read the end of the diary. I had a few pages to go; Will admitted to having stopped when Baker threw Kitty over for the girl with more money. I had this thought that he would read out loud to me and it would all be very English Country House Party. It was a good thought. But my copy was (somewhere) in London; Will's copy was (somewhere) in London. Bronwen's copy, we learned when we found her and the (s)mother having tea in the West Parlor (Will actually called it the West Parlor, suggesting there is an East, North, and/or South), had been eaten by one of the Labradors. Two, actually. "They shared," Bronwen said proudly, patting the nearest dog on its drooling head. She thought for a sec. "Try the library. There should be an old family Bible there. It might at least tell you who Katherine married."

I think Will and I both had a pretty good idea who Katherine married. I didn't think it would make me feel any better to see Lord Chilham's name in ink.

We went down a few corridors and across miles of ocean, road, and tundra to the library. What a place. Shelves floor to ceiling, tall enough that there are actually ladders on runners that go back and forth from wall to wall. Have you ever known me to go all goofy over anything other than a guy or the perfect pair of jeans? Okay, maybe a hamachi roll at Hikaru . . . I felt like Belle in the Disney movie.

Will took the six thousand books on the left; I took the four thousand on the right. Most are hardbacks. Most have leather binding and gold lettering. The paperbacks are pretty impressive, too. I pulled out a copy of *Brideshead Revisited* and opened it. The inscription said, *To Chaz. Couldn't buy the hardcover, you old Scrooge? Always, E.W.*

"My great-grandfather Charles," Will explained, completely unimpressed by the presence of Evelyn Waugh. "The one with the flowerpots. Probably never bought a hardcover book if there was a paperback available."

After a while, it was like being in the tenth store on a shopping trip. Everything was starting to look the same. I found myself only noticing the colorful books. "Hey. *Waverley*. I've heard of . . ."

An old copy of Walter Scott's *Waverley*, bound in red leather. I gotta say, my heart started beating a little faster as I reached for the book. It felt smooth and a little cold as I slid it out. And there,

there it was: a tartan ribbon tucked through the book. There were other things tucked between the pages, too: several folded papers, a single dried and blackened flower, and a piece of a playbill. From the Theatre Royal, Covent Garden.

"Uh, Will. I think I might have found one of Katherine's books." I carefully opened one of the folded sheets. The lines were written in very bold, very masculine printing.

A Riddle for Miss Percival, by An Admirer

My first is in the Lanes but not the Plants.
My second is in the Song and in the Dance.
My third you'll find at Court but not at Home.
My fourth comes when you Walk but do not Roam.
My fifth is in the Skies and in the Rain.
My six begins not Bliss, yet ends the Pain.
My seventh is in Whole but not in Part.
My eighth is in your Head but not your Heart.
When joined together, you shall surely see
Our lives have always been; So shall we be?

Will had been reading over my shoulder. "Oh. Right. I remember that. Couldn't figure it out."

Okay, so I gloated just a little. I am very good at puzzles. I'd figured out that one in no time.

"You find the letter that's either in one or the other, or in both." I explained, resisting adding a "duh." "The first one's easy. There's no E in 'Plants.'" (You with me here, ladies?) "Then, only N is in both words . . ."

Edison would've been proud of the lightbulb that went off over Will's head.

Figured it out yet?

E-N-T-W-I-N-E-D.

"Our lives have always been. So shall we be?"

It gave me a little tummy tingle the first time I read it. Now, standing next to Will, holding a two-hundred-year-old book and a two-hundred-year-old love letter, I got full-on butterflies. I looked up at him, at that perfect mouth and even more perfect skin and blue blue eyes, and wished like I'd never wished before (pony Prada parents-back-together Adam were nuthin' compared to this).

Gentle Readers, he kissed me.

He tastes like ginger ale, too.

He kissed me in the middle of the library and I kissed him against the huge antique desk and, after a few minutes, when my legs were totally weak, we moved the action to the squashy, tufted leather sofa.

"Wow," I gasped when we finally came up for air. "Wow."

"I agree. Let's do it again." We did. After a while, he flopped back against the cushions, grinning. "I have wanted to do that since . . . Well, maybe not the *first* time I saw you."

I remembered the first time. Best not to think too much about that first view he would have had of me coming at him across the BM floor like a human windmill. "You did?"

"Since you offered me tea in your flat. Especially when you told me you wanted a satellite for your birthday. In the Royal Academy, at Hatchards, standing in front of that bloody Napoleon statue. I wanted to kiss you last night, but you went all spastic on me just at the moment."

I remembered and winced at the memory. "Not my finest moment. I was thinking of . . . Hey!" Bad thought. Bad. And then, what's a worse thought?—that there is a girlfriend, or that there might not be a girlfriend but I might totally ruin the Moment by asking?

Like there's any contest. I asked. "What about your girlfriend? The very *bella* Bella."

Well, ladies, as it happens, the very *bella* Bella has had very dubious girlfriend status since India. They fought endlessly through Italy, almost split up three times between Venice and Jaipur, and called it quits at the Delhi train station. He was relieved ("It had been pretty awful for a few months"); she apparently had second thoughts during her time in Greece ("She started calling all the time when she got back, wanting to *talk*"), and even I understand how hard it can be to completely, totally close the door on something that had been going on for so long and was, at least for part of it, good ("So much *history* . . .").

"You asked me," he said. "You asked me how long we'd been together and I wanted to say we *weren't* together, but she was back and calling and you were so bloody cool, Cat. Like a cat. I couldn't read you . . ."

Cool like a cat. Oh, stop laughing, Jen.

Turns out I was right: he didn't have a clue that I liked him. Gotta remember to tell Consuelo. Crap. Totally forgot to tell Consuelo about the fight she and Bayard never had.

Forgot everything for the next hour or so.

"Come on," Will said eventually. "There's something I meant to show you before." He held my hand all the way upstairs.

Boys' rooms are always kinda strange, no matter who lives in them. Either they're filled with dusty sports trophies, or the walls are covered with posters of scowling, diamond-grilled rappers or swimsuit models (I hate to admit Adam had one of each), or the technology cords cover everything like colorful snakes. They all smell like socks, the level of stinkiness determined, I think, by the resilience of whoever does the cleaning.

Will's room does have a very faint sock thang going, but

otherwise it's good. No posters, no trophies, no cables. The only definitive boy-was-here display is a group of tin soldiers on top of a glossy old table. There are a lot of books, a few framed maps and paintings on the walls, a very slick laptop, and even slicker plasma-screen TV. A big, tiled fireplace takes up the middle of one wall; a big, modern-looking bed takes up the one opposite. I didn't want to spend too much time looking at the bed.

So, I'm thinking, What if he wants to . . . I mean here, now . . . There's a real bed but no flowers or "I love you" or . . . Right place, wrong time? Right time, wrong place? How about anyplace. Another time.

He did that mind-reading thing. "As much as I have thought about it, Cat, about you—as much as I intend to keep thinking about it and you, this isn't the time. Or place. So relax." And he sez he can't read me. I must have looked and sounded like a deflating balloon. "A little less visible relief would be nice for my fragile ego."

So I kissed him, to show him his ego had nothing to fear, and he was the one who had to (gently) disentangle us after a few more minutes.

"I thought you'd like to see that." He pointed to the painting on the wall above the desk.

I took a closer look. "It's Katherine!"

I'd seen the b&w photocopy, with the diary, but that was like seeing a kid's clay model of the Golden Gate Bridge. The portrait isn't all that big, but it's amazing. I gotta go look at more of Turner's stuff. She was really beautiful: rose-and-ivory skin and incredible topaz-colored eyes. I could even see a little of the modern-day Percivals there in the masses of dark hair and determined chin.

"I don't know if it's incredibly sweet or kinda creepy that you have this on your wall."

Will shrugged. "She came with the room. In fact, she was right there when my great-grandfather lived here. He wrote about it in a letter to my great-grandmother before they got married. Says that's why he first fell in love with her: she reminded him of the girl he'd grown up looking at. I think maybe this was Katherine's room when she lived here."

Ever get that dizzy feeling when something weird-but-good happens? Between all the smooching and the letter in the *Waverley* and the picture, I thought maybe I would sit down for a sec. I opted for one of the two armchairs near the fireplace. It creaked so loudly that I spent a tense moment waiting for it to collapse under me.

"That chair," Will said, "once supported Lord Byron's arse. Of course, it might have been the other one—" He laughed as I very carefully and gingerly levered myself out. "Oh, for God's sake, Cat, it's just a chair. Far more interesting things have probably happened on pieces of our furniture than on that one. Sit."

Instead, I wandered over to look at the soldiers. They were old and well loved; some were missing their weapons, some bits of their paint. Will leaned past me and picked up a particularly battered one. "The Duke of Wellington. Probably made a few years after Waterloo." He chose another. This one was smaller, rounder, and was wearing a sillier hat. "Napoleon."

He handed them to me. They were cold and heavier than you'd think, and I had this image of generations of little Percivals banging them against each other in endless battle. "Did these come with the room, too?"

"Nope, but they've been handed down from Percival son to Percival son for at least a hundred years. There's this cool but weird thing in my family: for the last hundred and fifty years, every male Percival has had one son and one daughter. No more, no less."

Okay, smack me, but of course I thought it: I could live with that—one boy, one girl.

I dunno if Will was thinking the same thing. Probably not. They never do. He was probably thinking about whether we could both fit in one of the Byron chairs.

We could. At least until his phone went and we both nearly jumped out of our skins. It's just too easy to forget there are other people in the world when you're with a guy who kisses like he does.

"My dad," he said, looking at the screen. "Dinner's ready. He made ham and farm greens."

Dinner was fine. The rest of the evening was mahvelous. Will has asked me to pass on a message to you:

✦ *Will here. Just a few things I feel I ought to set straight: since Catherine won't let me read her blog, I have decided it's only fair that she refer to me in all future posts as Prince William, His Studliness, or 007.*

✦ *She has promised to keep certain details out of print.*

✦ *I think she's f—well, pretty bloody amazing.*

✦ *I will be very, very good to her for as long as she'll let me.*

✦ *I promise.*

24 June

I do not know what I would do in these terrible days without Nicholas. He has come to us each morning after he has been to Whitehall, with whatever information he has been able to gather. There is little.

We know the battle began near midday on Sunday last, began, I imagine, just as we were returning home from services at St. James's. It ended near midnight, near the time that I set aside <u>Waverley</u> and extinguished my candle. We know the fighting was fierce, and both sides felt certain of both victory and defeat over the many hours. We know that thousands of men fell, and that our forces were victorious.

I feel disloyal to my country, but what is victory when I do not know if my brother is among the men who fell?

We received a letter this morning, and our hearts leapt. Upon opening it, we saw that it was not news we wished to hear. Charles had posted it two days before the battle.

Brussels, June 14

My Dearest Family,

I have too little time to write, and too much to say. It has been confirmed that the enemy has moved, and is within twelve miles of where I sit. Hence, we, too, shall move. After all the waiting and the anticipation that slid into complacence and ennui, the time for battle has surely come. I am not frightened. I have done this before; I know what to expect. And in knowing, I also know how important it is for me to send this letter. I can think of little worse than to meet any sort of misfortune and not have taken even these mere minutes to send you my boundless and grateful love.

Also, I must beg an indulgence of you, Kitty, and ask you to deliver a message for me. I have not time to write another letter, yet things must be said. Try not to be angry at either me or the party to whom I will ask you to speak. Our attachment developed quickly and simply. We had not been in each other's company more than a half-dozen times before we realised how nearly incomprehensible it was that we had ever <u>not</u> known each other, or loved. She is my second half, and I hers. We agreed to keep our attachment silent until my return, so that we might have the joy of telling each of our families when gathered. I am such a blithe fellow; when not actually facing battle, I conveniently forget what battles truly are. Now, with only the certainty of violence ahead, and no certainty of ever seeing England or those people I love again, I regret that. So, Kitty Kit, say aloud, "Yes, Charles, I promise not to be angry and to deliver your message." Go on. Say it.

I made Mama stop reading and did as he asked, speaking the words aloud.

Now, please, when next you see Luisa Hartnell, tell her this: I <u>shall</u> return to her, and when I do, I will not leave again. Yet, and I wish I did not have to write these words, should I breathe my last on a Belgian field, it will be with gratitude for having had even a day of her love. Tell her not to mourn long, but to be happy for the time we had, and when she is old and grey and sitting surrounded by grandchildren, to remember one man who loved her well and not nearly long enough.

For you, Mama, and you, Katherine, I have not adequate words. You have been my cornerstone, the core upon what the best of me is built, and the Home to which I have always cherished the return. Pray that I shall have one last such return from war and no more to it.

Yours ever,
Charles

Luisa. Charles loves Luisa and she him. I thought, for the merest instant, that I should be angry for the secrecy, for the fact that they must have met in private, perhaps even in the middle of very public places, and found themselves so connected that the rest of the world, that <u>I</u> disappeared. Yet I am not angry. What better connection to have, than my brother and my dearest friend?

I have not wished to go out in the days since we received word of the battle. I have thought it best to be home at every moment, in order to be here for the <u>one</u> moment when that all-important missive arrives. Mama has urged me to go; Nicholas has done the same. Luisa came this morning, as she has done every day. Now that I am aware of her circumstances, I am awed anew by her kindness. Always it has been about my worries. In retrospect, I know now that she has been paler of late, and has certainly grown thinner even in a mere few days. Still, not once did she require comfort from me, only offered it. Tonight I shall accede to Mama and Nicholas's urgings and attend the Stuarts' party. I shall give Luisa Charles's message. I do not think I shall be very merry, but I expect I shall not be alone. Among those celebrating England's victory are many like me, still waiting for news of brothers and sons and husbands who were part of it.

When I told Mama of my intentions, she wholeheartedly approved. Her own health has not been helped by this waiting, but she rallied and will, I believe, be well enough to accompany me.

"Shall you feel easy in the company of Mr. Baker and Miss Northrop, should they be in attendance?" she asked after we had sent off a note to Nicholas.

"Oh, certainly" was my reply. Oddly enough, it is true. I have thought so little of Mr. Baker in the last few days that I was almost surprised to have to do so now.

He bruised my heart in his way—as did Papa in his—but had no power to break it. I do not think I care to sit and have a cosy chat with him, but I believe I will be able to be in the same room and feel neither fury nor sorrow. A little sadness, perhaps, for the loss of my romantic plans. They made me quite happy. Mr. Baker did, perhaps, for a short and illusory time, but I think could not have in the end.

We have not heard from Papa. He is too angry. Nicholas has seen him. He says Papa is desperate, too, for news of Charles. We are a shattered family, but a family still, in pieces. That is something.

Becky has arrived and wishes to know which dress I shall wear tonight. Oh, what does it _matter?_ I do not care how I appear. Well, perhaps a little. I have yet to wear the pale green with embroidery. I shall be Spring, bearer of life and hope and good things in the air.

(the clock has just chimed half-two)

I do not know what to write first. What a night it has been. I suppose writing things in order is the best way to go about it.

Luisa cried when I read Charles's letter to her. Then the first words out of her mouth were a plea for forgiveness. Silly, lovely girl! _When_ Charles comes home, I shall make him marry her _immediately_ so we may be sisters.

Mr. Baker and Miss Northrop were not in attendance. Winnie Stuart told me with great glee that she made certain they were not invited. She bounced while telling me, then quite left the ground after saying, "Just wait until you see who _has_ just arrived!" She would not tell me, but confessed, "I must view him from afar. I fear that if I were to try to speak to him, I might do something awful like forget his name or _my_ name or, God forbid, poke him or bump him or _spit_ upon him in my excitement!"

With that, she hurried off to compose herself in some quiet corner.

I thought perhaps Walter Scott himself was in attendance, as I could think of no one else who would set her off so.

I mentioned the matter to Nicholas when he brought me a glass of lemonade. We had settled ourselves at the edge of the party, neither much caring to dance or to chatter. "I would not know Scott if he were to tread on my toes," he mused, "but I think perhaps I have just spied . . . Ah, yes. I have heard he and James Stuart are friends . . . Come along, Katherine. I am going to quite cheer you up."

I confess I did not know how, but I accepted his arm, and even allowed myself to step those few inches closer to him than might be entirely seemly, but which allowed me to feel his comforting warmth and solidity. He guided me through the crowd, toward a gentleman who was standing, back to us, chatting with Winnie's brother. At first, he was wholly unfamiliar, but as Nicholas led me around and his face became visible, I felt my steps falter a bit. It was a familiar face to anyone who read London's society news and the illustrations that accompany it.

"I cannot!" I whispered fiercely. "Nicholas, I—"

"Oh, stop. You are charming and you are especially lovely this evening. Now chin up and smile. Or look bored, whichever you feel better suits the moment. He is merely a man with a very, very good way with words. Ready? Good. Byron . . ."

The poet turned. At first, his handsome face was cool, unwelcoming. I imagine he is much besieged by fawning attention, and it appears he does not relish it. Upon seeing who was addressing him, however, he smiled broadly, making it very clear why he is considered so handsome. "Everard!" he cried. "Damn but if it isn't good to see you!" His eyes lit on me. "And in the company of a fair lady, no less. Should I be offering congratulations?"

I felt my face flame. Nicholas, however, laughed. "I do not believe Miss Percival would have me even if I possessed half of your smoothness of tongue. Miss Percival, allow me to present Lord Byron, wit extraordinaire. Byron, this is Miss Katherine Percival."

"Miss Percival. It is a great pleasure. I apologise if I inadvertently insulted you by suggesting a connection with my pitiful friend here. He has an air of arrogant satisfaction about him. I had thought perhaps the Fates have at last taken pity on him and put him in the path of something splendid."

"You are too kind, my lord. I know little of Fates," I said without thinking, "but Sir Nicholas is frequently inclined to put himself in the way of a Fury or two."

"Ah, yes, indeed he is. I have had my own encounters with their kind, usually in search of a Grace. I am always in search of Grace, it seems."

"Fates and Graces, sir? They are not to be found in England, I think. I believe you possess an affection for the Mediterranean. Perhaps a holiday in Greece?"

"Not a bad idea, that. Are you a traveler, Miss Percival?"

"Only if one counts very long drives on very muddy Somerset roads. No, I am not, but I should like to be."

"A reader, then."

I am certain that only I heard Nicholas's very faint snort. In fairness to him, I do not believe he intended to make any noise at all. "I am becoming one," I said, giving his ribs a quick poke with my elbow. "I should be certain to have a good book upon my person at all times."

"Except those muddy drives."

"Most especially those muddy drives," I countered. "If I cannot have Odysseus's Aegean waves or Childe Harold's Channel, I can at least make use of Somerset's gulleys."

"Well, invoking both Homer and my humble self in one clever speech. You seem to have a fine mind, Miss Percival."

"I often have my doubts on that, sir," I returned. "What I had was a very fine governess."

Byron laughed. "You are outdoing me in my own game of words, Miss Percival. I cannot have that. No, no, don't you dare look down in modesty and denial! I cannot have that, either. So . . ." His marvelously blue eyes narrowed and he was silent for a long moment. Then: "I shall leave you with this:

> 'Now this mortal bows before thee,
> To admire and adore thee,
> Left in awe of wit and beauty,
> I salute the Grace that you be.'"

With that, he bent over my hand, all boyish charm and undeniable appeal. I fear I might have stayed right where I was, giggling like a schoolgirl, had Nicholas not taken my arm, bade our farewells, and firmly led me away.

"Close your mouth, Katherine. You are pulling your fish face again."

I bit back a retort, closed my mouth, and looked up to see if he was annoyed with me. On the contrary, his eyes were bright with amusement and, I dared to imagine, affection. "One day," he said cheerfully, "Byron shall be old and grey and dottery as anyone, and perhaps by then he shall have lost the ability to make everyone he meets fall under his thrall. Until then . . . Come and dance with me, Katherine."

It was but one short dance before the sight of Mama's weariness had us leaving for home. One dance where he only held my hand for the briefest of moments, and we had no time to speak at all. Still, I was very sorry when it ended, sorrier still when he bade us a good night at our door. Mama thanked him for the escort, then stepped inside. I lingered on the stoop.

"I must go," he said gently. "There is more to be done tonight."

"But you will come back?" I asked. I needed the reassurance that, no matter what, he would never leave me completely. I know I sounded like a frightened child when I demanded, "We will always know each other, will we not, Nicholas?"

In the faint glow of the hall light behind me, his face was so familiar, yet possessed then a softness that was not familiar at all. "I cannot imagine it being otherwise."

"We are . . . friends?"

"Dear friends." He touched my cheek fleetingly, then walked halfway to his carriage before turning back. "Some might even say entwined. Good night, Katherine."

And he was gone.

Entwined.

That was Nicholas. Thomas Baker offered me fields and cowpats in his words. Nicholas Everard gave me the earth, moon, and stars in his.

I think I have been a very foolish girl indeed.

My world is more than a bit off-kilter tonight, and I a bit dizzy. It is not all bad, however. It should not surprise me at all that I am in love with Nicholas Everard. What surprises me is how long it has taken me to admit that I have always been a little bit in love with him.

The idea that Nicholas might feel as I do? That is the greatest shock of all.

Say Hey (I Love You)

I hate packing. I really really hate packing.

I hate leaving. Always. I tend to get entrenched wherever I am. Even Whole Foods.

By this time tomorrow, I'll be winging my way back over the Atlantic toward Philadelphia. There are only two reasons why I am not, at this moment, chaining myself to the big wrought-iron gates at Percy's Vale.

One. You're all waiting for me at home, and I've missed you like crazy. Now, while you can deny it all you want, I am perfectly aware that the quiet Chinese-delivery-and-video night Keri sez she and I are going to have at her house Friday is a ruse and a crock. I can smell a surprise party from three days away. Alex, I know as a fact that your Pappous's birthday is in January (remember who slogged through the snow to Paper on Pine last year in search of the *perfect* card to go with the Wii you all gave him?) and there is no family celebration. Nice try, Kel, but no one is protesting *anything* in D.C. this week. JenJen, I thank you for not giving me a silly excuse, but the going mysteriously incommunicado thang was pretty weak. Sophie, the shop closes at 7. You won't be working. Djenan, while you get the most points for creativity, I remind you just whom you were trying to fool. I invented the need-to-stand-in-line-for-tix-but-still-might-not-get-them excuse to avoid more than one unappealing evening.

Two. The BM has pull with BA and apparently likes to impress visiting Americans with it. Hence the (s)mother and I will be flying back business class. Think big squashy armchairs, scads of legroom, goody bags that actually have *goodies* in them, and independent video screens with seventy-two options for my viewing pleasure.

So this is it, goils, the last entry in Cat's Cat-astrophic Cat-aclysmic Cat-atonic Summer Blog. I could just end there, That's All She Wrote, but would I do that to you? Actually, I would, of course, but I hate packing, and I'm not meeting Will and the crew for another hour, so I have some time to kill.

I can't really think about leaving Will right now. Or the London gels. Or Cadbury's or the orange sofa or *Eastenders*. I figure I'll cry a lot and you guys will give me Häagen-Daz and go to TLA for videos and eventually I'll be just fine and I'll e-mail and Skype and I will come back. When I can.

I know I've been less prolific than usual in the last two weeks. No surprise, huh? Of course, I promised Will that I wouldn't share too many details here. Note: I didn't promise not to share exactly the right number of details once I got home.

I will share this, since Soph has informed me that the last page of Katherine's diary was unreadable. Sorry about that. Will and I were ... multitasking ... while I was scanning. So, here it is:

1 July

There is still no news of Charles. I have looked hard for a second magpie whenever Nicholas walks with me in the Park, which has been much of every day this sennight, despite the rain. I cannot abide being inside. Nor can I bear to think of how these days would have been without him.

How odd it is to think how much has changed since I arrived in London mere months ago. How I have changed, in nearly everything I want and admire and believe.

Today, I believe this. I believe Charles will come home. I believe, too, that if I am very, very fortunate, and he does not change his mind about me, I shall marry Sir Nicholas Everard and be very, very happy.

Bummer, ain't it, that she never got to tell us what happened to her bro?

Well. Will found this in an old *Debrett's Peerage*. That's kind of a who's who of English aristocracy. It's pretty cool if you like that kind of thing. Consuelo's in the newest one. So's Will, of course, since his grandfather is the current Lord Chilham. Which means Will's dad will someday be Lord Chilham, which means . . .

Anyway. His Studliness had a brainstorm and got his hands on an 1840 edition. Here's what he found:

Chilham, Baron. (Percival.)

CHARLES SAMUEL SPENSER PERCIVAL, 6th Baron.

Born April 2nd, 1791; succeeded his cousin, who died without issue 1828; entered the army 1811, made Captain 1814, retired 1815: married (1816) the Hon. Luisa Jane Hartnell, daughter of Baron Hartnell of Howth, and has issue living,

The Hon. William Nicholas Percival, b. 1817,

The Hon. Mary Katherine Percival, b. 1821.

Residences: Chilham House, Odstock, Wilts; Percy's Vale, Cadbury, Somerset; 108 Half Moon Street, London.

Will is descended from Charles and Luisa. Which means Katherine is his great-(insert proper mathematical number of extra "greats" here)-auntie.

Pause for sloppy, sappy sigh.

So, as I prepare to return to the land of substandard chocolate and fab friends, I leave you with the question of the day:

What would you rather have, O My Friends: a good beginning or a happy ending?

To: will_percival@mayfair.eng.
From: overnon@thewillingschool.org
Date: December 19
Subject: Kiss Me Thru the Email

Yes, Mr. Percival, I am studying extra-hard for my AP History and English exams. And stop nagging—I'll have my Glasgow and St. Andrew's applications done in plenty of time. Besides, remember Dr. Furball from the BM? Turns out he's actually one of the UK's premier scholars in the field of 18th-century Gaelic Literature and holds some honorary St. A's chair called Sconce or Scone or something. He told Mom he didn't think it would be necessary (can you say 4.3 GPA in Brit?), but that he'd be happy to grease the wheels anyway.

Consuelo sez hi. She's going to Bali for the holidays. Imogen's going to Norway. Elizabeth has family coming in from Jordan. Her cousin broke off her engagement and is trying to get into the London School of Economics mid-year. Economics. Ick.

Interesting tidbit for you. While perusing my Byron book for the English exam, I came upon this:

Stanzas for Music (1816)
There be none of Beauty's daughters
With a magic like thee;
And like music on the waters
Is thy sweet voice to me:
When, as if its sound were causing
The charmed ocean's pausing,

The waves lie still and gleaming,
And the lulled winds seem dreaming;

And the midnight moon is weaving
Her bright chain o'er the deep,
Whose breast is gently heaving
As an infant's asleep:
So the spirit bows before thee,
To listen and adore thee,
With a full but soft emotion,
Like the swell of Summer's ocean.

Middle of the second stanza seem at all familiar? Looks like maybe Byron knew he had something when he composed those lines to Katherine on the spot, and built on them. I gotta say, this version is better, but then, he had some time to work on it. I think she would have loved it. Maybe she did.

I hope you're sleeping, dreaming of . . . well, me, of course. You'll get this when you wake up.

I'll be there tomorrow, at the BA Arrivals Gate. I'll be the one wearing the great big goofy grin and no lipstick. I've stocked up on mistletoe.

Vive les vacances!

Love,

>^..^<

(moi)

Cat's Playlist: Songs to Blog By

1. "Transatlanticism"—Death Cab for Cutie
2. "Who Knew"—Pink
3. "Why Does It Always Rain on Me?"—Travis
4. "Help!"—The Beatles
5. "Someday My Prince Will Come"—Etta Jones
6. "Ain't No Sunshine"—Bill Withers
7. "I Want Candy"—Bow Wow Wow
8. "Smiley Faces"—Gnarls Barkley
9. "Say"—John Mayer
10. "Eh, Eh (Nothing Else I Can Say)"—Lady Gaga
11. "(What's So Funny 'Bout) Peace, Love and Understanding"—Elvis Costello
12. "I Can See Clearly Now"—Johnny Nash
13. "Rich Girl"—Gwen Stefani
14. "Stronger"—Kanye West
15. "I'll Take You There"—The Staple Singers
16. "Hide and Seek"—Imogen Heap
17. "These Streets"—Paolo Nutini
18. "Beautiful Girls"—Sean Kingston
19. "Sad Story"—Plain White T's
20. "Cannonball"—Damien Rice
21. "Last Words"—The Real Tuesday Weld
22. "Viva Forever (Radio Edit)"—Spice Girls
23. "Live Your Life"—T.I.
24. "Happy Birthday"—The Ting Tings
25. "You Can't Always Get What You Want"—The Rolling Stones
26. "Falling Slowly"—Glen Hansard & Markéta Irglová
27. "I'm Yours"—Jason Mraz
28. "Say Hey (I Love You)"—Michael Franti & Spearhead
29. "Kiss Me Thru the Phone"—Soulja Boy